Wish You
Were Here

FLORIDA
2
BOOKS

Wish You Were Here

KAY DEW SHOSTAK

August South
PUBLISHING

ISBN: 978-0-9991064-2-6

Library of Congress Control Number: 2017918943

FICTION: Women's Fiction / Small Town / Florida / Beach /
Contemporary Women / Georgia

Text Layout and Cover Design by Roseanna White Designs
Cover Images from Shutterstock

Published by August South Publishing. You may contact the
publisher at: AugustSouthPublisher@gmail.com

To my Aunt Alice Faye

You always encouraged my reading.
The books you gave me are still some of my
most treasured possessions.
Especially the Kay Tracey mysteries
(written in the 1930's and 40's).
When I open those old hardback books,
I remember the early joy of reading all over again.

Thank you

Hello, everyone. This is Pearl Manningham and I've placed this note here at the beginning, which may help you or may not. But do not complain about not knowing what's happening if you pass this to move right into the story. If it were left to the other people in this subdivision, or whatever it is we are now, you'd go into this book blind. My background as a teacher will not allow me to do that.

As you might've noticed, this is Florida Book 2. Yes, there was a Florida Book 1, which most of you will remember. You may also remember that we were abandoned during the recession by our housing developer, Caleb Mason, who ran back home to Georgia and died. Car crash or something. His lawyer brother, Jameson Mason, dumped our mess of a subdivision onto Caleb's second ex-wife's lap. (That should tell you the type of people we are dealing with here.) Her name is Becca Sue, and with her arrival, all hope was lost.

Becca Sue spent most of her summer drinking and sleeping with Magnus Llord, a man older than her father. She didn't even improve when her stepchildren were foisted off on her. Then the children's grandparents from up north, the Worth Family, (yes, that Worth family) got involved and we found ourselves part of a so-called "Grand Experiment." Our planned upper-class, adults-only subdivision is now part junk yard, part farmland, part construction, part trashy businesses, part—well, you get the picture. Oh, and our delightful new name is Backwater.

So, you've been warned. Now, I'm going to go lie down. Florida gives me a headache.

1

"Seems kind of bare with all the decorations gone," I say, perched on the edge of Miss Bell's couch. She keeps saying it's *our* couch, or *our* refrigerator, but it's not. I just live here. For now.

Miss Bell sighs as she looks around. "Yes, but it's a good bare. A 'new start' kind of bare. I think I missed this feeling of a new start, fresh and empty, as much as I missed having all the decorations up. It's been years, ever since Mr. Bell died, that I got to put up all my Christmas decorations." She nods her white head at me. "Thanks to you, we had them all, Becca Sue."

"Oh, Miss Bell, it's the very least I could do. You letting me live here and all. Plus, I liked it. It was like living in Walmart at Christmas with all the lights and stuff."

Miss Bell laughs. "Oh, maybe a tiny bit better than a Walmart, don't you think?" She tips her head at the sound of the doorbell. "Who's that, do you think? You mind getting it?"

I'm already walking across the carpeted floor to the entry way. It's still pretty light outside, but it gets dark so early this time of year. The front porch is already in shadows. "Hi," I say to the woman standing there.

"I'm looking for Virginia Bell."

"What about?" With all the activity in Backwater since the summer, we get a lot of salespeople. Usually, however, they stand back from the door and have a shirt or truck that lets you know what they're selling, like frozen food or magazines. Plus, they don't usually come this late. But I've gotten pretty good at sending them on their way. At my old house next door, I just didn't answer the door. But Miss Bell says that's rude.

Instead of smiling real big and explaining what she's selling, though, this one looks putout. "Who are you?" she demands.

This is why it's better to just not open the door. So I start to close the glass door as I say, "It's late. Thanks, but no thanks."

She raises her voice, "Tell Virginia it's Mimi."

Behind me I hear Miss Bell gasp. "Mimi? Oh, Becca Sue, let me see." She's come up behind me, and as I step back so she can see, Miss Bell clasps her hands together. "Oh, Mimi! It *is* you!"

This stranger named Mimi pulls the glass door open. "Virginia, so good to see you."

They hug. I take the moment to give Mimi a look. She's tall and thin, and she has a very strange accent for someone from around these parts.

Miss Bell asks her, "What are you doing here?"

Mimi answers as they separate from the hug. "January is cold in Wisconsin, so when you have relatives in Florida, why not hop in the car and visit?"

Miss Bell looks around the woman. "Oh, Drummond's with you, right?"

Drummond?

"Of course. He's just finishing up a call in the car. Let me go hurry him up." As she steps back out the doorway, she turns to me. "We have some luggage you can help with."

Miss Bell's mouth opens, but I put my hand on her arm and shake my head. "It's fine. I'm happy to help." However, before following the woman walking down the sidewalk I ask, "So these are relatives of yours and it's okay if they stay here? I mean, she mentioned luggage."

"Of course. I just... I haven't seen them in years!" She pushes at me to follow Mimi. "I'll go fix up the room at the end of the hall."

Mimi waves me around to the rear of the big SUV, which is packed full. There's a man sitting behind the steering wheel talking on his phone.

"Wow, y'all brought a lot of stuff," I say.

"You don't need to carry it all in tonight. You can start with those." She points to two big rolling suitcases, bigger than any I've ever seen. She moves to messing with some smaller bags, and so I jerk on the handle of one of the huge suitcases until it comes tumbling out onto the sidewalk. As I pull up on the handle and start towards the house, she gives me a tote bag to carry in my other hand.

Mimi follows me in carrying a *small* satchel and a *small* curved pillow. I guess the man will bring in the other big cases. Although even as I think that, I know who'll be lugging in all the heavy stuff in.

Mimi stays in the house to help arrange things, and the man, Drummond I assume, stays on his phone call in the front seat of the vehicle. After each load, I wait for the tall woman with the strange accent to tell me that's enough, but she never does. Miss Bell goes from looking happy to looking concerned by the time I announce I've emptied everything out of the rear of their SUV.

Miss Bell clasps her hands. "Well, that's good. You sure brought a lot for just a visit."

Mimi sniffs and unwinds her soft, gray scarf, which matches her boots and sweater. It was hard to plan with the different weather. Sure doesn't feel like January, does it?"

Didn't she say they flew?

She lays her scarf on the back of the living room couch and asks, "What are you doing for dinner tonight, Virginia? We are starved."

Miss Bell and I look at each other. I say, "We had dinner earlier. Just soup and some leftover biscones we froze after the last market in the fall." Miss Bell's combination of biscuits and scones were a big hit at the Backwater Market we started last summer on the empty lot next to her house. It was just the beginning of our subdivision becoming a real community.

Mimi sniffs again. "Well, I suppose that will be good enough for us, too. Let me go tell Drummond."

As she leaves the house, Miss Bell picks up the abandoned scarf. "It looks like they're planning on staying a while, doesn't it?"

I nod. "Yes. They should have the big room I have. I can change with them or . . ."

"Nonsense. They should've let me know they were coming. I don't believe I've seen them since Mr. Bell died."

"Miss Bell, well, I didn't think you had any children."

She twists up her face, and her eyes get shiny. "Yes, well... Oh, Drummond!" she exclaims as she opens her arms up and heads to the entryway.

A tall man with dark hair strides toward her. His hair is thick and swoops over to one side. He looks to be older than me by a good ten years, maybe more. He's wearing a stiff dress shirt and a long coat that looks much too warm for Florida, even in January. He bends down to hug her, and Miss Bell is openly crying now.

They sit down on the couch I'm standing behind.

"You look just like your father. He was so tall, too." She touches his hair and tucks it back, holding her hand on his head. "And his hair was thick like this, but not ever this dark."

As they laugh and hug and talk, Mimi comes to stand next to me. I try to smile with her at the sweet scene, but there's no smile on her face. "Is the soup warming? I don't smell it."

"Oh, no, but I'll get it on. Tomato, okay? Or we have chicken noodle?"

She doesn't answer, just waves a hand at me and goes to sit on the other side of Miss Bell.

Okay, then.

In the kitchen I open two cans of tomato soup into a pan and turn it on. Getting the rest of a meal together, I set places for them to eat at the kitchen table where me and Miss Bell eat. As I think about it, I realize they must think I'm her help. Maybe a housekeeper? Or a nurse assistant? I mean, what else would they assume? Surely not that I own the entire development and am living here while my old house becomes a clubhouse and my new home is being built.

It's been a strange few months, I can tell you. I found out my ex-husband, Caleb Mason, owned this development on the day of his funeral last summer. He had a new baby on the way and two kids from his first marriage, so his brother Jameson thought getting me out of Piney and all of South Georgia would be a good idea. I was real mad at Jameson at first, but he was just protecting me. I think. Well, I hope. Then Roger Worth, the real estate tycoon and grandfather of Caleb's two older children, decided to invest in the subdivision and we became our own town, Backwater, Florida. We are now a "multi-use community" (Roger had me practice saying that, because I'm the manager of Backwater. Well, kind of. I just do whatever Roger tells me to.. Folks here are getting used to everything, well some of them are. They all bought here when it was a luxury retirement community, so the little shops, condos, and our farmer's market aren't a hit with everyone. But it's better than a half done subdivision with no lights, bad roads, and empty lots with cows on them every other house!

I laugh to myself when I realize how silly Drummond and Mimi will feel when they find all this out. Miss Bell has probably already told them while they've been talking. The three of them are still sitting on the couch when I walk back into the living room to tell them their food is ready. Drummond jumps up and walks around the couch.

He holds his hand out to shake mine. "We didn't get to meet. I'm Drummond Bell. Virginia says you'd be happy to change rooms with us? Obviously makes more sense for us to have the larger room with outside access and our own bathroom. I appreciate you making us dinner, when I understand you've already eaten."

He holds up his hands and says, "Guess I should wash. Nice to meet you." He walks down the hall and then into my room. He looks back at me. "Okay if I go ahead and use our bathroom? Thanks."

He's one of those people who ask a question, already assuming the answer. Mimi walks into the kitchen and comments, "How quaint. We're eating in the kitchen."

Miss Bell moves next to me and whispers, "Thank you for being so sweet. They're just surprised to find you here." She blinks and looks around. "I think they believe you are in my employ. I'll let them know. You don't really have to move rooms."

Grasping Miss Bell's arm, I look down into her eyes. "No, don't say anything to them, about, well, about Backwater. It's all so embarrassing. Just tell them I'm a friend, okay? And he's exactly right, we should change rooms. Besides, I've been wanting to go visit up in Piney. While they're here would be a good time."

The way her face melts into a relieved smile lets me know I said the right thing. I give her a quick hug and pat her on the back as we walk into the large kitchen. Mimi looks up and sniffs at the spoon of soup she's holding. "Becky? This is canned soup? Well, I'm not really asking, I looked and saw the cans in the garbage. Virginia does not need to be eating regular canned soup. There is much too much salt in it for her. For any of us, as a matter of fact."

Miss Bell drops her head, and I rest my hand on her back. "You're probably right. I'll leave y'all to visit and eat while I go move my things." I turn away, but then I hear behind me. "Becky? Be sure and change the sheets and towels, too."

"Yes, ma'am!" I say, maybe a bit louder than necessary.

As I pass her husband in the hallway, he grins at me and shakes his head. Then he whispers, "She really doesn't like to be called 'ma'am.'"

I smile back, but make a mental note to call her ma'am every chance I get. After all, it's only polite, right? 'Cause I was raised right. Oh, well, never mind.

We all know that's not true.

2

"But she doesn't have any children. I've heard her say so myself," Pearl says—again.

Ruth rolls her eyes, holds her hands up, and repeats herself, too. "I'm just telling you what Becca Sue told me."

Pearl stands up from the King's dining room table. "Then let's go meet these people. I'm not one for sitting around wondering." She removes gloves from the pockets of her heavy winter coat. As she pulls them on, she says—also again, "I told George it would still get cold here. We are at the very northern point of Florida." She looks at Ruth. "Well, aren't you coming?"

"Eason has a doctor's appointment, and he wants me to go with him. For a doctor he is the biggest scaredy-cat about going to one. Maybe he just knows what all can go wrong."

Pearl sits back down. "But he's okay, right? Nothing serious?"

"Of course. He just can't get over that cold everyone had at Christmas. Aren't you glad the holidays are over? Grandkids are wonderful, in moderation."

Pearl laughs. "Yes, but at least yours were in *your* home. Sleeping in a teenager's room is the worst. They mope around looking so putout and their rooms... well, their rooms smell. One step in my grandson's room and I'm taken right back to raising my own teenagers. And not in a good way."

"Is there a good way?" Ruth joins her laugh. "I better get ready to go."

As Ruth opens the door, Pearl asks, "So Becca Sue still sitting over at her new house every morning?"

"Yes. She keeps telling the contractors there's no hurry." Ruth rolls her eyes. "We found out when we moved down, you just can't say that to people here, they believe you. At this rate she'll never move in."

The sound of car doors down the road causes the women to step away from the door and look that direction.

"Looks like Miss Bell is going somewhere with her company. Guess our visit will have to wait," Pearl says.

Ruth shivers and hurries back inside the house. "It's cold out there. I'm closing the door. Talk to you later."

Pearl waves and wraps her scarf more snugly against her neck. "Back home, fifty degrees would've felt like spring," she says out loud. At the street, she turns left toward home.

At the top of the circle around the lake, she slows down to examine the progress of Becca Sue's home. She turned over the model home she was living in so it could become a clubhouse as originally intended. Now, though, neighborhood association fees wouldn't pay for it, it would be like a *real* clubhouse with dues and fees. Pearl wasn't the only one opposed to that part of the plan, especially since Roger Worth had made it plain that that meant anyone who paid the fees could join. *Anyone!*

Becca Sue's new lot had never been properly cleared, which was part of the delay. Workers were having to work around the trees and vegetation, because Becca Sue expressed some backwoods idea about it being a cabin in the woods.

Pearl shudders. A cabin. In their lovely, dignified neighborhood. Becca Sue wanted log walls and a real fireplace. As a rush of wind hits her from off the lake, Pearl speeds up and shakes her head at the construction site. "Well, I guess you can take the hick out of the woods, but you can't take the woods out of the hick."

Her hurried stride stalls as she reaches the top of the loop.

"Ooh, there's a car in Magnus' driveway." A driveway that's been empty since he left last summer. She hurries again, looking to her left like she's checking out the progress on the two-story townhomes being built there.

As she passes the car, though, she swivels her head to check the license plate. The plate makes her stand still. "New York," she whispers. Another rush of wind chills her and she decides to see what George knows first. Hurrying up her own drive-way, past the brown hibiscus bushes and brown grass, she wonders why no one ever talks about *this* Florida. The half-dead, too warm to snow, too cold for flowers time of year. "We should've moved farther south or not at all!" she says—again. Then pushing open her heavy front door, she yells over the dogs' excitement at her being home, "George? George, some-one is over at Magnus'. New York plates."

"Hello Pearl," a voice purrs from the hallway.

Shoot. She should have checked before blabbing her mouth. "Oh, Magnus. You're back. Is, uh, is anyone with you?" She bends down murmuring to the dogs, Freddie and Scooby, and looks past Magnus as George wheels his chair out of his office and up behind his old friend.

"Do you see anyone with him? Is there any coffee left, or did you pour it out like you usually do?" George wheels past Magnus as he complains. "She has her one cup and lets me have one, then any extra she throws out before I lose my mind and do something crazy like have a second. C'mon, I'll make a new pot."

Magnus leans down to kiss Pearl's cheek. "I see he's de-lightful as always. How are you, Pearl? And, no, Sybil did not come with me."

Pearl pulls off her coat and takes it straight to the closet. She talks over her shoulder as she hangs it, buttons it, and wraps the scarf around another hanger. "I didn't think you were coming back this soon. How are things at home, I mean, back in New York? We haven't lived there in three years, yet I still call it home. Settle down, puppies!"

"Wishful thinking, I'm sure," her husband says from the

kitchen. "Pearl, where are you keeping the coffee filters now? Only thing I use in this kitchen, and I bet you've put them out of my reach."

She bustles in and reaches into a cabinet above the coffeemaker. Without saying a word she puts the stack into an empty space in the drawer her husband has open, but not before peeling one off and placing it in the empty coffee basket. "Here, I'll do it. You go entertain Magnus."

Magnus laughs from the doorway into the living room. "You two sure make marriage look enticing."

George throws a hand up to dismiss his friend. Pearl, however, perks up. "Marriage? Are you thinking about marriage, Magnus?"

She perks up even more when he doesn't laugh, but looks serious and shrugs. He turns and follows George into the winter-bright living room. The morning sun is to the front of the house, so the lake is in shadows, but with solid walls of windows and glass doors, it's always bright. Pearl once thought this was a good idea, until she realized she didn't care for sunshine all that much.

After starting the coffee pot, she moves to the living room, picking up the dogs to hold on her lap. "So what brings you to Backwater? It can't be the weather. It's awful, just gray and brown, cold at night and then humid and sticky by noon."

"Yes, perfect for golf." He smiles at his hostess. "Tell me, Pearl, you don't like the summers here, you don't like the fall with the trees not turning colors, now winter is gray and brown, so is spring your favorite season here?"

She sets the small dogs down and then waves her hands, palms facing him. "Heaven forbid! Spring without lilacs or daffodils? And having to wear sunscreen and sunglasses before Easter? No. Never. I'll bring the coffee out."

George sighs, then he and Magnus laugh at Pearl's familiar laments. "I'd try to blame it on her getting old and crotchety, but she's been like that since we met. The kids and I just laugh about it." He wheels closer to his friend's chair. "But back to you, before she gets back in here. How are things with Sam? Are you two talking?"

Magnus stares down at his hands for a moment, then looks up. His eyes meet George's intense stare. "We talk some. He's lived his whole life without a father. Doesn't seem to be anything he missed. I went back to New York to try and get to know him. I mean, we have thirty years to catch up on." He pauses, then sighs. "Finally got tired of waiting for something to happen, so took a road trip down here. I'm ready for a change, some kind of change." The two men pull back as Pearl enters with the tray of coffee cups. Then he continues in a louder voice. "Looks like we have townhomes going up across the street. Are they already sold?"

Pearl huffs as she sets the tray down. "The man who is building them plans on living in one of them and renting the other. Retiring across the street from *rental property*! It's just too much." She points out the window. "And see there, at the top of the lake? That's the roof to Becca Sue's cabin. A true cabin in the woods." She sits down and takes a sip of her coffee. "Do you ever talk to her? Becca Sue?"

Magnus only grins and sips his coffee.

Pearl shakes her head at him and tsks. "You are such a lawyer."

George speaks up. "And besides, *I'm* not retired. Still writing every day."

"You know what I mean." Pearl sniffs. "Did George tell you his last book stayed on the *Times* bestseller list longer than any of the others? People apparently still love all that thriller spy stuff." She sniffs again and rolls her eyes.

"Apparently they do, and thank God, because as long as they do, I have a reason to go in to my office and close the door. Which I must do now." He reaches out a hand as he passes his friend. "Magnus, I assume you're headed to the golf course?"

Magnus shakes George's hand, then stands and picks up his coffee cup. "Yeah, see if I can get in some games this week and find out who's around. Thanks for the coffee, Pearl. I don't have anything at my house yet. Why don't we all have dinner at Sybil's restaurant tonight? That seems to be going well."

Pearl wrinkles her nose. "It just seems so, so common, to eat in our own neighborhood. But you probably want to check it out for Sybil, so I guess we can. Right, George?" she asks her husband's back as he whirrs down the hallway.

He shouts, "I don't care!" Then entering his office, he shuts the door firmly behind him.

"See what I put up with?" Pearl leads Magnus to the front door.

He chuckles. "Like I said, you make marriage look enticing."

"Magnus, tell me honestly. Are you thinking about marriage?"

He grabs her upper arm and leans close. "Only if we can get rid of George and you're willing."

Pearl laughs and shoves him out the door. "In your dreams!"

As the door clicks shut behind him, Magnus takes a deep draw of fresh, warm air. Then, whistling, he strides down the driveway. His whistling is choked off with a laugh when he realizes he's whistling "Here Comes the Bride."

3

It would be funny if I wasn't so tired. Neither Drummond nor Mimi lifted a hand last night with changing the rooms *or* the sheets *or* the towels. After Miss Bell went on to bed, I was informed that me calling her *Miss* Bell was entirely inappropriate and very Southern. (Don't think they find *very Southern* a good thing at all.) Mimi spoke very slowly and very clearly, so now it's Missus Virginia Bell, Mr. Bell for Drummond, and Ms. Bell for Mimi. I could hardly wait for her to finish so I could say, "Yes, *ma'am*, Ms. Bell!"

Then this morning I was greeted with a note telling me meals were to be served in the dining room from now on. Starting with breakfast at 9 A.M.

So I left the house by 8 A.M., thinking the real Miss Bell could explain things to them.

However, after a walk to my cabin, I got cold. And well, how would Miss Bell explain everything to them? And she's been so nice to me. They'll only be here a little while, right? So...

"Good morning, Mr. Bell. Everything is set up in the dining room. Can I get you some coffee?" I say as I stand next to the real Miss Bell in her kitchen.

"Yes. Thank you. Ms. Bell will be out in a minute. Good morning, Virginia. How did you sleep?" But he doesn't wait for an answer, just head on into the dining room.

Miss Bell leans on the counter next to me, shaking her

head, and then she rolls her eyes. "I am telling them at breakfast that you do not work for me. If you don't want me to, I won't mention all the other stuff. But this is ridiculous."

I pat her hand and whisper. "Okay, that works for me. Plus, I'm heading out to Piney this afternoon. Give you and them some time to visit. Now go sit down, eggs are almost done."

"Okay, but have you even been back to Piney since you moved here?" Miss Bell asks.

"No. I don't really want to go back now, but feel like I ought to. I'm staying at the hotel and not telling anyone I'm coming. Through the holidays, I told Momma I'd come up after. So, this is as good a time as any. Now go sit down."

"But Becca Sue, it might be hard..." She begins, but I cut her off as I brush past with the bowl of scrambled eggs and basket of toast. "It'll be fine. Go on and sit down."

She sighs, but then Mimi strides into the dining room. My last task is taking her coffee, then I sit down at the table, too.

As her guests' mouths drop open at my joining them, Miss Bell says, "Becca Sue does not work for me. We are partners in the market and friends. She's staying here while her house is being built."

Drummond's forehead wrinkles. "But why didn't you tell us last night?"

Miss Bell and I shrug with smiles, and I speak up. "It was all so hurried that there was no time to try and explain things then. And I'm going to go see my folks up in Georgia for a few days, so that'll give y'all some time to visit."

Mimi pushes her plate back and sips her coffee. "But, Virginia, who takes care of you? Who, well, who does everything here?"

"I don't need a lot done. And my friends take care of me. My friends, like Becca Sue," she says with a warm smile directed at me, then her smile becomes wider, and not quite as genuine, as she turns to Drummond and Mimi. "And now that you're here to help me, it's a perfect time for Becca Sue to visit her parents. This worked out perfectly!"

I stand up and, taking a piece of toast and my coffee, I walk towards the kitchen. "I'm going to pick up a suitcase from a friend, and then I need to pack."

In my new, smaller bedroom, I sit on the bed and take a deep breath. Sleep last night was full of dreams of when I was married to Caleb and we lived in his parents' house. They treated me like the help, too, which I thought was all I was due. Scary how quickly I fell right back into the old routine when those two showed up last night. It took a while, but people here in Backwater, for the most part, treat me different. I haven't felt so bad about myself in a long time. Now I *really* don't want to go to Piney.

Maybe it'll be better with a friend. Maybe I can talk Ashleigh into going with me.

"My wife told me you were coming. Something about borrowing a suitcase?" Carlos is in the garage and the door is up, so I walk inside.

"Your wife is correct. How are the newlyweds?"

Carlos shakes his head. "Something is wrong. I can't stop smiling. Go on in the house, she's in there."

After their Christmas wedding, Carlos and Ashleigh moved into a little house not far from Backwater. It's old and run-down, but they love it. They love it more when the weather is warm because their heat doesn't really work. Or maybe it's that there is no insulation and some of the windows don't quite close.

"Hey, chica, don't take your coat off. I'm in the back bedroom."

At the end of the short hall, I find Ashleigh pulling things out of the closet. "Here's that suitcase. I meant to get it out earlier, but well, you know my husband." Ashleigh still has on a silky nightgown, covered in lace and light blue ribbon, barely long enough to cover her ample behind.

"Ash! Okay, we know. You and Carlos are having sex. Lots of it. Good for you. But put on some clothes. Aren't you freezing? It's freezing in here."

She shrugs and then picks up a flannel poncho from the pile of things at her feet. "That's why we keep having sex. To stay warm." She pulls the poncho over her head. It falls to her knees. "This is kind of cute. Think I bought it in high school." Looking around her, she sighs. "My mom and dad brought all this over from their basement. I mean, it's all my stuff. But, well, I kind of wanted them to keep it over there." She steps over the piles and then pushes me ahead of her and across the hall. "I have to get dressed for work. Tell me what's the all-fired hurry about going to Piney."

We talk while she gets dressed in a little room off their bedroom. It's not actually another bedroom, but as Carlos' and Ashleigh's mothers keep pointing out, it would be a perfect nursery. Once Carlos and Ashleigh got serious in the fall, they decided they didn't want to wait to get married. They set the ceremony for the weekend before Christmas, and it was in my old house, which had been sitting empty since the first of October when I moved out. Construction to turn it into a clubhouse hadn't begun, but it was clean and empty and big enough to hold Carlos' family. They all came from New York.

There was much crying at first as they shared their plans and Mrs. Jimenez lamented her son moving so far away. His sisters told Ashleigh not to worry about it as she always gave her only son, the baby of the family, whatever he wanted. Soon she would be demanding Ashleigh marry him right this very minute and get him settled in Florida! They were right. Now, Mrs. Jimenez believes Carlos needs a baby to be happy, and she has found an ally in Ashleigh's parents.

"I can't go with you. I have work and, well, Carlos." She grins. "He needs me."

"No, he just wants you," I correct. "But, I know. It's so last minute, maybe next time."

She looks at me, then tilts her head. "What's wrong? You worried about going?"

"I wasn't, but then I had all these dreams about Caleb and his mother last night."

"Jameson? Any dreams about Jameson?" she asks.

I jump up at that. "Gosh, it's cold in here. Thanks for the suitcase. I'll go out through the garage."

She follows me, and as I pass Carlos, I roll my eyes at him. "You two are too much."

He laughs. "What can I say? She can't keep her hands off me." And as if to prove his point, she comes up behind him and nestles into him.

Ashleigh yells at me as I get into my car. "Call me, I want to hear what happens. And tell Jameson I said hello."

Over last summer, Jameson went from being The Enemy in the development his family palmed off on me, to being a friend. He was even kind of my date for Ashleigh and Carlos' wedding. Kind of. Seeing as I was married to his brother, he obviously wants to take things slow. Backing down their sand driveway, I lick my lips and smile. Yeah, Jameson might've shown up in a dream or two last night—but I need to concentrate on driving right now.

4

Soft lights at the foundation of the building shine up into short palms, and the lighted walk to the front door helps with the early evening darkness. The only thing that lets you know it's not just a regular home is the painted wooden sign hanging over the fake windows where the garage door used to be. Another light illuminates the sign that simply says, in large open script, "Sybil's." Below that single word is the line, "A gathering place."

Instead of a normal front door, the sidelights have been removed and a large, leaded glass door has been installed. Walking up the sidewalk, Miss Bell looks through the glass door and points for Mimi and Drummond. "See, through the back windows, across the lake, you can see Becca Sue's old house. It's going to be the clubhouse."

Carlos opens the door just as Drummond reaches for it. "Mrs. Bell! Wonderful to see you again. And you brought guests!"

"Oh, Carlos, I haven't seen you since the wedding. You were so handsome. Oops, you still are, of course!" Miss Bell laughs as she begins to shrug out of her coat.

Carlos helps with her coat as she makes introductions. "This is Drummond and Mimi, all the way from Wisconsin." The older woman leans closer to him as he lays Mimi's coat across his arm and asks, "So? Is the sex as good as Ashleigh promised?"

"Virginia!" Both Mimi and Drummond exclaim.

However, Carlos only laughs and then winks at Miss Bell. "You know that Ashleigh, she keeps her promises! I'll put your coats away. There are some open tables, sit wherever you like." He nods as he steps to the side. "And nice to meet you. Welcome to Sybil's."

Miss Bell moves into the main room, large and softly lit with stone tiled floors, warm orange walls, and turquoise tablecloths. There's sparkle from candles and their reflections glint off glasses and all the windows. The large glass doors are closed due to the cold, but through them, the guests can see lit torches lining the lake and the patio. Drummond leads them to a table in the corner of the room, and as they get situated, Miss Bell speaks to a few of the people at the dozen tables in the room.

As soon as they are all seated and looking at the menus, Drummond clears his throat, then bends his head closer to Mrs. Bell. "Virginia, who is that young man you were so rude with at the front door?"

"Rude? Rude with Carlos? Oh, no, he's not like that. He's a very good friend of mine, and well, you'd have to know his new wife. Just adorable. A larger girl, but so pretty and sweet. Of course everyone knew they would have a satisfying sex life, but I couldn't resist needling Carlos. Now, let me tell you, the pasta items are their specialty and they are good, but I love their crepes."

Mimi sniffs and says, "You sure have some unusual friends. First that maid, and now the local cook." She looks down. "Very limited menu."

Miss Bell rolls her eyes. "Of course, look how small this place is. It's like the old restaurants you'd find in the neighborhoods in cities. You remember, Drummond?"

He pats her hand. "Remember? I was forced to move to Wisconsin when I was only a child." He stares at Miss Bell with his mouth drawn tight. She opens her mouth, but nothing comes out.

Eventually the older woman nods and then bows her head.

The table is silent until a waiter appears and takes their orders. As he heads back to the kitchen, Magnus and Pearl enter the main room, following George's wheelchair.

"Oh, Mrs. Bell, I was going to visit you this morning, but you were leaving," Pearl says as she comes up to the table. Drummond stands, and from her seat, Mrs. Bell introduces everyone.

Pearl tips her head and her eyebrows wrinkle. "Are you family?"

Again, Mrs. Bell's mouth opens, but nothing comes out immediately.

Mimi speaks up. "Just visiting. You know how cold Wisconsin can be in January." She then lifts her wine glass, twists her face away, and takes a slow sip, dismissing them all.

Drummond takes his seat and smiles, tightly with no teeth showing, again, at the three. Magnus turns quickly and walks off, while Pearl stammers for something to say. George pushes buttons on his wheel chair, which makes it back up, then he looks directly at Miss Bell. "Virginia, call me if you need anything."

She only lifts her head at his words and smiles a bit. George heads toward the table where Magnus waits, saying over his shoulder, "C'mon, Pearl."

Pearl finally follows and gets to the table bursting to talk. She begins before getting fully seated. "Becca Sue said she thinks that's her son and daughter-in-law! They seem awful and like we're not good enough to be her friends."

Magnus asks. "When did you talk to Becca Sue?"

"I didn't, I talked to Ruth who talked to Becca Sue. They do seem rather cold, don't you think?"

George shrugs. "Who cares? I'm having the mushroom ravioli. Let's not wait to order, I'm hungry. Oh, Sybil."

"Hello, welcome." The tall woman places one hand on her lean hip, which is jutted out a bit. "Glad you've joined us this evening and hope everything is to your liking." She's moved on to the next table before George and Pearl say a word. Magnus is staring at his menu.

Pearl hits his menu with the back of her hand, and Magnus looks up. "What?"

"You said Sybil didn't come back with you."

Magnus tilts one eyebrow. "She didn't." Then he goes back to reading his menu.

This time Pearl grabs the menu out of his hands. He sighs and folds his arms on the table in front of him. "Yes, Pearl? You have something else to say?"

George just shakes his head at his wife, which she ignores. "Yes. Yes, I do. Are you and Sybil still together? You were together all fall, right?"

Magnus shrugs. "Sometimes. Thought she'd help me get close to my son, but she doesn't want to share him. It's a closed chapter."

Pearl starts, then stops. "But you said you are thinking about marriage?"

He grabs his menu out of her hands and closes the conversation with two words. "I am."

5

None of this looks familiar. Except it all looks like home. Like South Georgia. Which, I guess it is since I did pass that Welcome to Georgia sign a bit ago. So while it may look familiar, it's not. I don't remember seeing any of it last time.

Last time. First of all, it was dark. And I was crying most the drive, coming straight from the funeral like I was.

Everybody knew Caleb drank more than he should. Maybe it was that he was getting older, but it was beginning to show. The drinking, that is, and that was pretty embarrassing for a guy like Caleb Mason. For his family, too. Maybe if his big truck hadn't been in the shop getting fixed from the last wreck, him getting hit by that other car wouldn't have been enough to kill him. But he was driving some small car. Turns out it belonged to a worker on the farm. Paid the guy five hundred dollars to borrow it for the night. Crazy thing is, after all his close calls and wrecks, the one that killed him wasn't his fault. Girl ran a stop sign and hit him right on the driver's door. She was fine. Didn't even have to go to the hospital.

It took a while for folks to find out what had happened since it was late and he wasn't driving his car. He never did carry a wallet much. He always said they couldn't take your license away if you didn't have it with you. Besides, he was Caleb Mason, and once he moved back from New York, he rarely left Piney. He liked being where folks knew who he was.

Momma called me from the diner the next morning. I'd been sleeping on the couch in their trailer since Caleb moved Audrey into the house. Audrey's daddy had told her she had to go live with the Masons since she was carrying a Mason baby. Which makes sense, I guess.

But me and Caleb were still on pretty good terms, and it worked okay me living in his house until I couldn't. I mean, I was there for Maggie and Cab if they needed anything. The cook and housekeeper did all the work, but we got along good all there together. But of course, it wouldn't work with Audrey, too. So, I moved home, 'cept Daddy had moved into my room in the trailer and that meant I had to sleep on the couch. I didn't care. I didn't care about much of anything, but since I'd been there for a month, Momma had started talking about how I needed to get a job and find my own place.

I was still asleep when she called me that morning.

Momma said Caleb had been in a car wreck and had died last night. That he'd been out near their hunting property on a backroad. She said they didn't know why he was way out there. And all by himself, too. Then she had to go, said the news had the diner full and getting fuller.

We hung up and I just sat there. Thinking.

Caleb dead? But he couldn't be. Just couldn't be.

I mean, he'd been fine when I was with him last night.

The backroad I'd driven from Florida widens and suddenly there are those big gas stations and every kind of fast food you can imagine. Which all means I'm getting close to the interstate. Piney is a good twenty minutes from here, but there are no hotels in Piney. (Well, none that I'm going to stay at. All I need is to take a bunch of bedbugs back to Miss Bell's.)

Whoever thought of putting a hotel behind the Cracker Barrel is a genius. As I get ready to open the car door, I stop. I've never checked into a hotel before.

I call Ashleigh real quick. "Hey Ashleigh, I don't need anything special to check into a hotel, do I?"

"What? Are you there yet? *Is there even a hotel in Piney*?" she asks.

"No, well, no, there's not a hotel, but yes, I am here. Not Piney, but out by the interstate at Tifton. But I've never checked into a hotel. Do I need anything special?"

"Just a credit card. Your drive okay?"

"Yeah. Wish you were here. It's kind of lonely."

"Plus, if I was there, you wouldn't have to check in, right? We both know I'd do it for you."

I smile and laugh a little. "Yeah. I know. I'm supposed to be getting braver. Okay, I'll go in there like you are standing right behind me. And you know what?"

"What?"

"After I get into my room I'm going over to the Cracker Barrel and I'm not getting take out. I'm going to sit at a table all by myself and eat."

She groans. "Aw, now I want Cracker Barrel. Have fun and get the chicken fried steak and broccoli casserole. I've got to go. I'm heading to my mom's to watch CSI. Too cold over here to watch TV, and besides, Carlos is working."

I get out of the car, collect my roller bag, and march into the hotel pretending Ashleigh is right behind me. She tells me all the time if you act like you know what you're doing, people just naturally think you do, but I'm having trouble acting anything but excited. Me, checking into a hotel all by myself. Crazy!

Everything is shiny and smells like carpet. Not dirty carpet, just carpet. The man and woman behind the counter are both staring at me and smiling. Not mean smiling, just smiling. Then the guy says, "Welcome to Tifton. How can we help you?"

"Can I get a room?" Then I catch my breath and blurt, "I don't have a reservation or anything. Do you have—"

"No problem, ma'am," the lady says with an even bigger smile as she drops her head and starts typing. "How will you be paying?"

"Oh!" I stand my bag up and my purse around, reaching for my wallet. Opening it, I lay it on the counter. Pulling out my credit card I have to rub my lips together to keep from smiling too big. This feels so grown up. "Here you go!"

"And here you go," she says as she presents a little folding envelope, lays it on the counter, and begins pointing at it with her pen. She says something about a Wi-Fi code and then points at a little map before folding it back up and handing it to me. Turning and reaching behind her she pulls a sheet of paper from the printer and lays it on the counter for me to sign.

"Do you know your license plate number?"

"No, why? I can go get it."

"No, don't worry about it. We don't always get them, especially when it's not the weekend."

"Well, I don't want to get in trouble."

They both laugh out loud, call me ma'am, and tell me it's all good. Then they say they hope I have a good afternoon. And they go back to looking down at whatever they are working on behind the counter.

"Excuse me, but I need a key, right?"

The lady tilts her head and frowns. "Isn't it there?" She points and then holds out her hand toward me. She motions for me to hand her the little envelope. "Yes, it's in there. She pulls out a little credit card thing and then pushes it back where it was, folds the envelope, and holds it out for me. She's not smiling anymore.

I open the envelope and look at the card. It's really warm in this lobby and my throat is awful dry. When I look up, I blink to keep my eyes as dry as possible. "But, don't I need a key for the door?"

"The card is your key." Then she goes on to explain about the card and a slot on the door and about the backdoor needing the key, but I can't. I just can't hear what she's saying, so I nod, tuck my head down and walk away. Luckily I'd already seen the elevators so I didn't have to ask where they were. Although she probably drew them on that little map.

The wheels on my suitcase clack so loud on the tile floor. Probably should've picked up my suitcase and carried it. Everyone has to be staring at me.

At the elevator I stand close to the doors so no one can see me getting ready to cry, but just as they open, the guy from the desk touches my shoulder. "Ma'am? Can I tell you something?"

Now what? I bite my lip and turn to him.

He sticks his arm in the elevator to hold the door and bends his head down toward me. "I'd never stayed in a hotel when I got this job." He shrugs and smiles at me. "Matter of fact, I still ain't. Yeah, I work here, but I've never spent the night here, or in one anywhere. You have fun, okay?"

"Okay," I promise as I walk into the elevator. By time I turn around, the doors are closing and he's gone. That was nice of him. But I can see right now, there is now way in heaven I can go sit at the Cracker Barrel and eat by myself.

6

"I'm about ready to go," Becca Sue says on the other end of the phone. "What are you doing this morning?"

Ashleigh hears the telltale gurgle of a coffee maker in Becca Sue's hotel room and answers, "Talking to you. Did you get a good room? You mentioned the elevator, so what floor are you on?"

"Third, top one. I can see down the interstate, but nothing real good to look at."

Ashleigh says, "Well, go look out in the hall."

"Why? It's just a plain old hall. The room is nice, but the hall is awfully bare. Seems like they'd make it prettier, but then I guess—"

Ashleigh rolls her eyes. "Go look out in the hall!" she shouts into the receiver.

"Okay, okay." The door opens, and there stands Becca Sue, still wearing her slippers. "Hey! What are you doing here?"

Ashleigh stands in the hall with a suitcase, grinning. "I'm here to make sure you don't go to Piney looking like that." She shakes her head as she bustles her full-bodied self into the room. "And I knew it. You did McDonalds drive-thru for dinner last night, didn't you? Told Carlos you'd chicken out of going to eat at Cracker Barrel."

Becca Sue picks up the hamburger wrapper and empty fries container off the desk and throws them in the garbage can. "I was tired and wanted to watch TV while I ate."

35

Ashleigh rolls her eyes and throws her suitcase up on the one unused bed, which is still neat and tightly made. As she unzips her bag, she talks. "I went over to Miss Bell's last night to look in your closet, and look what I found. All your nice clothes. They were left in Florida and that," she emphasizes with a sharp point at her friend, "is what you planned to wear to Piney."

Becca Sue looks down at her old jeans and big flannel shirt. "Well, yeah. Guess I didn't really think about what to wear. These are just Piney clothes."

Ashleigh stands in front of her and places both hands on her shoulders. "But you are no longer the Piney Becca Sue." Ashleigh rubs her hands on Becca Sue's sleeves. "You wore this before you lost weight, didn't you? It's huge."

"Yeah, I guess. It's comfortable."

"And the clothes I brought you, that we bought together, they aren't comfortable? I've seen you wear them, and you've never looked uncomfortable."

"But that was in Florida."

Ashleigh walks to the coffee maker and hands the cup of coffee to Becca Sue. "Here, sit down and let's talk." Ashleigh sits in the chair from the desk and scoots until it faces the chair beside the window where Becca Sue settles.

Becca Sue gestures at the suitcase laying on the bed. "Are there any clothes in there for you?"

"No," Ashleigh says. "I'm just here for the morning, drive was only a little over two hours. Anyway, Mom made me realize last night what a big deal it is to go home for the first time. Especially for you. You really are a different person than the girl who showed up on Oyster Break last summer."

Becca Sue sips her coffee as she stares at the cars flashing by on the interstate. Finally she mumbles, "But I won't be different in Piney. They know me."

Ashleigh leans over and plucks at the hem of the red and gray flannel shirt. "This? This is really who you are? Honey, if you want to wear this, then that's fine with me. But I want everyone to know who you really are. Becca Sue Mason, mover and shaker of Backwater, Florida. All I'm asking is that you think about it and go back to Piney how you *want* to go back. Not how they expect you to return."

Becca Sue sets her coffee down on the window ledge, then folds her arms across her chest. Finally she asks, "Did you bring that green sweater?"

Ashleigh hefts herself up from the desk chair, and after digging in the suitcase for a minute, she holds up a kelly-green cotton sweater.

Becca Sue smiles, untucks her hands, then rubs them on her old, baggy jeans. "And that probably wouldn't look that good with these jeans, would it?"

Ashleigh shrugs and smiles. "Just in case you thought that, I brought those navy corduroy pants we got at Target. However, there is one new thing I picked up on my way here." Ashleigh lays down the sweater and reaches into an orange plastic bag. She pulls out a shoe box and hands it to her friend, still sitting beside the window.

Becca Sue sets the box in her lap and takes off the lid. Nestled in the tissue paper is a pair of those boat shoes rich people wear. Her eyes are blinking when she looks up at her friend.

Ashleigh announces. "The Holy Grail of shoes in Becca Sue Mason's world—official Sperry Top-Siders. Leather tops and white bottom with leather ties. I went completely old school for your first pair."

"But, I don't know if I can wear them. They don't seem like..." Her voice slides off as she lifts one out of the box.

Ashleigh empties the suitcase into the drawers in the hotel dresser as she talks. "Honey, they are just shoes. But to you, I've got a feeling they are going to be like Cinderella's slippers. You don't have to wear them today, or even on this trip. But I want you to remember that you now own a pair of boat shoes. You are *that* kind of person."

She stops unpacking and puts both hands on her hips. "Even if you don't believe it, or feel it, that is how *I* see you. And, honestly, aren't I the only one that matters?" She laughs big and snaps her fingers. "Now let's get this show on the road.

We are both going to be on the road, in opposite directions, by one o'clock. I have to be home to cover the school board meeting tonight for the paper. Plus, you know Carlos doesn't want me all tired out when he gets home." She laughs again and winks.

Becca Sue finally laughs, too. "I know, I know. Your husband is a stud."

At 1:33 Ashleigh gets in her car and heads south, and Becca Sue gets in her car and heads northeast. Becca Sue wears the navy corduroy pants from Target, a white button-down shirt, and over that, the bright-green, cable-knit sweater. Her hair has been refashioned from an ordinary ponytail into a thick braid, which hangs down just past her shoulders. Her lips are tinted with a touch of berry, as for the first time ever she bought colored Burt's Bees lip balm instead of clear after they had lunch at Cracker Barrel. On her feet...

On her feet she wears her old tennis shoes. The boat shoes are safe and secure, wrapped in their tissue paper inside the closed shoe box, on the night stand beside her bed in the hotel room.

But one day. One day...

7

"Hey Momma," I say as she comes out of the kitchen at the diner.

"Honey! Let me put this down," my mother says as she motions to the tray in her hand. She bustles to a table near the window and unloads the tray, placing the plates and bowls in front of a young couple sitting there. She talks with them for just a second, then holds up a finger at me as she passes by again. She sets the tray down on the counter as she swirls by, lifts up a bottle of ketchup from an empty table behind me, and then takes it to her customers. They are the only table with folks actively eating since it is nearly two p.m. There are four men at another table with papers and coffee cups spread out between them as they talk. Seated alone at the table closest to me is a girl in a waitress outfit like Mommas. She's filling salt shakers and talking on her cell phone.

"Here, sit down. I won't hug you 'cause you know I smell like fried onions." She motions us to a booth near the kitchen door. "I can keep an eye on things from here. So, what are you doing in Piney?"

"Thought I'd come see how y'all are doing. You know, since I didn't come home for Christmas or anything."

Momma dumps the sugar and fake sugar packets out of their container and starts sorting them. "Yeah, it was different, wasn't it? Before, even when you were with Caleb, we got to see you. But it was busy here, so not much time to worry about it. The new owner I told you about, the good-lookin' one?" She glances up at me, so I turn my silent nod into a word. "Yes." It's hard to focus on what she's saying because I'm so distracted by her fidgeting. Momma is downright gifted at sitting still. Daddy fidgets a good bit, but Momma is like a cat. She moves fast when she wants to, but when she stops, her whole body stops. Daddy's step-momma, Irene, says instead of a cat she's more like a snake sunning on a rock. And, yeah, that might be about more than her not fidgeting.

She looks back down at her busy hands. "Well, he's the owner, but he lives most of the time up in Atlanta, some of the time in Piney with his wife, Pepper." Momma rolls her eyes as she says 'wife,' then she adds, "They have some fancy ideas and it's got this place almost too busy, if you know what I mean."

I look around at the empty restaurant. "Doesn't look that busy to me."

"Oh, not now, but you should see the mornings. And the weekends are awful, just awful. Packed."

"But, Momma, how's that a bad thing?"

She taps her fingers on the table, then slides the newly organized packet container next to the bud vase holding a bouquet of silk daisies. "Guess it's not all bad, but I liked when it was just our regulars, not all those tourists or whatever." She straightens the salt and pepper shakers, then flutters her hand just above the table. "Not that an occasional new face wasn't welcome, but this is... never mind. How are you? You look good. Still keeping off that weight, I see."

"Oh, yeah, it's been busy in Backwater." My words come out in a stream, filling her in on my new house and living with Miss Bell, but my mind's not on them. I'm watching Momma fiddle with her hair, her collar, dumping out the sugar packets again and putting them back like they already were. Suddenly, she scoots out her end of the booth.

"Honey, I've got to get back to work. Can I get you something? Just see you back at home, later? I get off at three-thirty, and I'll bring some fresh fried chicken for dinner, okay? I'll see you then." She darts into the kitchen, leaving me with the rearranged sugar packets and not just a little confusion.

I slide out of the booth. At the front door there's a chalkboard sign about being sure to check out South Georgia Shoppes next door. Now before, I would've avoided a place like that like the plague, but after working with the Backwater market, seeing how other people sell things is really cool.

The chalkboard inside, and the even larger and fancier one outside, points me to the left, where there's a very large and very old building. Obviously this building has been here all my life, but I don't remember ever seeing it. Now? You can't miss it. The old stone building has been painted a creamy white, and the big barn doors on the front are shiny black. They are pulled back and in the opening hangs a dozen pots of bright red geraniums, which match the enormous pots, also full of red geraniums, along the front sidewalk. The doors are so large, I can walk underneath the hanging pots of flowers and still have two feet of clearance, even though I'm almost six feet tall.

There's a skylight inside which lets in natural light, along with tall windows on the sides. Adding to this is rows of lights that keep the building from feeling like a big old stone building. It feels more like, like a mall, or something you'd find in a fancy tourist town like Oyster Break. This is so not Piney. And yet—it is.

Booths of old stuff, almost like a flea market, are next to booths of baked goods and homemade wares like soap and jewelry. There are lots of people around, but most seem to be working in their booths. And I don't recognize any of them, which feels strange. It's even stranger when, near the end of the third row, someone calls my name.

"Becca Sue? Hey there! Thought that was you." I finally recognize the older woman coming towards me as one of my high school teachers, Mrs. Fulbright. She exclaims, "Look at you! You are doing good down there in Florida, I hear from Maggie. She's so lucky to have you for a stepmother."

She pulls me to her in a hug before I can stop her. Hugged by a teacher? "Hey, Mrs. Fulbright. Y'all off school today?"

The tall woman laughs and grabs my arm. She talks as she leads me forward. "Sweetie, I retired last year. And wasn't it just in time? That darlin' Pepper opened this place, and look, my own booth!"

She's showing me the items for a few minutes before I make the connection. "Everything is about books and authors."

"Of course," she says. "I did teach English for thirty-five years. I'm acquiring quite a name for finding unusual books and every cute thing on the internet that has to do with books." She can't contain her joy when she says, "People come all the way here just for my little shop. I have regulars!"

She grabs my arm, and we start off again. "Let me introduce you around. Monday is the day we try to restock and straighten up after the weekend. Weekends are a tad intense. This place has done wonders for Piney." She suddenly stops and exclaims, "That's right! Maggie says you've opened a market down there in Florida." Then she leans close to me and whispers, "You do know that Maggie Mason near worships you. She and Cab came back from their summer with you changed people. Cab has straightened up and is flying right, and Maggie is head of the yearbook committee! Can you believe that? She was always so quiet and shy, but not anymore. Cab even has a booth reserved here for Mason Farms, but his grandmother won't allow him to open it. Pepper is holding it for him because she'd love to have the Mason's stamp of approval. Maybe you can help him? Yes, that's a wonderful idea. You can help him."

"Well, I won't be here that long."

She shakes her head at me. "He can call you. You know these kids with their phones."

Wait, I guess that means I'm no longer one of the kids. Hmmm.

She continues to lead me around the shops, talking a mile a minute. Some of it does ring a bell, Cab asking me questions about the farm vendors at Backwater Market and Maggie enjoying school for the first time. But did all really start with their summer in Florida? In Backwater?

Finally back at the front doors, I tell my old teacher I have to go. Walking underneath the pots of geraniums, Mrs. Fulbright shouts my name again. "Becca Sue, really hate to hear about your father. He's in our prayers."

At least I think that's what she said. By the time I turn around, she's off talking to another vendor. Daddy? I can't remember last time we talked, he doesn't like to talk on the phone and he's been busy with a new job. At least I think it was something like that. Daddy's kind of hard to nail down. He and Momma like not being pinned down to anything, including each other. They only have me because they didn't know they were pregnant until it was too late to do anything without folks knowing. Everyone around Piney, and the surrounding counties, know Rick and Brenda Cousins are always up for a good time. Why they don't get a divorce, nobody knows.

I'd meant to go through downtown and drive around before heading to the trailer, but I'll do that tomorrow. Momma's car is no longer in the diner's parking lot, and she said she'd bring hot fried chicken home. Plus, she'll know why folks like Mrs. Fulbright are praying for Daddy.

8

"Becca Sue and I usually only have some crackers and cheese for lunch, but then we usually like a bigger breakfast. Shame she left yesterday before she could make us some biscuits and gravy. She can't cook much, but some things she's perfected." Miss Bell looks around the dining room. "Hard to believe she's only been gone one night. I do miss her." She sighs as she takes a spoonful of the takeout soup Mimi had ladled into her bowl.

"Virginia, she's a young woman. Don't you think she deserves to get out of here occasionally? You can't expect her to stay here here caring for you." Drummond clears his throat and adds with a frown, "Hope she doesn't feel she has to hurry back because we aren't taking good enough care of you."

"Oh, no. I would never expect her to rush back! Surely she knows that." Miss Bell looks at Drummond and mimics his frown. Then her face lightens. "But what about the party? I want folks to meet you," Miss Bell says across her dining room table.

Mimi's voice is hard. "We're not here to socialize."

Drummond pats his wife's hand. "The thought is nice, Virginia. It would be good to meet your neighbors. These lots are so large I'm sure you rarely get to see them yourself."

"Oh, pshaw!" the older woman says with a chuckle. "They worry about me so much that they are always dropping in on me."

Drummond's face scrunches in concern. "Why do they worry about you? Are you not okay?" He sighs. "This *is* a rather large house for you to maintain. I know Father worried about you being here alone."

"He did?" Miss Bell's face echoes his concern. "He never said that to me."

"Oh." Drummond shrugs. "Probably didn't want to worry you."

Her voice trembles and her eyes collect tears as she agrees. "He was like that. Never wanted me to worry."

Mimi softens her voice a bit, but it still feels harsh in the quiet room. "Wonder what he'd think about all this Backwater Market stuff?"

Her husband smiles. "Oh, Father would've probably loved it at the beginning, but then he'd be ready for his privacy and quiet soon enough."

Mrs. Bell looks up at him, her head cocked to the side. "Oh, I hadn't thought of that, but you're probably right. He didn't like a fuss." She pushes her lunch plate back from the edge of the table. "Thank you, Mimi, for the sandwich and the soup, but I'm just not hungry. Think I'll go lay down for a bit." Mrs. Bell stands, but then with her fingertips pressing on the table top she asks, "So you don't want me to have a party?"

Drummond smiles and shrugs. "If you want to, it's fine with us. Right, Mimi?"

Mimi's smile is still tight. "Of course. I can even arrange the caterer."

"Oh, that's right. Usually Becca Sue would handle all that. Her friend Ashleigh knows everyone in town. Wonder when Becca Sue is coming home? I should call her."

"That's all right, Virginia. Mimi and I will handle everything. You go rest." He hesitates, then adds, "And I wouldn't bother Becca Sue when she's with her family. We'll take care of everything. After all, we're *your* family."

"Yes, you're probably right." After a deep breath, she admits, "I am tired." Her halting steps take her past them as she says, "It's so good you came to visit."

Mimi raises her eyebrows at her husband, and her voice is sweet as she agrees. "We only want to make sure you're okay. You're our number one concern. Have a good nap and we'll clean everything up from lunch."

The older women turns. "But you shouldn't be having to clean up. You're my guests."

Drummond stands as she's talking and leans to kiss her cheek. "No, we're family and just glad to be here."

He sits back down and they listen to Mrs. Bell's shuffling steps down the hall. When her door clicks shut, Mimi leans forward and whispers, "Did you hear from the Greens?"

Her husband crosses his long legs and taps the side of the table with his finger. "Yes. They sent a counteroffer."

Mimi's already large eyes bug out more, and she leans even closer to him. "And?"

"It's not good, but Jim's going to work with it." He stops talking, and holds his hand up at his wife. "Don't start..."

She smacks his hand as she stands. "Good luck dismissing me like that. It's my father's business you're losing. Or have already lost, for all I know. I'm going for a walk to that little place we had dinner last night to see about this party I now have to plan." She zips the warm-up jacket she's wearing and marches toward the front door.

"Um, what about the lunch dishes?" her husband asks.

"Virginia will do them later. I went and got lunch. *You* could clean it up, but I'm not sure you're capable."

As the glass front door softly closes behind her, Drummond looks at the table before he slowly rises. Lifting his coffee cup, he turns away then walks to the living room. "Planning parties and taking naps, I'm the only one doing any real work here. Why should *I* clean up?"

"George? You in your office?" Pearl shouts as she comes in

the front door. "George? There you are," she says as she opens his office door. "I know you're working, but I have to tell you. Whew, I'll sit for just a minute." She flops in the chair beside his desk. "I was taking the dogs down to the spa to get cleaned up for their playdate and guess who I ran into?"

She pauses, and he finally looks away from his computer screen. "Pearl, we've been married over forty years, surely in all that time you've realized I don't play guessing games. Especially when I'm in the middle of writing."

"The woman who was with Mrs. Bell last night! Her name's Mimi, and she seems very nice. We should have them over for drinks some afternoon." Her words fade off as she stares at nothing. Abruptly, she looks up and continues talking. "They are having a party. This weekend. Which night do you think would be best? Mimi wanted my advice."

George shrugs and types a few lines.

Pearl keeps talking and asking questions.

George keeps typing.

"Perfect!" she exclaims as she bounces up from her seat. "It's all worked out." She leans over and hugs her husband around his shoulders. "You are such a sweetheart to let me interrupt your work like this, but you are always so much help. Anyway, I can't sit here with you all day, I have work to do while the boys are at the spa." As she's leaving the room, she throws out, "We can discuss what we'll wear later."

As the door clicks and silence surrounds him again, George cracks a smile. "Honestly, I believe I might get more written while she's talking than when it's quiet."

"Aren't you cold?" Carlos asks as he pulls a chair out for Mimi to sit in.

She rolls her eyes. "This is practically spring, hell, summer in Wisconsin."

He joins her laugh. "Exactly. Keep wondering if I'll get like the other northerners after I live here a while and think fifty degrees is freezing. So you're visiting from Wisconsin? I moved here from New York."

"I can hear it in your accent. I'd like a glass of wine and then I need to talk to someone in charge about catering," she says as she turns the lunch menu to the wine selections. "A pinot noir," she says looking away from him and out towards the lake.

"Absolutely." He backs away, and in the kitchen he steps to the door of the small office to the side. "Sybil? There's a lady here who wants to talk about catering. Think she would prefer to talk to you rather than me. She's the woman visiting Mrs. Bell. They were here last night."

Sybil stands and then shakes her head at him. "When are you going to get used to married life and quit being so happy? You are in danger of losing your New York edge. People think you're just a silly waiter." She rolls her eyes at him. "See? Like that. You look goofy." As she passes him, she leans to him and whispers, "But I've never seen you look so happy and I'd give my right arm if my son was half as happy as you."

Carlos nods. "Me too. I miss Sam."

Sybil stands straighter and sniffs. "Get back to work. You know dinner hour comes early here."

His face folds into a grin, and he says louder than necessary, "Early dinner means I get home sooner to warm up my freezing wife. Yes, ma'am!" Hearing the southern twang slip into his *Yes ma'am*, he bursts out laughing. "My New York mother is going to kill me!"

9

"There's a spa for dogs," I say with my mouth half-full of chicken. "I'm not joking! That's what it's called. What everyone calls it. Miss Pearl will say, I'm taking the dogs, no, *the boys*, to the spa. They get cleaned up and, get this, she pays for them to stay extra to play with other dogs and it's called their play-dates." I swallow my food. "Momma, this chicken is delicious."

"Mr. Johnson, Bruce, kept the menu the same when he bought the diner. Only way to keep Mel cooking." She says that as her crossed leg bounces and she shifts in the chair at her little dining table. Mama is tiny and takes good care of herself. She still styles herself after the 1980's Madonna. Think that's why I never tried real hard with my looks, not possible to compete with her. Now, though, she's not looking up to her normal standards. And she's acting strange.

She eats like she's not even tasting the food. I know she eats this stuff at the diner all the time, but she usually wallows in *whatever* she's doing. She makes eating a bowl of cereal look like she's eating hand-churned peach ice cream. Makes you want cereal. "Momma, you okay?"

She doesn't answer. Just keeps bouncing, squirming, picking up fried chicken crumbs up with her fingers and shoving them in her mouth. "This spa for the dogs? Is it near where your house is going to be? I'd like to see that when I'm there next time."

"It's on the other side of the lake from me. There's some other shops going in like one with olive oils, which I don't understand, and then some offices. An insurance guy and repair place opened in that area, too." I scoop out another spoon of fried squash as she gets up to go to the sink. "Oh, speaking of shops, I went to that big, new place next to the diner. When did that open?"

Running water in the sink, she doesn't turn, just speaks up. "Halloween? Yeah, about that time. The market is why the diner is so busy on the weekends. It gets pretty crazy."

"Saw Mrs. Fulbright, my English teacher in high school. She has a booth there." Momma's back stiffens when I mention Mrs. Fulbright, but she keeps her back turned to me. "Momma, she said she was praying for Daddy."

Momma shuts off the water, but keeps looking out the little window above the sink. She's still for moment, then she turns and opens up the refrigerator. "Yeah, Rick's been sick." The refrigerator door hides her face so I wait, but she doesn't close the door or move.

"Sick? Daddy's been sick?"

"Yes, in the hospital sick, but he's coming home soon."

That brings me to my feet. "He's still in the hospital? What's wrong?" I lightly push the refrigerator door, and it swings shut, leaving Momma staring at its harvest gold door.

"It's his heart. He's going to be okay, but..." she turns to me, "how did you know?"

"Know? I didn't know anything. Still don't know anything. What happened?"

She waves her hand at me. "Just one of those things, but by time they did surgery it was a little more involved, so he's been in the hospital now about two weeks."

"Two weeks! And you didn't call me? I've talked to Daddy and he didn't mention anything like surgery! Just said he was starting a new job. Is he going to be okay?"

Momma takes a deep breath. "That's what they say. And it was supposed to just be a little procedure, but you know your daddy likes to keep things complicated." She kind of laughs as she picks up the dishrag and starts wiping down the counters. "He's supposed to come home end of the week, but, well, are you sure you didn't know?" She turns to me and shakes her head. "You turning up like this, just out of the blue. He didn't want me to call you. And you'll tell him I didn't call, right?"

"Right. But you *should've* called me."

She dismisses me again with a wave of her hand. "Naw, it's all being handled, but since you're here..." With a shrug, she pauses for a moment.

I reach out to lay my hand on her arm, but she sways around me and starts clearing the little table. So I pull my hand back and pick up my plate. "Okay. What do you need? Get things ready here for Daddy to come home?" Then I look around. "Oh my gosh, Momma, this place is spotless."

Being hungry, and used to ignoring the state of the trailer, I hadn't paid much attention when I got here. Plus, there was Mel's fried chicken waiting. Every flat surface shines, the windows are clean for the first time since I can remember. Even the rug at the door isn't covered in red-clay foot prints. And the refrigerator I thought of as so gross I didn't eat food out of it looks like it just came off the Sears showroom floor. A sniff only finds faint hints of our meal, but mostly lemon and clean.

She takes another deep breath and leans her hip against the counter. "Yeah, apparently I can clean. Had hoped I'd never have to display that talent outside my closet."

"Is the rest of the trailer like this?" I ask as I step down the narrow, panel-lined tunnel. The bathroom is first. It looks nothing like the one I grew up with. Same for the two bedrooms. "This looks like a brand new trailer."

In only a couple strides I'm back in the kitchen. Momma has her cigarettes in hand. "Let's step out on the porch so I can have a smoke."

"You don't smoke inside anymore?"

"No, your daddy needs to quit, and I'm going to try. But no promises. I gain one pound and I'm back to smoking."

We both put on our coats and step out to the front porch. The woods are quiet and everything is still like it gets sometimes right at sunset. Most the trees are bare, but several hold onto their dead, light brown leaves, which stir and rattle in the breeze. The sky is pink with touches of light blue. We sit in the two lawn chairs at the edge of the deck.

"Can we go see Daddy at the hospital?" I ask.

"He's being taken care of there. What I'm concerned about is later. When he comes home." She takes a long drag, and it's hard not to cough myself as she pulls it deep into her chest. Then releasing it, slow and steady, she looks at me. "Wasn't going to call you. Your daddy was clear he didn't want to bother you, but seeing as you showed up, I'm calling it a God thing and going with it."

"Okay, what? Anything you need."

"I need you to come back when your daddy gets out of the hospital and stay for a while." She stares me down, daring me to back away from my offer.

"Oh. Of course. He'll need someone here to help him recover. But won't he need a nurse?"

"I'm going to be his nurse."

"So, what do you need me for?"

"Mr. Johnson, the new owner at the diner, says my spot won't be open when I get back if I take off that much time. Up until this afternoon I was just planning on quitting and finding me another job later. But you know jobs aren't that easy to come by in Piney. Especially jobs where I can make decent money and that I really like. Like I said, it's getting busy. And law knows getting tips from them Atlanta people shopping next door is like taking candy from a baby."

"So you want me to stay here with Daddy? Okay, I can do that."

"No, here's the thing. I know your daddy's never been real private about his parts, but he's insistent that I'm the only one that's going to help him dress and such. He's been a real handful at the hospital, trying to do everything himself. There's no way he'd agree to you nursing him.

"So, I don't get it. What do you want me to do?"

You'll take over my shifts at the diner. Shouldn't be more

than a week or two." She takes another drag and speaks as she releases the smoke. "You said anything. If you don't want to help, no problem, but you asked what I needed. That's what I need." She turns to stare at me. "You said anything."

As the pink fades from the sky, I nod. "Yes, I did and I can see how Daddy wouldn't be keen on me nursing him. But Momma, I've never been a waitress. I don't think I'll be good at it."

She sighs. "You probably won't. But you'll be good enough to hold my spot. You can work hard if you have to, right? Law, its cold out here. And your daddy can't know anything about this until it's already happened." She walks past me, the old boards creaking in the cold. "Come in soon, don't freeze out here."

The door closes behind her. It's quiet and still again, but darker.

Much darker.

10

"**B**ut you've only been gone two nights," Miss Bell says into her phone. "Is everything okay there? Don't come rushing back for me. I'm fine. We're fine. Just fine." Clutching her robe around her, she lowers herself into the chair beside the sun-filled bedroom window while she listens.

"Oh my, Becca Sue. Yes, of course, you must be there to help your parents. Your poor father. But he'll be okay?" Her head bobs as she listens more. Then she takes a deep breath and asks, "So you think you'll be *here* through the weekend, at least? Because we're having a party. Mimi's handling everything, so you don't have to worry a bit. Just come and relax and have fun. What time will you be home today?"

Miss Bell ends the call after the young woman answers and lays her phone on the table beside her chair, talking to herself. "I don't like Becca Sue spending time back in that little town of hers. I don't like it at all." She stands and walks toward the closed door. When she reaches it she stops, lays her ear against it and listens, then whispers, "Maybe they're still asleep and I can have a cup of tea in peace."

Quietly, she turns the knob and pulls the door open. She jumps a bit as the heat kicks on with a whoosh that sounds loud in the silent house. She tiptoes down the hall and into the open living room area where the large ceramic tiles are washed in muted sunshine. The lake is covered in a layer of fog and wisps of it float in her backyard. "Oh!" she exclaims as she steps closer to the back windows and sees Drummond sitting in a chair facing the back of the house.

"Good morning. Hope I didn't scare you. I'm just sitting here enjoying the fog. I've never thought of Florida as having fog. Always just think of it as blazing hot."

"I didn't realize you were awake. Is Mimi up?"

"Oh yes, she's gone for a run. I heard you talking on the phone. Who's calling this early?"

Miss Bell nods, ignores his question, then turns to walk toward the kitchen. "Can I make you a cup of tea? Or coffee?"

He stands. "I'll come help you."

In the kitchen they work at getting cups, heating water, collecting tea bags and spoons and sweetener. Sugar for Miss Bell. Splenda for Drummond.

Picking up his cup and saucer, he motions towards hers. "Can I carry that for you?"

With a tight smile, she shakes her head. "No, I believe I'll take it into my room. Thank you."

She picks up her saucer and cup and, leaving the kitchen, turns to the left. Behind her, Drummond heads back to the chair in which she found him. Before he sits, and before she reaches her doorway, he says, "Wonderful how big this house is. Everyone gets their own space. Plenty of space."

Miss Bell smiles her same tight smile, enters her room, and closes the door. She sits her cup down on the table beside her chair and drops her shoulders. "He's right. It is a big house. A very big house. And I'm selfish to begrudge him my chair looking out at the lake. A different view every so often can be a very good thing." Properly admonished, she settles in her chair, intentionally not noticing the lumps, and looks out at the bare trees on the next property. And the cows standing around them. Cows that reduce the tax rates on the empty land, something she and Becca Sue keep meaning to look into.

"Yes. Cows can be as peaceful as the lake." Taking several deep breaths and a sip of her hot tea, she adds, "But I can't help but think what they smell like when I watch them." With a wrinkled nose, she closes her eyes and works on her tea, with only an occasional moo to break the silence.

"How's Eason?" Pearl asks as she steps through Ruth's big front door. Without waiting for an answer, she adds, "I'm thinking of getting a golf cart. We've all talked about getting them, so why haven't we?"

Eason pipes up from his office off the main room. "So we'll get some exercise. Golf carts are too easy. And, by the way, I'm fine!"

Ruth rolls her eyes. "Ignore him. He's been a bear lately."

Pearl lowers her voice. "Is he feeling badly? You said he was having tests done?"

With a glance towards her husband's office, Ruth pulls her friend into the kitchen and then across the shiny black tile floor, into the windowed alcove where a round table sits. Pearl's eyes are wide by time they get there.

However, Ruth only shrugs her shoulders a bit and says, "He's fine. Those tests were just his annual physical."

"Then why are we whispering? And why is he being a 'bear' as you put it?"

"Because he, well, he... oh, never mind. So there's a party this weekend at Mrs. Bell's? George told Eason you've talked to Mrs. Bell's company. Who are they?"

Pearl slumps into a chair at the white painted table. "I don't know. She's not very talkative, just didn't answer my questions. Ignored them like I never asked. She's rather cold. And he reminds me of a politician. Always says the right thing. I did find out his name is Drummond."

Ruth walks toward the kitchen sink. "Want a cup of coffee? And don't tell me about how you only have one cup and you've already had that. We all know you go by the coffee shack when you walk the dogs."

"Only sometimes," Pearl protests. "But yes, if you've already got it made I'll take a cup. A small cup." She sniffs. "Just trying to help the Coffee Shack lady get on her feet. How did you know I have her hide my coffee in a smoothie cup?"

Ruth sits both mugs on the table and grins. "I didn't."

Pearl laughs. "Okay, caught me. But I just don't think it's good for George to have too much caffeine. He's cranky enough as it is." They drink their coffee and gaze out at the fog-laced lake. Then, having held it in long enough, Pearl announces, "So, the real news is that Magnus is back."

"I saw lights over there last night," Ruth says. "So? What's happening with him and Sam and Sybil?"

Pearl sighs. "Who knows? She's back too, but they aren't together. And get this, he's talking about getting married!"

"Married? To whom?" Ruth demands. "Not Becca Sue."

Rolling her eyes and sighing for effect, Pearl answers, "For all I know. He thinks he's so mysterious, but he's really only annoying." With another round of rolling eyes and woebegone sighs, she finishes, "Becca Sue will probably be all over him when she finds out he's back."

"Now, Pearl, Becca Sue's been doing really well. I think she's completely over him."

Just one more heartfelt sigh, and Pearl stands up and walks away from the table. "That would be wise, but putting 'Becca Sue' and 'wise' in the same sentence is the very definition of ridiculous. Mark my words, she'll be sprawled all over his fancy couches in no time." She sits her empty coffee cup in the sink and walks toward the front door with her friend following her. "I need to go see Mimi, she wants my help with the party."

Ruth leans against the painted column in the entrance as Pearl buttons up her coat and twists her scarf around her neck. Both women glance up as Eason's raised voice on a phone call carries from his office. Ruth coughs and scurries to open the front door, speaking louder than necessary. "Okay, well, let me know about the party and if I can help with anything."

Out on the sidewalk, Pearl pauses and chews on her lower

lip as she wonders out loud, "What in the world was Eason talking about?"

11

"Wait'll Maggie finds out you're coming back to Piney—" I interrupt Jameson. "For just a bit. Not to stay. Just to help Momma keep her job."

"I know, but she'll still be excited," he says as he brushes crumbs off his dark gray suit coat.

We're sitting in the front seat of his big SUV that still smells new, so I keep breathing in that smell. He's on his way to work and I'm on my way back to Backwater, so we decided to meet at AJ's. AJ's is a gas station that sells biscuits. It sits about ten miles outside Piney towards the interstate and makes a perfect meeting place. There's nowhere to sit inside the restaurant, it's strictly take out. In the summer there are picnic tables to sit at, but this time of year everyone just eats in their car.

Taking a sip from my water bottle, I shake my head. "And you can't tell Maggie no ways. Momma says the only way for it to work is if Daddy doesn't know anything until I'm already there. I'm coming back Monday, working the afternoon shift with Momma, and then Daddy comes home from the hospital on Tuesday."

"You're staying all the way out at the interstate? Your momma works some awfully early shifts at the diner."

"No," I huff. "Momma about had a fit that I stayed out there last night. She never worried about what folks thought before, now she's all like, 'What'll folks think, my only child staying at a hotel!' I don't get what she's worried about, but guess I'm staying at the trailer." Running my thumbnail along the lines of my corduroy pants, I watch my hand and feel the heat from the sun on my shoulder. The heater is running, and the car is nice and warm. Jameson reaches over and puts his hand on top of mine, which is still on my thigh. Suddenly the car isn't just warm, it's hot. I keep my head down, staring at our hands, and wait for him to say something while a trickle of sweat runs down my back.

My hand is large, so none of Jameson's hand is actually touching my leg, but it feels like it is and my eyes are glued to it.

"Becca Sue, Maggie's not the only one looking forward to seeing more of you. All these months of texting and talking on the phone, it's really good to see you."

Still can't look up. "It's nice to be friends," I manage to squeak out.

He turns in his seat and leans toward me. The car is so big that I'd also have to lean towards him if anything's going to happen, but I don't move a muscle. He lifts his hand off mine and moves it onto my shoulder where lays it on the back of my neck. His other hand grabs the hand that has just been un-covered. As he massages my neck, I swallow and finally look at him.

Thank God we are here in this car in the middle of AJ's parking lot on a sunshiny morning. He's got everything inside me humming. We've flirted a bit on the phone, but sitting this close to him and him looking at me like that. Oh...

He lifts my hand to his mouth and kisses the back of it. "Becca Sue," he says and my lips part because I'm breathing so heavy. "Becca Sue, I plan on wooing you like you deserve when you come back next week," he whispers as he kisses my hand again and lays it back down on my leg. He gives my neck one more gentle squeeze and pulls away from me. "Now, I have to get to work, and you need to get on the road."

My legs are wobbly as I get out of his car. He meets me on the other side and walks me to my car. I hurry and get in so I don't grab him right here in the parking lot. My daddy is not supposed to know I came to town and me jumping Jameson Mason in AJ's parking lot would be all over Piney before the biscuit crumbs fall off my sweater.

Jameson motions for me to lower my window, and when I do, he leans in quickly and kisses me before I know what's happening. Then he straightens up and walks off to his car. Rolling the window up, I can't help but smile.

I've never been wooed before.

Driving over the bridge onto the island, I laugh to remember I didn't even realize I was on an island when I moved here last summer. My laughter fades when I remember Jameson was the last person I talked to before that drive, too. We were in a little office in the funeral home, and we were signing papers. I hadn't been allowed to go to the graveyard for Caleb's burial or the big gathering at Caleb and Jameson's parents' house. I'd walked down to the schoolyard and sat on the swings and thought about things and waited for my ex-husband's brother.

Jameson had explained the afternoon before Caleb's funeral, when he came to find me at Momma and Daddy's trailer, that he had an idea that would let me get away from Piney for good. He told me about the house in Florida, plugged the directions into my phone, told me to pack up whatever I wanted to take, and then asked me to wait for him to come back to the funeral home after the burial and the reception.

Boy, if last summer anyone would've told me Jameson Mason would be kissing me, and that I'd like it, well, I'da called them crazy. He was always so mean, well maybe not mean, but cold. Miss Bell says that's because he always liked me, but I was married to his brother. Miss Bell thinks me and Jameson would be good together. She really didn't like me being with Magnus. She liked Sam, but she says now that she knows he's Magnus' son, that I should forget him, too.

She'll be tickled that Jameson wants to 'woo' me. She likes old-fashioned words like that. Turning left onto the road to Backwater, I roll down the window. It feels like spring, even though lots of brown still fills the forests on the sides of the road. Up in Georgia, only a couple hours away, there is more gray, as the trees are all bare. Except for the pines, of course.

I park in my old driveway and get out of the car. My office (that is still weird to say) is where the dining room was in my house. Right to the side of the front door. Mr. Worth had it turned into an office first thing. Really he just moved in some file cabinets and two desks. One for me, and one for him to use when he's here. I still mainly do whatever he tells me to. But I'm getting the hang of things. Working out construction schedules, doing background checks on people who want to open a business here, keeping the maintenance crews busy, and promoting Backwater. He told me I could do it, and apparently I can, since he hasn't fired me yet.

Work vans are parked out front, and, like I assumed, the front door is unlocked. I step into my old home and turn to the left to swing into my office, but I come to a quick stop. "Mr. Drummond?"

"Oh, Becca Sue. Back already?" He unfolds from where he was bent over the filing cabinets, but his hands push at the files in them.

I sit my purse down on the chair next to Mr. Worth's desk. My chair is on the other side of where Miss Bell's relation is looking in the filing cabinet behind my desk. "What are you doing?"

"Just being nosy," he says as he slides the drawer closed and walks toward me. As he passes, he says, "Glad you're here. You can take over the party from Mimi. She's used to paying someone to do things like that." He looks around where the old living room was. Now the open room is empty except for boxes of tables and chairs and bathroom fixtures. "This place is shaping up. I need to speak to the workers out back." He turns to the back doors and adds over his shoulder, "I'll let Virginia know you've returned." Then he's gone.

I hurry to look in the file drawer he had open, but I can't tell which file he shoved back into place. Nothing seems messed with or unusual, but I can smell his yucky cologne. It's too minty and makes my nose itch.

They need to go back to Wisconsin. Soon.

Sliding into my chair, it doesn't take long to get busy. I didn't plan on working today, thought I'd be in Piney. But if I'm going to be up there all next week, and maybe longer, I've got things to do. Everything is quiet as all the work is outside in the pool area today, so I don't even look up until my stomach growls so loud it startles me.

"Was that your stomach?" a familiar voice says from around the corner of the office doorway.

Now my stomach clinches. "Magnus?"

"Sure is, darlin', and I come bearing gifts." He saunters into my office with a basket. A basket that is noisy. Glasses tinkling, paper crinkling, and, wait, meowing?

As I stand, he sits the basket down on my desk. There's the glasses, big margarita ones, and they're all nestled in clear, crinkly paper, and there's what's causing the meowing. A tiny gray and white kitten. He, or she, is batting the cutest paw at the ribbons hanging down from the handle.

"Oh my word, Magnus. A kitty? What's its name?" I weave my hand inside the shiny paper and find his little head. He pushes into my hand and then starts climbing up it. When he finds my sweater, he makes more progress, so I cradle him against my arm with my other hand. Pulling him out, I bring him to my chest. "Is it a boy or a girl?"

Magnus leans up to also pet the sweet thing and says, "It's a boy, and its name is whatever you choose."

"Why? Is it mine?"

Magnus cocks his head and smiles. "It's the least I could do, right? You like him?"

My eyes well up and I start to sniffle, but not in an allergy way. "Oh, I love him. What should I name you?" As I rub noses with my kitty, I can't help but be aware that Magnus is standing much closer to me than I ever planned to let him stand again. But... he brought me a pet. So I ignore him and focus on what's in my hands.

Magnus puts his hand on my back as he looks over my shoulder at his gift. Just as I stiffen and start to move away he sighs and says, "You told me you'd never had a pet."

"Really? I told you that?" I try to remember telling him that. It's true, but I don't remember ever thinking about it. I never expected to own a pet, so why would I mention it?

He puts a finger under my chin and turns my head to look at him. "Honey, you weren't complaining or wishing, you never do that. You just said it as a fact of life one day. It made me sad. Every girl should have a pet, at least once."

I swear to God, I could go to bed with him right now.

However, he moves away and picks up the basket. "Are you done with all this?" He waves at the paper-filled desk. "It is happy hour. Come show me your new house."

We walk along the lake, ignoring whomever might be sitting on those screen porches wrapped in blankets, watching us. The sun is still up, but just barely, by time we reach my cabin.

Finally released from my arms, the kitten pounces around the concrete slab floor. I lean some boards across the doorways so he can't escape, but he's happy playing with the scraps of wood and loose papers lying around.

"See, it's all open. The kitchen is over there against that side wall. All this will be the living room and there's a guest bedroom back there. I don't know why I need a guest room, but the builders and Ashleigh say I can't build just a one-bedroom house. Then upstairs is going to be my room. Wanna see?" I ask as I turn and see him standing looking out the window cutouts across the lake.

He laughs. "How did you do this? It should be ridiculous, a cabin in the woods here. In this subdivision. Even with the leaves off the trees, this feels secluded. Private."

I pause on the bottom step. "Well, I didn't do it. Roger made it all happen."

He comes toward me and picks up the kitten as he's trying to follow me up the stairs. "But I can tell, it's all your idea." He talks to the kitten and in a playful voice says, "Why yes, Miss Becca Sue, we sure would like to see your room."

When I look for a wink, or his usual smirk, he's focused on the cat. "Come on then," I say as I move up the unfinished wooden stairs.

And I was not stomping.

12

"Oh you *are* home!" Miss Bell greets Becca Sue when she comes in the front door. Miss Bell is seated in the living room, but she gets up to hug her housemate. "Drummond said you were at your office earlier today. Poor girl, you've been working all day after driving from Georgia?"

Becca Sue sits her suitcase down and smooths her hair that's come untucked from the braid Ashleigh put it in yesterday at the hotel. "Some. It got kind of late."

Mrs. Bell gives her hug. "Oh, will this winter never end? It feels like it gets dark right after lunch."

Mimi and Drummond laugh from the living room. "Winter? Try Wisconsin in January," Mimi says. Then she continues, "Drummond says you want to take over planning the party since you're familiar with everyone here. Fine by me. Plus, should the guests of honor be hosting their own party?" She laughs again and Becca Sue looks down at Miss Bell.

Miss Bell whispers, "I think she's a little tipsy."

"I'm going to put my stuff away."

The small woman reaches up and gives her another hug. "I know you were only gone a couple nights, but I missed you." She lowers her voice back to a whisper. "You don't have to do the party if you don't want to. I'm fine either way."

Becca Sue smiles. "Of course I want to help with the party. It'll be fun. Now, I want to get unpacked and changed. Take a shower." She's halfway down the hall when Mrs. Bell calls out, "Did you hear Magnus is back?"

Yanking the rubber band out of the tail of her bedraggled braid with the hand not dragging her roller suitcase, Becca Sue mumbles, "Yeah, I heard," as she shoves her door closed.

Mimi purrs, "Who's Magnus? He's come up in a couple conversations today. That Pearl woman said he needs to be on the guest list for Saturday, but she said it with both eyebrows arched like it meant something. The restaurant owner refused a call from him while we were meeting, and when she saw who was calling, she said his name like she smelled something bad."

Miss Bell stands behind the couch, but she doesn't say anything for a moment. Long enough for Drummond to take notice and look up from his phone. He scowls and asks, "What's the name? Magnus?"

Miss Bell fiddles with the buttons on her sweater and finally says, "Yes, that's it. I'm going to make a cup of tea. Anyone else interested?" She steps toward the kitchen. Drummond gets up and follows her.

In a loud whisper he says as he enters the dimly lit kitchen, "Think my wife could use some coffee." He sets the coffee to brewing while the older woman puts her tea pot on to boil. Then leaning against the counter, he fold his arms and asks, "Magnus is a funny name, is it his first or last?"

"First."

So does this Magnus, wait, what kind of last name goes with a first name like that?"

Miss Bell rolls her eyes as she reaches into her box of tea bags. "Llord. His last name is Llord."

"And he lives here?"

"Yes. He's been back in New York for a few months."

"Oh, so that's why people are talking about him, he's just returned. Must be a pretty popular guy."

Miss Bell frowns. "Well, he likes to think so."

Drummond gets a coffee cup from the cabinet. "So I assume this Magnus Llord person will be at the party?" With his back to her, he waits for her answer.

Miss Bell's sigh is partially hidden beneath the whistle of the tea kettle, but her quiet "I suppose so" is what he's obviously waiting for because as soon as she says it, he walks out the other door of the kitchen mumbling about making a phone call.

"Guess I'm supposed to take his wife her coffee," Miss Bell says looking at the empty cup sitting beside the coffee maker.

"There. I told you something is really wrong with Eason," Pearl says as she hangs up her phone. "George, didn't I tell you?"

Her husband lays down the book he's reading beside the fireplace and agrees. "Yes, you did tell me that, but I can't believe Eason wouldn't have mentioned it to me. It's probably just you letting your imagination get away with you again. But what is your newest bit of evidence?"

"That was Ruth. She wanted to ask if it would be okay if their son Bradley could be included on the guest list for the party. Bradley was just here at Christmas. Why in the world would he be back already unless his father was truly and honestly sick?" Pearl shudders and pulls the soft blue throw farther up her shoulders.

George shrugs. "Not like Bradley always has a lot to keep him occupied with his job, since he's not usually tied to an office."

"It's just not good for young men, or young women for that matter, to not have a profession. To not have something that ties them down to the real world. Like our children. A nurse and an engineer. Good and steady, or like myself, a teacher."

"Not like their old man, a writer. Can't get much more untied to the real world than a fiction writer," George says with a laugh. "Never thought about it but maybe that's why our kids are such stick in the muds."

"They are not stick in the muds, just good solid people. Bradley King, on the other hand, seems to always be involved with a new scheme."

"They are not schemes. He's an investor, a very *smart* investor. He makes more than both our children and his brother combined."

"Well, his marriage is rocky."

George grunts. "True. But those things happen. He has two kids, twins, right?"

"Yes, wonder if they'll be with him." She thinks for a moment, then sniffs and shakes her head. "No, I'm sure Ruth would've mentioned if she was going to have to be watching the twins. One is a handful at two, but two two-year-olds? Heavens!"

They both stare at the fire in the white marble fireplace for a bit. With fake gas logs and a thermostat starter, it's no work and makes the early nights cozy in the big, glass-walled room.

"Maybe I'll see if Eason is available for lunch tomorrow," George says as he picks his book back up.

Pearl snuggles deeper in her blanket, reopens her *Coastal Living* magazine, and smiles. "What a wonderful idea."

"How is he? Do you think he misses me?" Becca Sue asks with the side of her face pressed to her phone, sitting on her bed at Miss Bell's.

"He's busy exploring my coffee table right now, but I'm sure he misses you. Come up with a name yet?" Magnus stretches out on his wide, olive-green couch and lifts the kitten off the table, onto his lap.

"No. Maybe I should've brought him with me here. Miss Bell probably wouldn't care."

"Probably wouldn't, but didn't you say she has guests? Just make sure nobody's allergic. But, hey, whatever you want. He's all yours."

Becca Sue stares around her new room, small and cramped with her stuff she hadn't found a place for yet. "No, I'd be afraid of him getting into something until I get things put away. Plus, where would I put a litter box? Does he know where it is at your place?"

Magnus laughs. "You should see him. He's found the tassels on the pillows. Hey, hey, don't tear it up. He sure is feisty! Yeah, I showed him the litter box, it's in the laundry room. He did his business and came out like a champ. Although it has a cover so I didn't actually see him do his business, but he looked awfully proud of himself."

"Oh, I miss him so much. Where would I put his litter box here? It'd be easier if that Drummond and Mimi weren't here. Shoot."

"Honey, don't sound so sad. I probably should've waited to get you a kitten until you were settled in your house."

Becca Sue sits up straight. "No! He's my kitten. He was meant for me. It'll all be okay."

"And you can always come over here anytime to play with him," Magnus offers.

She rolls her eyes and smirks. "Oh, of course I can come over there anytime. To play."

"Tomorrow. Come over tomorrow morning."

Becca Sue's chin juts out. "And I should bring champagne for mimosas too, right?"

Magnus chuckles and says to the kitten, "Let go of my pillow, you rascal. Sure. Mimosas are great."

Becca Sue stands up. "Of course they're great. Just like last summer—"

He interrupts, seeming to not even hear her, "I won't be back until around two in the afternoon, so you should probably give the little guy some lunch. I'm looking for the pamphlet they gave me at the pet store, but I don't see it. I'll pick up some more kitten food, too, when I'm out. Oh, look! Becca Sue, he's heading to the laundry room. Well, I'll be, he marched right into his litter box. I'll leave the screen door on the porch unlocked in the morning when I leave, so just come on in."

"Okay." She sits back down on the bed, listening to Magnus wander around his house talking to her kitten. "And, um, you want me to leave it unlocked when I leave?"

"Sure, but I need to go. I didn't put out any water for him. You sleep tight, okay?"

"Okay." Becca Sue lays down the phone, but continues to stare at it. "Okay," she says again, but this time it sounds more like a question.

13

"Let me see him," Ashleigh says as she comes in through Magnus' screened porch. "Oh lord, he's adorable!"

"I know," Becca Sue agrees as she cuddles her tiny friend under her chin. "You want to hold him?"

"Screw cat hair, give him to me. Wait, let me take off my jacket." Ashleigh pulls off her gray wool blazer and lays it on the back of a chair. "You don't think he'll pick my blouse, do you? Here, give me that throw." She takes the jewel-toned throw Becca Sue offers her from the back of the couch and wraps it around herself. "Now, give him to me." She coos at the kitten as she walks around Magnus' living room.

"Sit down," Becca Sue invites. "This is the most comfortable furniture in the world." Two couches face each other, one deep olive green and the other dark red. The floors are covered in layers of rich carpets. Chairs just as deep as the couches are gold, and all the fabrics are luxurious.

"I've never been here, you know. He's paid some designer a pretty penny," Ashleigh says as she perches on the edge of a chair. "What's this sweetie's name?"

"I don't know. Nothing seems to fit. I think he wants down."

"I agree," Ashleigh says as she puts the squirmy kitten on the floor. They watch him prance around in the morning sunshine and Ashleigh sighs. "I want a baby so bad I can't see straight."

"A baby? Not just a baby kitten? I thought it was your mother and Carlos' mother that wanted a baby."

"Well, they do. But I do, too. Carlos and I decided to not use birth control since we're both ready, so should be any day now that I'll have an announcement to make." She stands up and folds the throw. "However, right now I have to get to work. Have to cover the town planning meeting this morning."

"Well, you sure look pretty."

The large woman pulls her blazer on over her white satin blouse and gray wool skirt. She takes a bow. "Thank you. Catch more bees with honey, my grandma says, and I need some good quotes so this story won't be so boring. Can I go out the front door?"

"Sure, let me get the cat. Make sure he won't run out." With the kitten scooped up, Becca Sue opens the heavy front door and Ashleigh passes her by, but then turns.

"You didn't sleep here last night, did you?" she asks.

"No! I haven't even seen Magnus today."

Ashleigh studies her friend's face. "You seem a little too comfortable here."

Becca Sue rolls her eyes and steps back inside. "Go to work. You're crazy."

As the door seals shut, Ashleigh walks to her car talking to herself. "I might be crazy, but, girlfriend, you've slept with a guy for a lot less than a cat." She settles in the car seat and looks at herself in the rearview mirror. "But then, haven't we all?"

"So I hear Bradley's coming to town," George says as Eason settles into his chair. One of the four chairs at the restaurant table has been removed to accommodate George's wheelchair. Facing each other, they both have a view of the fogged-in coastline through the old window beside them.

"Yeah," Eason says. "Kind of nice this time of year to have everything to ourselves, isn't it? Summer we couldn't possibly get this table for lunch. I'm having clam chowder. You?"

"Order two. But I'm not doing the buffet. Just want some fried shrimp and hush puppies. So, how are you, Eason? Bradley coming back so soon because of your health?"

The tall, white-haired doctor laughs and eases back in his chair. "Ruth warned me Pearl was all concerned and had put you up to this lunch."

George smiles and nods, then raises his eyebrows with a quick tip of his head.

"I'm fine. Just my routine physical and everything looks good. I told Ruth her worrying about nothing is what got Pearl's imagination working. Bradley is just coming to check out a business opportunity in Backwater."

George's full face wrinkles, then settles. "Really? Bradley is interested in Backwater?"

"Two cups of chowder. We'll order when you bring them," Eason says to the waiter. "Yes, one of his partners works with Roger Worth, so he's heard all about us. Of course, when I mentioned it..." he shrugs. "Working out just like Roger thought it would." He leans forward, elbows on the table, and lowers his voice. "Talk is that once the local economy picks up, the county is going to put some of the restrictions and taxes back onto Backwater. The time to invest is now. Get grandfathered in so when things change, you're already set."

"What kind of business is he talking?" George's low voice mimics his friend's.

Eason straightens up, looks down at the table, and shakes his head. "It's not ready to talk about yet. Ah, here comes our soup."

As the cups of chowder are placed on the table, George hands his menu to the waiter and orders a fried shrimp basket. Eason chimes in with the same. While George blows on his spoonful of soup he watches his friend. Then he says, "Maybe I should talk to Bradley."

Eason winks and grins as he puts his spoon into his mouth.

Then digging in for another bite, he says, "Don't tell this to my Boston daughter-in-law, Olivia, but this is the best chowder I've ever eaten."

"Is she still your daughter-in-law? Thought they were getting a divorce."

"She's mother to two of our grandchildren. Besides, divorce isn't final. Ruth has a plan."

"Ruth? That sounds more like Pearl. You think there's any hope?"

"Always hope in a mother's heart, I guess. You know Bradley has done well. Very well, in fact. But..." Eason scoops the last bite of soup up and shrugs as he eats it.

"But there's *well*, and then there's Boston Baets well," George finishes for him.

The doctor sighs. "Yes, old families like the Baets, with their money and foundations and names, are impossible to compete with. Especially when you're someone like Bradley who doesn't believe in competing. He only believes in winning."

"Is he interested in winning Olivia back?"

The waiter appears with their shrimp baskets, and both men make room on the table. Eason picks up a golden brown shrimp by the tail. "As I said, Ruth has a plan."

"Ruth, that's the stupidest thing I've ever heard. Miss High-and-Mighty Olivia isn't coming here. She'd rather die!" Pearl exclaims. "Matter of fact, I've heard her say those exact words: 'I'd rather die than go to Florida.'"

"But that was in the summer. Before she had two-year-old twins. You watch, she'll come."

Pearl rolls her eyes as she collects a bite of avocado and romaine from her salad. "This is delicious, but I can't enjoy it because I know the guys are eating chowder and fried shrimp at Walker's."

"Probably, but don't think about it. Tell me about this Mimi person. I'm stopping in at Mrs. Bell's after lunch."

"Shoot, I have my hair appointment or I'd go with you. *I* like Mimi. You know, she asked for *my* help with the party on Saturday, but then Becca Sue came home and took over. Mimi was rather dismissive the first time I met her, but she was probably just tired. Plus, we *were* with Magnus. You know he turns most people off."

Ruth nods. "He does at that. I so hope Becca Sue can resist him this time. He can be very relentless when he wants something. But, back to the party, it hardly seems like Becca Sue to take over anything. Especially a party. I *was* surprised to hear she was back yesterday. Rather short trip home, wasn't it?"

"But she's going back right after the weekend. Who knows with *those* people? I'm done with this," Pearl says as she places her fork on her plate. "I'll take the rest home and have it for lunch tomorrow." She waves at their waitress as she says to her friend, "I wish you good luck with Olivia and Bradley, but I just don't see it happening. Her family has been upset ever since they started dating. Her mother probably has a line of *appropriate* suitors in that fancy parlor of the *family* home as we speak."

Ruth takes one more bite then places her fork down. "Bradley should be here this afternoon, so we'll see. You know, Pearl, I find the older I get, the more exhausting being young looks."

14

"She's awful! So skinny and, just—just awful," Ashleigh says to Carlos as she lifts a pan of pulled pork out of the oven. "Is this it? Can I turn the oven off?"

"No, I need to brown the meringue on the banana pudding. Set that there and I'll get it in a minute."

She sets the pan down, removes her oven mitt, and leans against the counter. "Who would've ever guessed you'd be cooking up a Southern feast a year ago?"

Carlos kisses her neck, saying, "You inspire me. You bring out the good ol' boy in this Italian soul." He straightens up and fastens the top clasp on his chef's jacket. "The guests of honor didn't seem as thrilled when they heard the menu Miss Bell asked Becca Sue to order. Barbecue sliders, deep-fried catfish nuggets, slaw, hush puppies, deviled eggs, fried pimento cheese balls, and banana pudding for dessert. Your friend Mimi almost passed out right there in the living room when she saw it written out on the blackboard."

"I know. Like I said, she's awful." Ashleigh looks around Miss Bell's kitchen. "Can I help with anything else? Guess I need to get back out there and keep Mimi and Becca Sue from killing each other."

Arranging a platter of barbecue sliders, Carlos laughs. "Yeah, who knew Becca Sue had such a temper? What's she so mad about anyway? She had one of my helpers ready to quit today."

Ashleigh sighs and closes her eyes. "You *know* what I think it is. But Lord knows I won't mention getting laid to her again. 'Bout got my head bit off." At the kitchen door, she says, "Holler if you need any help. Or if I look like I'm about to slug somebody, *anybody*, including Becca Sue."

The large living room is half full of people. The day had turned mild, so with the patio doors open, guests wander outside, enjoying the waning rose and orange streaks of the sunset. Ashleigh swerves to the dining room to look at the food setup. Carlos' catering was adding some needed extra money to the family bank account and he enjoyed it, so it was a win all around. Sybil was happy to shift most of the catering jobs to Carlos, and the wait staff at Sybil's enjoyed the extra money, too.

Ashleigh turns back toward the living room at the sound of raised voices. "What now?" But then she laughs when she realizes someone has turned on the TV and the raised voices concern the playoff game. Drummond is cheering on his Green Bay Packers, who just scored.

"Green Bay's winning? Weren't they supposed to get trounced?" Ashleigh asks as she comes into the crowd around the TV.

"All that matters is the end score," Drummond says. Then he leans down to speak into Ashleigh's ear. "Your friend is pouting in her room."

She turns toward the hallway, muttering, "Great. Becca Sue, you've got Drummond Bell whispering in my ear."

Ashleigh knocks on the door and waits a moment before opening it. "It's about time to eat. Why are you in here?"

Becca Sue points at the suitcase on the bed, which she's filling. "I can't stay here one more day. Living here has been pure hell. I'm not leaving for Piney until tomorrow afternoon but might as well pack tonight. I can't take one more minute of Mimi and Magnus pawing at each other!"

"You coming out to eat? Just ignore them. Besides, they aren't actually pawing at each other. Seems more like Drummond and Mimi are infatuated with Magnus and his new found wealth. And he can be charming. I seem to remember someone falling under his spell last summer."

"Shut up."

Ashleigh comes on into the room and closes the door behind her. She doesn't come any closer to her friend. "She's a flirt. He's a flirt. You're not interested in him, right? Please tell me you are not interested in him."

Becca Sue doesn't answer, but shoots her friend a fiery look.

"Ignore them. Act like they're your mother and father. You sure learned over the years to ignore them when they flirted with every Tom, Dick, and Harriet around, right?"

"Whatever. Go back out there and help your husband. I'll be out in a minute."

"Okay." Ashleigh re-enters the hallway to find Miss Bell waiting there.

"Is Becca Sue okay?"

"Think so. Are you having fun?"

Miss Bell screws up her face. "No, Drummond and Mimi are ruining everything. They are both falling all over Magnus. Did you hear how much he inherited? I knew there were some houses his aunt left him, but apparently her death left him extremely wealthy. Hopefully it will get warmer in Wisconsin soon, and they will go back home."

"Really?" Ashleigh bites her lip and then takes a deep breath before asking, "Miss Bell, do you really think they're going to leave?"

The old woman suddenly looks frail. She reaches out a hand to touch the wall, but doesn't look up. "That's what Becca Sue asked me."

From the living room, they hear Carlos announcing the food is ready. Miss Bell turns that way. "Let's not think about any of that. Your husband has put on a true Southern feast to enjoy." She halts for a moment and half turns. "Is Becca Sue coming out?"

Ashleigh looks at the bedroom door. "She said she is. Maybe things will settle down once she goes to Piney. It's been a rough couple of days."

Miss Bell laughs weakly. "Tell me about it. You should try living with the three of them." When they get to the living room, she raises her voice and her hand. "Everyone, everyone, I'd like to say something before we eat. I want to welcome Drummond and Mimi Bell and hope everyone gets to meet them while they are here on their short visit. I'd also like to thank Carlos Ricci for the lovely food and drinks. Let's also welcome Bradley King to Backwater."

The tall young man quickly wipes his bored look away and smiles. He lifts his bottle of beer at Miss Bell and says, "Great to be here."

Miss Bell smiles back at him. "Everyone enjoy!"

"Good luck on that," Becca Sue snarks from behind Mrs. Bell and Ashleigh. "And hort visit? My foot!"

"There you are," Miss Bell says, then adds in a whisper, "I'm just trying to help them get the message." She grabs her young housemate's arm. "Come eat with me. Ignore them and try to behave. Come talk to that Bradley King. He seems like a nice young man. Besides, Magnus is loving how you and Mimi are fighting over him."

Becca Sue jerks her arm back. "I'm not fighting over that hound dog. He disgusts me. She can have him. It just feels... it feels... disrespectful to you." She says this as she pushes past them in the hallway. She leaves them to follow, but before they move much, Ashleigh bends down to the older woman's ear.

"I'm thinking her getting out of town for a bit isn't a bad idea."

Miss Bell nods. "I agree. I'm beginning to miss the Becca Sue that didn't care about anything."

"Yes!" Ashleigh exclaims. "That's what I was trying to explain to Carlos. I'm afraid she'll fall for Magnus, again, if only out of boredom." She shrugs and grimaces at Miss Bell.

The older woman returns her grimace. "I know. Me too. Sooner she leaves, the better. Then Magnus can be as big a fool as he wants."

They both shudder and join the line for the buffet.

15

Cold pimento cheese balls make a great breakfast when you're racing down the backroads of Florida. Racing away from a huge mistake. Oh, and coffee. Coffee and cold pimento cheese balls.

Miss Bell heard me leave. I know she did. She hears everything. Even she was too ashamed to face me.

Barely above the horizon, the sun shoots beams through the foggy pine forests. The bright light in my right window is giving me a headache. Yes, I'm sure it's the sun and not the pecan-flavored whiskey giving me a headache. Or sleeping on a wood floor. Or the—yeah, definitely not that.

"Let's walk to your cabin." That's all he said. That's all I had to do. I could've even said, "No, we're at a party. Maybe later. Another day."

Or I could've not taken the bottle of pecan-flavored whiskey from the bar when we left. Yes, that would've probably been a better decision. But now, it was *totally* him that figured out the fireplace worked, then went and got firewood. Yeah, that's not my fault. The blankets? Okay, maybe my fault.

I turn up the radio, although on a Sunday morning on the backroads of the Florida-Georgia line, the selection is preaching, gospel music, or old-time country. Old-time country works to keep me distracted and awake. Didn't get much sleep last night.

Neither did Bradley King.

16

"**D**addy! Daddy!"

"Hey, love bugs!" Bradley answers the two toddlers scurrying his way. "Morning, Mom." He scans the living room and kitchen as he lifts one, then the other, of the kids up. They jabber, and he vaguely responds as he carries them to the kitchen table where Ruth sits. "So, Olivia's here?"

Ruth nods, but doesn't look up.

One by one, he slides the kids down his legs and sets them on the floor. He rubs his hands over his dark beard and short hair as he steps to the counter. "Why'd she get here so early this morning?" He asks as he pours a cup of coffee. "Need more coffee, Mom?"

"No, thank you. Olivia and the kids got a ride on some friend's private plane to be here last night to surprise for you. However, weather issues delayed things, and they didn't land until early this morning. Still wanting to surprise you, I didn't tell you." She stares down her tall son, her words sharp. "How clichéd to have to say, *I guess the surprise was on us.*"

"Yeah, sorry about that." Bradley sits at the table, which is a sign for the little boy and girl dressed in matching green footie pajamas to come sit, too. As they scramble to climb up the other seats, he shrugs. "It just happened. Crazy that we were leaving the cabin when y'all pulled up. Figured I'd wait until you got the kids settled to come home. It's a shame we were trying to sneak out before light. A couple more minutes, and there would have been no problem."

"Honestly? No problem?" Ruth shoots up from the table. She brings a box of animal crackers to the table and gives each kid a couple. Then she goes into the living room, bringing back their sippy cups. "Olivia has gone for a run. You're father has gone back to bed. Son, had you even met Bec—her before last night?"

"No. It just happened. She seemed frustra—I mean, lonely, and we got to talking at the party. We were both kind of bored."

"But you came home last night after the party. You told us good night."

He rubs the back of his neck and stretches his shoulders. "Well, it was cold, and I knew y'all had that stack of firewood. So I came for that, and well, no need to tell you I was going back out."

"That doesn't sound like it 'just happened.' That sounds like there was some planning. And lying."

"Mom, c'mon. I haven't lived in your house in forever. I'm grown. You know about me and Olivia." He whispers her name as he looks at his toddlers who are having their own conversation about their assortment of crackers. They've taken advantage of the adults talking to pour themselves a small mountain of bears, tigers, and elephants. "Besides, you shouldn't have tried to surprise me. That's ridiculous."

"Your mother is not ridiculous," comes a gravelly voice from the hallway. "Ridiculous is what we had to watch walking up the street as we drove our daughter-in-law and grandchildren home this morning. All giddy about how they were going to be so quiet sneaking into Daddy's room to wake him up. But, no! There's Daddy coming down the street." He drops his voice to a murmur, "Wrapped in a blanket with another woman."

Grandpa gives hugs and kisses to the kids while Ruth pours him a cup of coffee and brings him a pill caddy. As he pours the morning's pills into his hand, he asks Ruth. "Did you tell him the rest?"

Ruth sighs. "No." She sits down. "I borrowed a condo from friends up in Savannah, on the beach at Tybee, for you and Olivia to have a getaway without the kids. Work on getting back together."

Bradley cringes. "Mom. That's sweet, but no. No, thanks. She can take it. I'll stay here with you and the kids." He stands up then leans forward on the table towards the twins. "Pancakes? Who wants pancakes? Daddy's going to take a shower and then come make pancakes for my sweeties."

The kids cheer, and their grandparents smile at them. The pancake promiser backs away from the table, then heads to his room. Inside, he closes the door and smiles as he takes off his shirt. "That worked out well. One fun night got me out of a weekend trip to hell with Princess Popsicle." He whistles and turns on the shower. "Florida is definitely agreeing with me." The whistling continues throughout the shower. However, as he's toweling off, it stops when there's a knock on the partially closed bathroom door.

"Are you done? Your parents put us in the room together."

He sticks his head out the door and greets his wife. "Oh, hi. I'll be done in a minute." He shuts the door and restarts his whistling. Finally, wrapped in a towel with his hair combed, he comes out. "It's all yours."

"Is the bathroom as trashed as the room is?" Olivia motions to the discarded clothes. She's still in her running clothes, which cling to her thin, toned body. She shakes her head as she passes, letting her long, auburn ponytail sweep from side to side.

"My parents don't have live-in staff, so we'll see how it looks when you've had to pick up after yourself a few days."

She stops so that they are nose to nose. Her voice is quiet, but clipped. "I will not be here a few days. Although, from what I and the kids saw this morning, their daddy doesn't really use this room either." She dismisses him with a sniff and a sharp turn toward the bathroom.

"No, hey, that was just—"

"Just a one-night stand? Typical," she replies, voice never raised above a whisper. She quietly presses the bathroom door closed.

Bradley whips off his towel, muttering, "Slam the door. Just once, slam the damn door!"

As if she's going to answer him, the door opens and she looks out. "Your mother and I decided we are all going to brunch. Please dress appropriately." She arches a sculpted eyebrow. "Although, is that even a thing here?"

She closes the door, and he realizes he'd grabbed his towel back up to cover himself. He throws it at the door with a curse.

"Sylvia should consider having a Sunday brunch at her place. It seems like everyone in Backwater is here today." Pearl greets the King family as they enter the dining room at the Ritz. "Oh, I better go. They have our table ready. We'll say hello later."

Olivia surveys the room and nods to several people. "Emerson, hold Mommy's hand. Phillips, get off your grandfather's shoulders and walk like a big boy."

Eason lets the boy down as he rolls his eyes at his wife, but keeps a light tone. "There you go, buddy. Want to hold my hand?"

The blond tyke shakes his head and answers, "No. Big boy." As the waiter leads Olivia and her daughter Emerson toward the ocean view windows, Phillips falls in behind her as do Ruth, Eason, and Bradley, bringing up the rear.

Ruth sits her purse in the chair assigned to her by her daughter-in-law and says, "I'll just say hello to Pearl and the others while you get the children settled." She tugs her taupe linen blazer into place and walks two tables over. "Good morning, George, Magnus."

"Good to see Olivia and the twins made it here safe and sound. Was Bradley surprised?" Pearl asks with an open face and what seems to be innocent interest.

Ruth decides Pearl doesn't know about the *other* surprise that greeted them on their arrival from the airport and relaxes. "Oh, yes. You can see they are all happy to be here."

Magnus leans over as if to look closer, then straightens up. "Oh, yes, that kind of happiness can't be hidden. The kids are cute."

Pearl echoes him. "They are adorable. Their names are...? Sorry, I know they're family names, but I forget."

"The little girl is Emerson, and Phillips is the boy, both have Baets as their middle name," she says as she rolls her eyes. They are almost three. Olivia said they'd be fine here for brunch, so we'll see." Ruth worries her hands and pauses as she looks around. "They are the *only* children here, aren't they? Oh, well, just wanted to say hello. Enjoy."

Her seat between Eason and Bradley is on the opposite side of the table from the children and Olivia. The children both have electronic tablets keeping them occupied, while Bradley and Eason are deep in conversation. Olivia is looking at her phone.

"Everyone at their table says hello."

Bradley stands to pull out his mother's seat. "Surprised to see Magnus here without his worshippers, that Mimi and Drummond. After all, it *is* Sunday morning."

Olivia looks up from her phone. "Magnus? Magnus Llord?" She looks to the right to see him over the children's heads.

Eason asks, "Do you know him?"

"Some. He was one of my father's lawyers a long time ago. I hear he no longer needs to practice law to make a living. He's suddenly quite wealthy."

Bradley smirks. "And when a Baets says you're wealthy, you must be out of this universe wealthy."

Olivia cuts her eyes at her soon-to-be ex-husband, then looks away. "Are we ready to order?" She locates their waiter and, when she catches his eye, waves him over.

Ordering completed, Ruth speaks up. "Olivia, we want to offer you and Bradley—"

"Just you. I can't leave right now," Bradley says with an apologetic shrug.

His mother continues. "Well, then, we want to offer *you* a beach house outside of Savannah for the next three days. We'll keep the kids."

Olivia gets still and then she asks, "How far is that from here?"

"Less than two hours," Eason answers. "It belongs to a friend, and it's very nice. We had thought it might be a good chance for you and Bradley..." His words trail off as both young people react to the thought.

"I could use some alone time. I imagine the beach will be quiet this time of year."

Ruth nods. "Yes, and we'd love the time with the children. Maybe if Bradley gets his work done here—"

"If Bradley goes, then I will not, and I'll just plan on returning home this evening. *With* the children."

Ruth and Eason's mouths droop.

Bradley shakes his head and leans forward. "No need for that. You'll have the house all to yourself. I'll enjoy the time with my parents and the kids. You're right, you deserve some alone time."

His wife nods, then reaches to the table for her phone.

Bradley meets his parents' eyes and shrugs. As the food arrives and they begin to eat, the only noise is the kids talking to each other and Olivia tapping on her phone.

Ruth sighs and says under her breath, "So much for my plan."

17

This time it's like I own this hotel.

"I know it's early, but I need to check in now."

"No problem, ma'am."

"Can I have a room not facing the interstate?"

"Of course!"

"What time does the breakfast bar finish today?"

"Eleven o'clock, ma'am, since its Sunday."

I even sighed a world-weary sigh as I punched the elevator button again. To us travelers, elevators are always *soooo* slow. The wheels of my huge suitcase getting stuck on the elevator door tracks started a little panic, but I just yanked it over. At the second floor, the elevator stopped, and two teenage girls are waiting.

"Oh no, it's going up?" They giggle and jump on anyway. "We'll just ride!"

They were still giggling when the doors closed on the third floor after the spectacle of me manhandling an uncooperative piece of luggage, my purse hanging open as I dig for my ringing phone, my loafer coming off in the hallway.

"Hello?"

"You left without telling the kitten good by?" Magnus purrs. Maybe it was the cat purring, maybe not.

I lean against the wall. "The cat. I did. I forgot."

And then we neither one say anything for several moments. I'm too tired to deal with Magnus.

"I'll talk to you later," I finally say. Then I hang up, find my room, work the door key on the first time, and fall into the room with all my stuff.

And cry.

Of course I missed the breakfast bar. Crying led to sleeping. By the time I opened the curtains to see what my non-interstate view included, the sun was full and bright. A small pond surrounded by pine trees and brown grass was on my right, and to my left was the parking lot of the Cracker Barrel. Just seeing that brown and yellow sign made my stomach grumble.

Didn't take more than ten minutes after waking for me to walk back through the lobby, headed outside. The afternoon warmth I expected wasn't there. I hadn't thought about the skirt and short-sleeved sweater I wore to the party last night not being warm enough. I had thought that it would look like I'd been to church, and in Tifton, Georgia that matters more than being cold.

Opening the doors to the country store section of the restaurant, I see that I'm right. Lots of church folks here. Didn't see anyone sitting at a table by themselves when I passed the windows, but well, yeah, I bet they do take out.

"Table, miss?" an older lady at the little desk asks.

"Oh, I don't know. I'm by myself, so..."

She lifts up a menu, steps from behind her podium, and opens her arm for me to step forward. She smiles real big and sounds like a Sunday School teacher when she says, "Got a perfect table just for you right by the fire. Warm you right up."

And before I know it, I'm seated at this little table with just one other chair in the corner beside the fire. She even shows me how to scoot my chair on the diagonal so I can look right into the huge fireplace. It smells so good with the wood smoke and the food that I almost start crying again until a cheery voice says, "Good morning! Can I get you something to drink? Some coffee or juice? Fried chicken is today's special, you know."

"I can still get breakfast right? Biscuits and gravy?"

"Sure thing, hon."

She's young and whip thin. Her short hair is a pretty red, and she makes me smile because she just look so happy. "Okay, I'll take some coffee and that first meal there on the menu with the eggs, sausage, and biscuits and gravy." She takes my menu, and as I watch her bounce off, I realize no one is staring at me. No one seems to care that I'm eating by myself. Holding my bare arms out to the fire, I remember something my grandma used to tell me: "If you had any idea how little other people actually think about you, you wouldn't mind 'em so much."

She always told me I sit back, letting other people tell me who I am. My happy waitress pours me a cup of coffee and then flits off, leaving me to stare into the fire. Grandma was my best friend, though when I'd say that, she'd always disagree. "I'm too old to be your best friend. Go find you a nice girl your own age." But she was my best friend up until she died the summer after seventh grade.

My phone ringing in my skirt pocket makes me jump, and when I pull it out, I can't help but grin. I do have a friend now. "Hey, Ashleigh. Guess what I'm doing? Eating at Cracker Barrel all by myself! And it's fine. Nobody cares!"

"So you've already left? I didn't tell you bye last night at the party because I figured I'd see you today! What was the hurry?"

"Um, yeah. Listen, my food just got here. Can I call you back in a bit? I'm starving."

"Sure, I guess. Enjoy."

I say "Bye," as I click the end button and lay my phone on the table. The empty table. The table with no food on it.

Guess lying isn't a good way to keep a friend, is it?

"You're right. She's guilty of something." Ashleigh stretches her stocking feet out from under the quilt to kick her husband at the other end of the couch.

"Told you she had a fire in the cabin fireplace last night. I just can't see her doing that alone." He unmutes the TV as the beginning of the afternoon playoff game comes on.

"But who with? Hopefully not Magnus, but who else? But Magnus in an empty cabin on the floor? Just can't see it." Ashleigh stares at her husband as he focuses on the TV. "What? What do you know?"

He shrugs and doesn't break his attention.

Ashleigh struggles around to sit up. "Who? What did you see? You know you're going to tell me. For love of jack, you're the one that started all this by telling me about the smoke."

Carlos sighs and finally turns to look at his wife. "You're not going to like it and it really makes no sense, but..." He takes a breath. "You know when you're catering you can watch folks and see things others don't see? Well, that Drummond Bell guy was really watching her."

Ashleigh shakes her head. "No, no way. He's so smarmy and, so, yuck. No way." She lays her head back down on the pillow and watches the singer destroy "The Star-Spangled Banner." With the last notes, she pulls the quilt over her head and groans. "At least Magnus isn't married." She pulls the cover down and sits up. "I spent so much time talking her away from Magnus last week, I probably pushed her right into that Bell creep's arms. Everyone knows she has no judgement in men."

Carlos interjects. "Well, except for Sam last summer. And we like Jameson, okay. Don't we?"

Ashleigh flings the quilt completely off and stands up. "Hell, we even like Magnus compared to Drummond Bell. But just because he was watching her doesn't mean anything happened. I know I keep saying she's frustrated, but him? Surely not. It could've been Magnus, right? Or she could've been by herself. She could probably start a fire in her fireplace. We don't know she was with a guy, right?" She demands an answer, standing between her husband and the football game. When he continues to stare straight ahead like he can see through her to the TV, she sits back down beside him. "Oh, no. Something else? What?"

"I was out at the garbage can when she came out the back door. She had a bottle in her hand, and she made sure no one on the back porch could see her. Figured she was sneaking out a bit early. I didn't want to put her on the spot, so I didn't let her know I was there. Then as I went back inside, I bumped into Drummond, and he had two red solo cups in one hand and a baggie of ice in the other. He grinned and said, 'Can't let a lady drink alone.'" Carlos pauses to watch a long pass in the game, but picks back up when the ball lands on the field. "So I laughed, assuming he meant his wife, but he continued right out the back door where Becca Sue had just went. And when I checked? Mimi was still inside the house."

Ashleigh lays her head against her husband's chest. "I'm so glad I'm not single anymore. Too many mistakes to make out there. Wonder if she'll tell me. Although, God knows, I wouldn't admit to sleeping with Drummond Bell."

18

The clouds are thicker than when I went in Cracker Barrel, and it's colder, too. Two steps into the parking lot, I turn around and go back into the store. On the far wall I'd noticed some fleece jackets, so I go straight for them. A tan one with black stitching and a black scarf attached feels great, so I just wear it to the counter. They cut off the tags, take my card, and I'm better prepared for the walk back to the hotel.

I'm not prepared for who's waiting in the lobby.

"There you are." Jameson Mason says as he folds the newspaper he was reading and lays it on the short table beside him. "You didn't call."

"Oh! Oh, that's right. I left in a hurry, kind of. When you called earlier I was driving and then I was sleeping. Sorry." He doesn't get up or say anything, just looks at me. "Oh! That's right. It's Sunday. We were going to dinner. Oh no. I just ate."

"Well, I didn't. So get changed and let's go. You can watch me eat," he says with a grin. "I'll wait here while you change." He picks up his paper and opens it.

Halfway to the elevator I turn around. He thinks I'm not dressed right? He can jump off a bridge. I march up to him and demand, "Why do I need to change? Where are we going? The country club?"

When he looks up he's surprised, but then he looks at my bare legs. "The club? No. Aren't you cold? It's going to be in the thirties tonight with snow flurries."

"Oh. The weather. Change because it's cold. Yeah, sure." Back at the elevator I sneak a look at Jameson. He's wearing casual pants and shoes and a navy sweater. His coat is lying on a chair beside him. *Wait, did he say snow? Oh my gosh, I haven't seen snow in forever.*

Rushing to change, I'm back in the lobby before he finishes reading the paper. "I'm back and better dressed for snow. Are they really calling for snow?"

He stands and laughs. "Yes they are. You're almost more excited than Maggie. She's been hoping for a snow day. Says she's going to stay up all night watching the news. Schools in Atlanta have already cancelled classes tomorrow. But down here? Don't think it'll happen."

Outside it's dark and blustery. We dart to his car, and we're pulling out of the parking lot before I realize what's happening. Something stranger than snow in South Georgia.

I'm on a date with Jameson Mason.

"Have you talked to Becca Sue?" Ruth asks her son as they leave the room where they just put the twins down for bed.

"Who?" Bradley whispers.

"Becca Sue. The girl, you know. The woman with the blanket."

"Oh, yeah, her. No, why?" He sits on the couch and grabs the remote, pointing it at the television.

Ruth closes her eyes and shakes her head. "What about Olivia? You remember her, don't you?"

"What? Olivia? No, I haven't talked to anyone. Haven't even looked at my phone all day." He flips channels as he settles further into the couch. "Where's Dad?"

"Probably in his office, still going over those papers you brought."

"This deal really has potential for Backwater. I think it'd be good for Dad to get invested in it."

"Does it mean you'd be here more? We'd love to have you and the children as much as we can get you." She lowers her voice. "Before Olivia's parents brainwash them." She looks for his reaction as he used to defend the wealthy and influential Baets family at every turn.

He doesn't say anything, but he also doesn't tell her she's wrong, so she pushes further. "What do you think Olivia will do after the divorce is settled?"

Shrugging, he flips channels again. After a long pause, he clears his throat and slides a look at his mother. "I know you don't like it, Mom, but I've got to get out of this marriage. And all the prenuptial stuff the Baets made me sign will make it all go pretty quickly. Lucky for me, my huge ego made me demand she sign everything. Who knew I'd actually have as much as I have?" He grins at her. "But now Olivia has to find a way to make some money."

Ruth gasps. "Oh Bradley, you wouldn't deny her or the children anything, would you? It's your responsibility!"

"Of course not, Mom. The alimony and child support is huge, plenty for a normal person to live on. But this is Olivia. She wants to live the way her folks live."

"Maybe she'll just stay with her parents."

"Not on your life. She eats, lives, and breathes to fight with her parents. It's her every waking thought. But in public? She's their biggest fan." He turns off the TV and lets the silence settle in. "Maybe I'll go see if Dad has any questions. If things work out, maybe me and the kids will get a home here in Backwater. This place is kind of cool."

He leans down to kiss her cheek as he walks by. "Thanks for listening, Mom."

As he enters Eason's study, Ruth sighs, and her smile grows cynical as she says, "Knew it wasn't all sunshine and daffodils in that family."

"Reminds me of the old spring break houses when we were in college," Olivia says into her phone. "But for all its rusticity, it's right on the ocean and has a fireplace and good stock of wine."

Her friend Jennifer laughs. "Your poor mother-in-law, thinking she was setting you up for a romantic reunion with her son."

"Seriously. This worked out better than I could've imagined." Olivia smooths her burgundy hair out across the back of the couch and takes a sip from her tall wine glass, then asks, "Have my parents asked about me?"

Jennifer scoffs. "No. They were lamenting all over the club about the twins having to spend time in *Florida* with their other grandparents. They were playing the martyrs to great effect."

"I'm sure they were." She lifts her glass up and looks at the fire through it. "Well, hopefully I'll be back home soon with some good news."

"I'm sure. No turning back now. Have fun and keep me updated."

"Oh, I will." Olivia hangs up the phone, but then looks up a number she managed to get earlier in the day. She presses that number, taking a sip of wine as the phone rings. With wine on her lips, she purrs, "I love having a plan."

19

No one knew I was coming in Sunday night. No one but Jameson. Just a quiet dinner. Just the two of us. Out of the spotlight of Backwater or Piney.

It actually started snowing as we drove the few blocks to the downtown area. I couldn't wait for him to park the car so we could walk in the flakes. They were melting as soon as they hit the sidewalk, but it was still so pretty. The restaurant was almost empty as it was a Sunday night, and most folks were home worrying about the weather. Jameson said we were okay since the temperature was still above freezing, but the man who came to take us to a table told us he might be closing early if the weather got bad.

Our table, at my request, was right by the front window so we could watch the snow. With our bottle of red wine and a melted cheese dip, we watched the snow and decided what to order. We bent our heads close together to read the menu by candlelight, and Jameson smelled so delicious. Everything was very cozy. Really cozy.

Then *they* knocked on the window. They being Piney.

As busy as last summer was with Jameson being engaged to the governor's daughter, his brother dying, getting stuck with his niece and nephew, then dumping Backwater into my lap—he apparently had time to be on a softball team. Yeah, who knew? And here they were at the window. Then in the restaurant. Then at our table.

"Caleb asked me to be the team manager before... well, before. Ended up liking it more than I thought I would. Besides, it wasn't a lot of work. You know, I got the shirts made, did the paperwork, that kind of stuff," he explained on the way back to the hotel later last night. Much later. Funny, but restaurants don't close early when they have a dozen guys sit down to order food and beer. Wait, did I say a dozen guys? Make that a dozen guys and one girl. Me.

Cozy, right?

Stretching in the hotel sheets feels good, but it's too early to be up. It was late by the time we got back to the hotel. The softball guys were on their way home to Piney from some international men's softball tournament in Florida. Just our luck they picked the same restaurant we were in. So much luck.

Going around the table in my head, I think of the ones I recognized and who recognized me. Several were in their late twenties, and they looked a lot younger than Jameson. A couple were right around my age. Caleb was the athletic brother, so I guess that's why Jameson was the manager. Funny, with them, his good ol' boy side came out. Didn't even realize Jameson Mason had a good ol' boy side. His brother Caleb was all about it, used it to woo women from Piney all the way up north where he married his first wife, Margaret. From what I hear, it gets old for northern women. Southern women? Yeah, not so much. We eat it up with a spoon and just live with the heartburn.

The softball guys finally hit the road for Piney, but not before making a big deal out of Jameson taking me back to the hotel. Never mind he said he'd be right behind them on the road home. It'll be all over Piney, probably is *already* all over Piney, that Becca Sue Mason and Jameson Mason were holed up in some hotel down by the interstate.

It's too early to get up, but I'm awake. I stretch again, roll over, and sit up on the edge of the bed. There's no snow on the ground. At least I don't have to worry about the roads. I'm worried enough about working Momma's shift with her at the diner. Shoot, she probably already knows I'm here.

At the door to the bathroom, I pause. I look back at the bed and sigh. "Jameson, don't you have to go to work?"

When I enter the hotel dining room, it smells like crispy bacon, but breakfast is just slices of canned ham, floating in, I don't know, ham juice? But the cinnamon rolls are pretty good and there's all the coffee you want. I'm on my second cup by time Jameson gets off the elevator, looking around the lobby for me. He's cleaned up, and even though he's dressed in his clothes from yesterday, he looks more pulled together than anyone else huddled in the breakfast nook off the lobby.

"Good morning," I say as he walks past my table. He only nods on his way to the coffee station. When he sits down, he can't meet my eyes. "You're embarrassed," I say, complete with rolling eyes.

"No. Not really," he whispers.

This is funny. "You were one of the boys last night. Big talk for you. Made sure to say we were coming back to the hotel. Several times. Looked to be enjoying all the laughs and winks."

He leans over his coffee, with both elbows on the table. "I was drinking. They were..."

"What? Egging you on? Making you feel like a stud bull? What?" My voice gets louder with each question. If he'd look up he'd see I'm laughing, not mad. But he stares holes in the table.

"Please, quiet down. People here might..." Then he does look up and surveys the room.

"People here might know you?" He looks at me now, but my laughing is gone. "Jerk." I stand up and gather my trash.

He reaches out and grabs my wrist. "No, I don't mean that. It's just, they were friends of Caleb's, you know. They expect, well, they expect..."

As he looks up at me, trying to get me to understand, I

suddenly do. "Oh my word, you want Caleb's rep without the morning afters. All the big talk, but no follow-through. Everyone in South Georgia knew Caleb was just a big hound dog. Me, especially. And he didn't care. That's the secret, you can't care what anyone else thinks."

I cover his hand on my wrist with my other hand, and shaking my head, I assure him. "If that's what you want, don't worry. I won't ruin your cover. Everyone in Piney now thinks you're banging your ex-sister-in-law. So be it." Turning away from our table, I walk to the elevator and stand there with my back to him. As the doors open, there's a hand on my shoulder and Jameson's head next to mine.

"But... we, we didn't do anything, right?"

In the elevator I turn and smile at him. "No, stud. We didn't do anything." The doors close, and I wish with all my heart I was headed home to Backwater.

Home. To Backwater.

That's kind of weird.

20

"What am I supposed to do for a uniform?" Becca Sue asks as soon as she arrives at the restaurant.

"Got ya one hanging in the bathroom, stall on the end," her momma says as she darts back into the kitchen. "Can't talk right now."

Becca Sue looks around at the busy restaurant. Almost every table is full, and the noise level is deafening. She avoids colliding with the waitresses darting here and there and escapes to the bathroom.

A wall heater is the only source of heat in the bathroom. It blazes a fiery orange, but doesn't spread a lot of warmth. She changes quickly in the cold stall. In the mirror, she shakes her head. Dark gold with a zippered front. It's snug, but it does fit. She wore her old tennis shoes, but her legs are bare and they're cold. "Didn't think about my legs being uncovered," she says looking down at the chill bumps spreading across them. She'd braided her hair extra tight at the hotel before she left, so taking a little water in her hand she smooths down any wiry strands that have escaped. "Okay, let's go."

A short girl with close-cropped hair, wearing the diner's uniform, says hello as she leaves the bathroom. "Oh, you're Becca Sue, aren't you?" She doesn't wait for an answer, but wraps Becca Sue's midsection up in a hug, with her own hard, beach ball-sized stomach in between them. "You are just an angel for doing this for your momma. Brenda has talked of nothing else but getting to work with her very own daughter!"

Becca Sue laughs. "Yeah, right." She opens her arms to get the girl to loosen her grip. "What's your name?"

The girl backs up and grins. "I'm Tina. I just love your momma. I gotta go to the bathroom, this baby is sitting right on my pee sack." She pushes past Becca Sue.

Taking a deep breath, Becca Sue moves to the end of the counter. Folks are leaving with no one taking their empty tables. Her mother spots her as she finishes up with a table of four women. Telling her customers goodbye, she goes behind the counter and comes to stand across from her daughter.

"Things will slow down now. These are the folks who came shopping for the weekend and are headed back to Atlanta. They all clear out by two on Mondays to beat the traffic back home. Uniform fits?"

"Yeah, though it's a little snug and kind of short."

Looking over the counter, Brenda Cousins shakes her head. "Naw, it's perfect, just like I told Maureen to hem it. It's the uniform her daughter used before she got married and moved off. They're real religious so they wanted it to cover everything up. Knew you were more interested in tips than keeping things covered. Come meet Bruce."

In the kitchen, Brenda pushes Becca Sue forward. "Bruce, this here's my daughter, Becca Sue, who's going to do my shifts for a couple weeks."

Bruce continues looking at the clipboard in his hand, then with a check and signature at the bottom, he tucks it under his arm and turns. He looks Becca Sue up and down. "Uniform fits. I hear you've never been a waitress."

He's big and muscular, wearing gray slacks and a black, short-sleeved shirt. His hair is steel gray and slicked back. He crosses his arms and waits for Becca Sue to say something. Finally when her mother shoves her with her elbow, she speaks up. "No, sir. But I'll work real hard. I know what this job means to Momma."

He cuts his eyes at Brenda and nods. "Brenda's a good one.

I would hate to lose her, so you just make sure I don't. I'm just going to pay your mother for the hours you work, and you two can figure the money out between you." He walks to the open office door, and they follow him. "Tips I don't concern myself with, so again, you two work it out." He lays the clipboard on the small desk and takes a black wool coat off the rack. Now, I've gotta get on the road, but I'll be back Thursday. Pepper will be around if you need anything. Oh, there she is now. Hey, babe, come here." The back door next to the office slams shut behind a petite blond woman.

"Honey, you haven't left yet? Traffic's going to be a bitc—oops, bear." Her blue eyes widen and her bright pink mouth broadens into a smile as she passes the two waitresses and wraps both arms around Bruce's neck. "Give me a kiss and you get out of here. Brenda can introduce me." She leaves Bruce's mouth pink, whether from the lipstick or the pressure, hard to tell. Brenda and Becca Sue raise eyebrows at each other.

With one more hard kiss on his cheek, the short woman slaps him on his almost nonexistent rear and shoves him to the back door. Pink lipstick marks and his goofy grin mark him better than a "hands off" sign. When the door closes, Pepper turns back to them. She looks Becca Sue up and down like her husband had earlier. "Y'all don't look anything alike! I love it! Not a teeny thing like me and your mother. You're a big girl. Pretty, too. Now, I've got exactly thirty minutes to get all this straightened up and get out of here."

She fiddles with papers while she talks and moves around behind the desk. When she looks back up she nails Brenda with her gaze. "Can you show her what you need to in thirty minutes while I straighten things up? Becca Sue and I are going to get a drink." Her brow drops and she looks at Becca Sue. "You do drink, don't you? So hard to know down here. Can't just assume it like you do in Atlanta."

Becca Sue nods. "Yes, but I think I'm going to need more than thirty minutes to learn all this."

"Bullsh—sugar," Pepper says as she plops into the big office chair. "Y'all go on. Close the door, too."

With the closed door behind them, Brenda closes her eyes. "There you have it. Bruce and Pepper Johnson. New owners of the Piney Diner and the South Georgia Shoppes."

Becca Sue whispers as they walk back through the kitchen. "But why am I having a drink with her? Is that normal for new waitresses?"

Her mother waits until they are back in the dining room, empty now except for two ladies at a table near the front door. She shrugs as she starts opening the cabinets behind the counter. "No, not normal at all. But then you're not normal, are you?"

"Oh, me being temporary, I guess. Still doesn't make sense, though."

"*Nooo,* that's not it. As of this time yesterday you would *not* be having a drink with Pepper Johnson. What happened between this time yesterday and this time today to change things? Think hard."

Becca Sue surveys the inside of the stuffed cabinets as she thinks, then she stops. "Oh. Oh, that."

Her mother smirks. "Yes, that. Sleeping with Jameson Mason changes everything."

How could I have been so flippant about it this morning? Leaning over closer to Momma, I whisper, "But we didn't do anything. He just drank too much to drive home."

Momma doesn't even give me a good eye roll. She just flips her hand at me and shows me the inside of the cabinets behind the counter. She won't let me get a word in edgewise, so by the time Pepper comes out of the office, Momma announces I know everything and am all ready for the morning shift. She grabs a bag out from under the corner cabinet and heads to the bathroom, so I tell Pepper to give me a minute to change, grab my bag of clothes, and follow Momma.

She's in the first stall, and she starts talking as soon as I enter. "Jameson Mason has been the biggest catch around here since he broke off his engagement to Cecelia Mattle. You don't dump the governor's daughter, and your chance at living in the governor's mansion, without everyone talking."

"But we're just friends, at least I think that's all," I explain. Again.

She answers that with a flush. When I come out of the stall, changed into jeans and a button-up shirt, she's at the mirror brushing her hair.

Her reflection looks at me. "Well, that would be a stupid thing to not know. If you want him, get him. He's a catch, and everyone knows he always wanted whatever his brother had."

"Oh, Momma. That's awful. He's nice, and we're just friends, right now."

Momma leans on the counter and turns to me. "Did he spend the night in your hotel room last night?"

I don't answer. My braid needs smoothing down.

"There." She stands up and goes to the door. "You made your time back in Piney awfully more interesting is all I gotta say. I'm going to go get your daddy, and we'll see you back at home soon. Irene's bringing over a pot of chicken soup for dinner."

The door shuts behind her, and I stare at myself in the mirror. Irene? Daddy's step-momma will be there? Ugh. She's not exactly my biggest fan. And sure doesn't help that my step-grandmother is Mason Farm's head bookkeeper. Ugh.

"Ready, sugar? I'll drive," Pepper says as I leave the bathroom. "Your momma said to just leave your uniform here since you didn't get it dirty today. Hang it in the office."

Tina is still on duty, and she lumbers off her seat on a stool at the end of the counter as I come near. "Here, I'll hang it up for you. You and Miss Pepper have a good talk, and I'll see you tomorrow. I'll be opening with you."

"What time should I get here?"

"I'll be here around five-fifteen to get the coffee going, but you don't need to be here until five-thirty," she says as she walks my uniform back toward the office.

Pepper is grinning at me from the counter. "Good thing you're staying with your folks working the early shift and all. Bet your love life will suffer, though."

I follow her out, and we turn towards the South Georgia Shoppes. There, between the two buildings, is a vintage pick-up truck. It's a big one with lots of shiny chrome. The paint scheme is old-fashioned aqua and white. Pepper has to pull herself up into her seat using the steering wheel, and even though I'm a 'big girl,' I struggle getting up into the completely restored interior, too.

"This is beautiful," I say. It has one long bench seat, which is pulled up as far as it will go for Pepper to be able to reach the pedals. It's as perfect inside as it is on the outside. "This is yours?"

"You don't think Bruce would be caught dead driving a pickup truck, do you?"

She backs it up and maneuvers easily between the buildings until we're out on the road. We only drive about a half-mile and pull into El Dorado, the Mexican restaurant that's been there forever. We get out and are barely in the front door before she's given an order for a pitcher of margaritas. The pitcher almost beats us to our table. Or should I say, "Her table." It's the only booth in the bar area. It sits right at the front window, and from it, we can see her truck. The only reason I know it's her table is the bartender shouted hello and said, "Miss Pepper! Your table is ready! You're early today."

She grabs my arm and steers me to the bar. "I'm breaking in a new waitress. You know Becca Sue?"

The young man reaches out his hand to shake mine. "Becca Sue, I'm Harry. You let me know if you need anything. Anything at all."

"Becca Sue's only back in town for a little bit to help her mother out. Our Brenda, you know her. Her husband's been in the hospital."

"Oh, you're Rick's daughter? That Becca Sue? Good to finally meet you. Your dad sure enjoyed his time in Florida. You need a bartender in that place of yours down there?"

I smile and shake my head. "Not that I know of. But, uh, thanks."

We get almost to our table when Harry calls out, "And Becca Sue? You tell Jameson I said 'hey.'"

"Oh, okay," I mumble.

"So, you and Jameson?" Pepper asks as we slide into the booth. "Weren't you married to his brother?" She pours the icy margaritas into our frosted glasses. She squeezes a lime into each of them and then takes a sip from hers. "Go on, have a drink. Where's our chips?"

Harry careens over to our table with a basket of tortilla chips and a bowl of salsa. "Here you go. Wait staff is still getting set up. Can I get you ladies anything else?"

Pepper grins at him. "No thanks, honey. We're all good." She lifts her glass and looks at me. "Should we toast our new friendship?"

We do, and then she settles back in the high, dark-red booth. "We have so much in common, Becca Sue. We should do a double date on Thursday when Bruce is back in town." She pulls her phone out of her purse. "I'm going to text him right now. Get it on his calendar." Still looking down at her phone, she says, "You know, I had my eye on the Mason boys early on. Saw they were ripe for the picking, but I was just a bit too young. Let's see, you were five grades ahead of me in school."

"Me? What school?"

Then she looks up. "County High. You think you lived out in the country, but you can't even see where I'm from from *your* front porch."

"You're from here? From Piney?"

She laughs and eats a chip. "Boy, you are out of the loop! Name wasn't Pepper, of course. Sara. Sara Walsh. Don't worry. We didn't know each other, so don't go trying to remember me."

"But you said we have a lot in common?"

"We do! Coming back to show these people what's what. Sleeping with Jameson Mason the night before coming back here and just *accidentally* running into those guys from here. Classic." She looks out the window, nods, and them slides her eyes at me. "There they are. You are a hot ticket. Unbutton that top button and put that chip down. Let's show 'em what we got."

I bend to look out the window. "Show who? What?"

"Becca Sue! You didn't tell us you were going to be in town!" Carol and Jessie. Of course I recognize them. They've been a hateful, awe-inspiring fixture in my life, in all of Piney, since the blessed days they were born. Like wouldn't a British person recognize the Queen of England?

"Hey, Carol and Jessie. Good to see you," I manage to say.

Carol is tall and has the same straight dark hair she had in first grade, parted in the middle and falling past her shoulders. Jessie's hair is short and curly, a little redder than I remember it. Jessie's also a little heavier than I remember. That does not make me smile. That does not make me smile. That does not... never mind.

Jessie bubbles over. "We're meeting the guys here for happy hour and dinner. Olé! Knew we had to come say hi to Pepper. And *youuuu*, Becca Sue!"

Pepper grins and reaches out a hand to them. "I'd ask you to join us until your guys get here, but we're just too busy catching up. Y'all have a good dinner, okay?" She dismisses them like I've never seen Carol and Jessie dismissed.

I try to stifle a giggle as they prance away like it was their idea. "That was weird! They've not said that much to me in all the years I've known them."

Pepper shrugs. "Their dear hubbies need Jameson to like them. So, if Jameson likes you... well, time's they are a-changin'," she sing-songs.

It's kind of hard to sip a margarita when you're grinning, but I manage. "But they weren't like this when I was with Caleb. We were even married."

"Honey, Caleb shot his wad with marrying that Worth bit—

girl. By time she got through with him, he had no power left, or pride. And you have to know he, well, he wasn't too kind around town how he talked about you."

Never had anyone come right out and say that. Well, except for Momma. "But how do you know all this? Why don't I remember you?"

"No one used to remember me. First of all, I didn't look like this. The boobs, the blonde hair, name, and personality are all thanks to my years in Atlanta. I was a serious book nerd in school. Left here for Georgia State the day high school ended thanks to a scholarship for poor, smart girls. Started that very day to work on my grand return to Piney."

"You *wanted* to come back?" This time I pour the margaritas.

"Of course! Doesn't every nobody from a small town want to go back and be queen of the place? Look at you!"

"Me? I'm only back to help my folks out."

She smirks. "Sure you are. The lost weight, the new clothes, salon haircut, getting Jameson Mason drunk so he can't drive home. All just a big ol' accident." She winks and takes a long sip on the straw in her drink before she drawls, "Whatever you say, sugar."

21

"Must say I'm not surprised Becca Sue left in such a hurry," Drummond says as he hands Miss Bell his empty sandwich plate before straightening out his newspaper to continue reading.

On her way to the kitchen, Miss Bell asks, "Why? She hadn't planned on leaving until the afternoon."

Drummond tips his head around the side of his paper to look at his wife and grins. "Just, well, just something I saw." He clears his throat and folds up his newspaper. By the time Mrs. Bell comes back to the dining room he's erased all traces of his grin and he looks serious. "Dear Virginia, she's not who I think you hope her to be. Please, sit down for a moment."

Straightening her back and standing taller, the old woman lifts her chin. "I know all I need to know about Becca Sue."

Mimi pushes out the chair beside her. "Here, sit down. You know we care about you, don't you?"

Mrs. Bell shakes her head at the offered chair. "I'm fine standing. I know you think you care about me, but, well, you've not been here since your father died."

Drummond catches his breath and then lowers his head. "Oh Virginia, I thought you understood. Just so much pain in remembering, and with my mother..." His words fade out as his voice gets thicker.

She drops down into the chair, then reaches out a soft hand to lay on his back. "Oh my. I'm so sorry, dear. Of course you care. Of course you do. You've had *so* much on your plate for *so* long. Poor thing. Of course, you had to take care of your mother, she needed you. I do understand. You are very important to me. Please forgive me, I just worry about Becca Sue."

Drummond keeps his head bowed. He sniffles, and she continues to pat his back. Mimi speaks up. "He does worry so very much about you, and we were surprised to find that young woman living here. I'm sure she's been a good friend to you, but we worry about whom else she's a good friend to." After a pause, Mimi says quietly, "Drummond, it's your duty to tell Virginia."

He nods, still looking at the floor, but then raises his head as he reaches out to take Mrs. Bell's hand. "I was concerned about her when I saw her leaving the party Saturday night. It was late and dark, so I followed her to her new home to make sure she was okay. I know you say this is a safe neighborhood, but you must admit you don't know everyone living and working here now. It's a very busy place these days. What if someone was living in her house while it's under construction?"

Miss Bell's face tightens in worry. "Oh, I hadn't thought of that. I'm sure she hadn't thought of it. We neither one are very security conscious. We often forget to even lock the doors at night."

Mimi tsks, and Drummond sighs. He says, "See? So when I got there she, well, she wasn't alone."

Miss Bell closes her eyes. "I was afraid of that. She and that man are like magnets. Can't stay away from each other. I so hoped Magnus wasn't why she left so suddenly!" She stands up. "That man is a nuisance. I'm going to bake some biscones. He gets me so agitated." She walks into the kitchen still muttering.

Drummond and Mimi look at each other and mouth, "Magnus?" Back and forth they talk in whispers until finally Drummond nods and calls out, "Believe I'll go for a walk."

Mimi stands, picks up the left-behind dishes and cups on the table, and carries them into the kitchen. Sitting the dishes in the sink, she asks, "So apparently it's nothing new? About Becca Sue and Magnus?" Her back is to the older woman, but she's still as she listens.

"Everyone knows." Miss Bell holds her finger and her thumb about half an inch apart. "They came this close to getting married last summer. That man just won't leave her alone. I don't want to talk about it. I'm actually kind of glad she ran off to Piney early. I don't think I would've handled this calmly. Magnus is *no* good for her! I don't care how much he begs to be in her life. But I don't want to talk about it!"

Mimi rinses her hands, then shakes them dry over the dirty dishes she'd deposited in the sink. "Maybe I'll see if I can catch up to Drummond. Feel like a walk myself."

"Dress warm," Miss Bell says sweetly, then mutters under her breath. "Magnus and Becca Sue back together. Ugh!"

"Figured you'd be waiting. It's true. They apparently were an item last summer. Virginia says they almost married. Claims he won't leave her alone," Mimi says in a rush as she catches up to her husband leaning on the fence next door watching the cows.

"Magnus Llord and Becca Sue? Makes no sense. Besides, it wasn't Magnus she was with, it was the King boy." He pushes away from the fence and joins his wife on the road. "Maybe Magnus was after her last summer because she owned Back-water, but now? He doesn't need her money. She's not even *got* money compared to his inheritance."

Mimi sniffs. "Maybe he just likes bigger girls."

Drummond lets that go and walks on. They are in front of the driveway to Becca Sue's cabin, and they both look towards it through the woods as they slow down. Mimi asks, "Wonder what he'd think if he knew who she was with Saturday? How can we play that?"

Her husband nods at her. "Just what I'm trying to figure out. You done walking? Think I've got Virginia ready to spring for a golf cart. Bet she's mad enough right now to go buy one. Let's go see."

Mimi wrinkles her nose. "Golf cart? I don't care about a golf cart. We're wasting time."

He puts his arm around her slim shoulders. "Baby steps. Gotta take baby steps. It'll all work out, but I've got to set things up." He turns them both around and then stops again. "Well, look there," he says staring at the two men standing under the front awning at the Kings' house. "Come on." With only a few big steps they are nearing Ruth and Eason's front yard, and he waves as he hollers out. "Hello. Just out for an afternoon walk. Much nicer than January in Wisconsin!" He laughs and drops his arm off Mimi's shoulders as they stride up the driveway.

Magnus and Bradley walk down the sidewalk to meet them. Both men wait where the sidewalk and driveway meet. Drummond shakes their hands and says, "Good to run into you both. From what I hear you two are the movers and shakers here, and I'm in need of a little business advice."

Mimi speaks up. "Don't you mean *we* need a little business advice? It is my father's business we're talking about."

"Absolutely. Yes, Mimi's father left her his whole business, but we're tiring of Wisconsin. Looking for some opportunities here. My mother passed recently, and we want to be closer to Virginia. Help her out. She's my only living relative now."

Bradley responds, "Sorry to hear that about your mother."

"Yes, sorry to hear," Magnus says.

Drummond bows his head and clears his throat. "Just so hard to stay there without her." Mimi pats his back and sighs.

"Well, I better get on home," Magnus says after the pause grows uncomfortable. "Good to see you both again. Bradley, we'll talk more later. Let me know how it goes with your dad."

Drummond peels off to walk beside Magnus. "I was just headed out for a walk, mind if I join you?" Over his shoulder he smiles at his wife and waves. "See you at home, dear."

Mimi nods and then reaches out a long arm to stop Bradley as he turns toward the house. "It's been lovely getting to know your parents. And so glad you got to attend our party. Hope you're feeling at home here."

Bradley looks at Mimi's hand clutching his arm. "Um, yeah, everyone seems nice. I better go inside. Mother has the twins."

"Oh, your children are here? I'd love to meet them." She relaxes her hold on his arm as she steps in front of him and heads to the front door. "And your wife is here, too? Oh my goodness, what a shame she couldn't come to the party, isn't it?"

Bradley chews on his bottom lip, eventually following Mimi to his parent's front door. "Olivia, my wife, isn't here right now." He reaches around her and opens the front door. Bright light welcomes them, along with children's voices. Loud voices.

Mimi smiles and claps her hands. "Oh, how delightful! Hope I'm not intruding, Ruth, but Bradley asked me in to meet the children. I hear his wife isn't here, though. Where in the world would she go that she could leave these precious babies?"

Ruth comes out of the kitchen and meets her son's questioning glance. Neither of them answer Mimi as both kids come running out to their father like they haven't seen him in weeks. Amidst the squeals, he introduces them both to Mimi.

Mimi bends down to their level and asks Emerson, "Where's your mommy, you pretty girl?"

Phillips screws up his face and throws himself against his father's legs. "Mommy! Mommy?"

Ruth reaches out and lifts the little boy into her arms. "Mommy's at the beach. Remember? You ready for dinner?" She looks up at Mimi. "Excuse us, but it's time for the twins to have dinner. Thanks for stopping by. Come on, Emerson."

Once again, Mimi reaches out and grasps Bradley's arm, stopping him from turning away from her. She shakes her head and exhales. "They are adorable. Just adorable. So good their mother, Olivia, I believe you said, can get away for a little break. I'm sure you could use a break also. Will you be joining her at the beach?"

Bradley studies her for a moment, then answers, "No. I have business here."

Mimi lowers her voice as she leans closer to the young man and tightens her grip on his arm. "That's so good to hear. We don't know what we want to do with the proceeds from the sale of the business and your mother has bragged about what a financial wizard you are. Can we make an appointment to talk to you? Tomorrow morning?"

As Bradley shakes his head and pulls back she interjects. "It would mean so much to Drummond. After losing his mother and... well..." She turns to look at the children seated at the kitchen table with their grandmother. "He's always had such a hard time, since his parents divorced when he was young..."

Her words fade out, and Bradley doesn't answer at first. He stares at his children, then nods. "Okay. Tomorrow morning. Ten. We can meet here in my father's office." She releases him, and he steps away. "I better go help with the kids' dinner. They can be a handful."

Mimi shoos him toward the kitchen. "Of course. I'll show myself out. See you tomorrow!" She pulls the big front door closed behind her and talks to herself down the sidewalk and driveway. "So, the young Mr. King and Mrs. King are having marital problems. Bet sleeping with the town floozy doesn't help. Or maybe that's the reason she's off by herself." Nearing the Bell house, she stops and leans on the fence where her husband waited earlier. "Might as well give Virginia time to get the dishes done."

22

Pepper drops me off back at the diner as the sky is blazing an amazing orange sunset to the west. Driving right into it, I drink in the wide open skies over the empty fields and let the beauty, the emptiness, and the margaritas keep me from thinking. As Daddy always said, "Thinking is overrated." Oh, yeah, Daddy will be home. And Irene. Oh, yeah. Irene.

Okay, too much thinking. Stop that.

Turning off the highway, the potholed road takes me through a bare cotton field, then up a little hill and into the woods. Momma and Daddy's trailer sits right on the edge of the woods with the creek down behind it. There's a couple other trailers on our little road and two houses. Friends of Daddy's. They were all gonna build houses out here, but, yeah, didn't happen for most of them.

Very little of the colorful sky is left by the time I walk up onto the wood decking and open the trailer door. "Hey, Daddy," I say 'cause he looks up immediately from his seat at the kitchen table when he hears the door opening.

"Sugar. Come here and give me a hug." I do and have to hold back tears when I feel that he is as thin as he looks.

"Where have you been?" my step-grandmother says from her post at the stove. "Brenda said you'd be here earlier, so we didn't wait on you. Good thing I didn't bring Maggie like she was begging me to. Sit down and have some soup."

"Yes, ma'am." I sit across from Daddy and beside Momma,

who is staring out the window facing the dark woods. "Daddy, you look good."

"I'm nothin' but skin and bones. Good to be home for some home-cookin'. Thank you, Mom," he says as Irene places his refilled bowl in front of him.

My bowl is empty, and I realize she's not serving anyone but Daddy. Nothing's changed. I get up and serve myself soup from the pot on the stove. "Can I get anything for anyone else? Momma?"

She doesn't look away from the window, just shakes her head. I pull open the oven. "Are there any more biscuits?"

Irene answers, "Didn't figure you'd want one. Figured you were trying to keep off that weight you lost. Looks like some of it has come back already." She sighs, picks up her half-eaten biscuit, and takes a bite. She's thin, real thin. You probably guessed that, right?

Daddy says, "Sugar, you can have rest of mine. I'm pert near full."

"No, thanks. I'm good." It's hard to slow down eating Irene's chicken soup. It is delicious. She's a fabulous, old-fashioned cook. I've heard that your attitude comes through in your cooking, and since she mainly cooks for my grandfather, Wayne, and my daddy, there's a lot of love in her food. Me and Momma get to eat it as byproducts of being related, and thank goodness her feelings for us don't come through her meals. "So, you said Maggie wanted to come with you? How is she?"

Irene beams. "Lord, that child is pure sunshine. She's so good to her grandmother and doing wonderful in school. She's gotten closer to her Worth family, and they are doting on her, too. She is just the perfect young lady. We're so pleased that her cotillion classes have given her so much confidence."

Momma turns her face full in front of her and says, sweetly, "Oh yes, dear Maggie grew so much more confident from her summer in Florida." Then she looks at me. "You helped her through such a rough time after losing her daddy. Oh my, Irene, you do know that Becca Sue and Maggie's grandfather, Roger Worth, are business partners? They get along famously!"

Daddy looks up and squints at Momma, begging her to stop. But we've all been here before. Stopping is not in the script.

Momma reaches out and touches her mother-in-law's hand. "And darling Cab, why, even Jameson says how thankful he is to Becca Sue for keeping him from following in his poor daddy's footsteps. Right, honey?" she asks me. Even when my mother tries to look innocent, it's just not possible. She was born guilty.

But I don't have to play. "So, Daddy, what did the doctors say? Are you going to need rehab or anything like that?"

He grabs onto the lifeline of my questions. "Probably not. Going to just take it easy here, and he said I should be good as new."

"If you put on some weight," Irene scolds. "I left three casseroles in the freezer, and another pot of chicken soup and a pot of vegetable beef soup in the refrigerator." She wraps her arm around his shoulders and squeezes. "Wayne says he'll be by tomorrow when the girls are gone. What time should I tell him to come by?"

She asks both me and my mother, but Daddy answers. "Ten a.m. would be good. Right, Bren? You can go do some errands or stuff, right? Bec, you'll be at work all morning, so that'll work. Well, I'm getting kinda tired," he says as he carefully stands up. "Think I'll go lay down now. Watch some TV."

"I'll get you settled," Irene says as he fully stands and heads down the hallway. "Y'all don't need to wait on me to clean up. I'll just visit a while with Rick."

We watch them shuffle down the hall, and then Momma picks up Daddy's remaining biscuit and breaks it in half. She hands me the bigger portion and then pops her piece in her mouth. "Meaner than a rattlesnake, but, law, that woman can make a biscuit."

"Hey there," I whisper into the phone after answering it quickly.

Jameson laughs. "You're whispering? Is everyone already in bed there?"

I straighten up and lean my elbow on the arm of the couch. "Yeah. Daddy's tired from his big day coming home. I have a really early morning, so I was trying to sleep, but wasn't there yet. What's up?"

"How was your first day back in town? Heard you were hanging out with Carol and Jessie and Pepper. Moved right into the popular crowd, didn't you?"

"No. I mean, I was with Pepper, but not Carol and Jessie. How did you hear that?"

"Oh, you know. People talk. But anyway, we're invited to dinner out at Carol and Buck's Thursday. Sound good to you?"

"Really? Um, I guess. But, ah, are you sure they invited me?"

"Honey, of course. Due to our night in Tifton, we are a thing now. I better let you get to sleep. Me and the kids are coming to see you for breakfast in the morning, so get your beauty sleep. See you soon!"

He hangs up. I make sure my alarm on my phone is set, again, before I snuggle back down into my blankets on the couch. The heat keeps kicking on, and it's loud, but keeps me toasty. Irene left before Momma and I had finished cleaning up the kitchen. Then we watched some TV, but Momma kept getting up every few minutes to check on Daddy. She only went outside to smoke once. Usually she chain-smokes and makes it almost impossible to sit with her for any length of time. So maybe she is quitting. Once Irene left Momma relaxed some, and we got along pretty good. She even offered me her bed, said she could sleep with Daddy. But the couch is fine. Plus, this way she won't disturb Daddy if she can't sleep.

Between the warmth and the cocoon of blankets, my eyes are staying closed longer and longer between blinks. Morning is going to come early. But then I start replaying the phone call. Jameson sounded weird. Happy. Too happy. Giddy almost. Can't wait to see Cab and Maggie tomorrow. Dinner. Dinner at Carol's house. Carol and Buck Lewis' house.

Great, now I'm definitely not falling asleep.

23

"Ashleigh, good to see you," Magnus says as he comes inside Sybil's. "Thought that was your car out front." He grins and purrs. "Marriage agrees with you, darling. You look beautiful."

Ashleigh stands up from her table. "Why, thank you, and good morning." She winks at him. "You're looking for me? Should Carlos be worried?"

He leans in to kiss her cheek. "Any man should be worried when he's married to a good-looking woman. But don't worry—everyone knows your heart is all his. Where is he? I don't want to interrupt your breakfast. I know the restaurant isn't open yet."

"He's in the kitchen checking in an order. We usually try to have coffee together here in the mornings, where it's warm. Our house is a little weak in the heating department. He'll be out in a minute. So, what can I do for you? Have a seat."

"The kitten. You know, Becca Sue's kitten? I'm wondering if you'll keep him a couple days. I need to take a quick trip out of town."

Ashleigh nods, then picks up her coffee. "I'd love to. So, a trip out of town. Will you be flying somewhere" She sips her coffee, her eyes never leaving his face.

"Ah, no. There's the groom!" He stands and shakes Carlos' hand as the young man enters the dining room.

"Good to see you again, Mr. Llord. Didn't get to speak to

you much when you were here for dinner. Can I get you a cup of coffee?"

"No, thank you. And please, call me Magnus. I really need to leave, just needed to ask a favor of your wife. And you, I suppose, as well."

"He wants us to watch the kitten while he take a short trip out of town," Ashleigh explains. Then she raises her eyebrows tellingly. "A driving trip."

Carlos laughs. "Hope you're heading south where it might be warmer. Who knew Florida could be this cold?"

Magnus grins and nods, but doesn't say anything.

Ashleigh asks, "So are you headed south?"

Magnus pauses, then answers. "Nope. North. Listen, I need to run, but is it okay if I bring the kitten over late this afternoon?"

"Sure," Ashleigh says. "I'll be home any time after three."

"Great. I'll see you then," he says as he waves at them both. In the little vestibule he remembers another question. He catches the door before it latches and pushes it open a few inches.

In the empty room, Ashleigh and Carlos' voices carry.

Carlos says, "You seem awfully happy. Didn't know you liked Magnus so much."

"Compared to Drummond Bell, I'm crazy about him. Obviously, Magnus doesn't know about her and that creep. And him chasing her up to Georgia is a good thing. Her sleeping with Drummond is a sure sign that Becca Sue has to be saved from herself. Oh, but wait 'til you see the kitten! Wonder if they ever picked a name for it?"

Magnus slides the heavy door shut and releases the handle so it makes no noise. He strides to his car with his head down, and after he gets in, he sits for a while with the engine running, staring straight ahead. Finally, he pulls out and drives away. At the opening of a row of new condos, he turns around and drives back past Sybil's, past his house, around the top of the lake, and pulls into the Kings' driveway. He gets out of the car barely before he's cut the ignition.

"Morning, Magnus," Eason King says as he opens the door. "Come in and have some coffee. Kids have been up for hours it seems."

Magnus walks in, and before he says anything, he sees the twins in their pajamas, lounging on the couch with their dad. "Looks like a comfy place to be."

Brandley looks up and grins. "It is. Do you need to see me?"

Magnus shakes his head and turns to Eason. "Can we have a word? In your office?"

"Sure," Eason waves him inside and then closes the door. "What's going on?"

"I think you have a good idea here, Eason, I really do. Might even get involved in Backwater somewhere else, but this deal here? Just won't work for me."

Eason frowns. "Now, Magnus, don't close the door on it. We need financing, and you need investments. You told Bradley that just yesterday."

"I know I did. And maybe we can work together sometime in the future, but right now it's not a good idea."

"But the way Florida law is, we need to move on it now. We can't wait."

Magnus steps to the door. "Tell you what, today's Tuesday. You work on other options for financing, and I'll make some decisions. Let's talk Sunday night. I'm going to be gone for a few days." He opens the office door just as Bradley walked up to it on the other side. Magnus puts his head down and maneuvers past the younger man. He leaves out the front door as Ruth comes out of the kitchen.

"What's Magnus doing? Is he okay?" she asks.

Eason sighs. "We're going to need other financing."

"What?" Bradley exclaims. "Let me talk to him." But as he pulls open the front door, he sees Magnus' car pealing out of the drive.

Ruth clears her throat. "Maybe it's a sign that you should just drop it. Drop it right now." She frowns at her husband and son and, after a quick look at her grandchildren, says, "You know how I feel about it. I'm with Magnus!"

The men watch her stomp back into the kitchen, then Bradley shrugs. "Guess it's good that I'm meeting with the Bells' this morning. We don't have time to mess around."

24

"Sure wish I could sit down and visit with y'all," Becca Sue says after she's hugged Cab and Maggie and they've slid into a booth. Maggie sits on the same side as Jameson.

He turns his coffee cup over so she can fill it as he asks, "How's your first morning been?"

She leans closer to the table and whispers, "Longest, fastest morning of my life, and it's still not even nine o'clock! Who knew all these people were up and eating breakfast this early every morning? Uh-uh, Cab. You're not drinking coffee. Are you?" When he nods, and Jameson shrugs, she fills his cup. "Maggie, what do you want? I know *you're* not allowed to drink coffee."

"Orange juice. And I want the French toast. No sausage or bacon. What time do you get off work?" She bounces a little in her seat.

Becca Sue's face is creased as she looks up. "Two, but don't know if I'll make it. I'm exhausted. Cab, what can I get you?"

"The number one, scrambled eggs."

Jameson speaks up. "Same for me, but with eggs over easy."

"Let me go put these in and get the orange juice. Be right back."

Becca Sue pours coffee for those lingering at their tables, digs out bills for rushed customers, and takes forever getting to the order window. She stops to remember where the order slip goes, then turns around and is filling a glass with orange juice as Mel hollers at her through the window.

"You have a pick up. C'mon, Bec. You can't leave eggs sitting here. There, that one and that one. Get on it, girl!" He shakes his head and mutters.

"Sorry, sorry!" Becca Sue repeats as she grabs the plates. As she pulls one towards her, the little bowl of hot grits slides off the plate and falls onto the counter, shattering and splattering hot grits on her. "Oh no!" she exclaims as the plate, left teetering on the edge of the window, bows to gravity and falls to the counter, then the floor, too.

Mel growls. "That was the sunny side up, right? I'm making another one. Go take that one and apologize. Wipe the stuff up in the floor so no one falls, got it?"

Tina darts up and throws a towel over the mess on the floor. "That's good for now. Take that plate to your table. You'll have to clean this up—I can't get down there with this belly."

Becca Sue's mouth is pulled tight and her eyes are shiny, but she delivers the plate to the right customer. After a deep breath, she apologizes to his wife and explains her breakfast will be right out. She pauses as she passes Maggie's table. "Oh, your orange juice. I poured it. I'll get it."

When she grabs the juice, she steps over the towel-covered mess to dart out around the counter. She sets it down in front of Maggie and then runs back to the window when she hears Mel call her name.

He speaks slowly, "Here's the new one. Don't spill it. And your other order is up, too. No, take the replacement one first." He shakes his head as she heads off again. "Thank God we're not busy this morning."

Tina smiles at him and nods in agreement. "Can one of the guys come clean this up out here? She's trying her best."

"Sure. I forget waitressing doesn't just come natural to most people. She's making *me* tired. But you're right, she's trying. DJ," he calls to one of the line cooks, "go clean up that spill behind the counter."

When Becca Sue finally delivers the plates to Jameson's

table, he grins and looks down at his plate. "Scrambled are okay."

"Oh, gosh, you didn't want scrambled. I wrote two scrambled. What is wrong with me?" Cab rolls his eyes, but keeps his head down, busy eating. Jameson just smiles and says, "Nothing is wrong with you. I like scrambled, too."

Maggie adds, "And he can have my bacon, so that'll make everybody happy. Right, Uncle J?"

Becca Sue sighs. "But you did want French toast, right? I got that right at least. And Cab, yours is okay, isn't it?"

He nods but says to his uncle. "Can't be late."

"That's right. We better eat up, but Maggie wants to know if she can meet you when you get off work. She could walk here from the high school."

"I can be here by two-thirty," Maggie says. "My last period is study hall, and I get out all the time to do stuff."

"Sure, sure," Becca Sue says. "I've got to go. Mel's hollering for me again."

Cab's head snaps up, and he stares at his sister. "What kind of stuff are you getting out early for?"

"Don't worry, I'm not like you. I'm not getting out to go drinking down at the creek behind the baseball field."

Cab holds up his egg-covered fork. "Not me. Well, not this year, Uncle J. Promise." He scowls at his sister. "Tattletale. So, really, what are you doing?"

She stuffs another piece of syrup-soaked French toast in her mouth and glares back at him. "Nothing," she mumbles.

"Ready, guys?" Jameson asks. "I've got to get to the office. Becca Sue didn't leave our bill, did she?" He takes another swig of his coffee and eats the last piece of bacon. When there's still no bill, he motions for Maggie to slide out. "I'll go get the bill."

At the counter, he talks through the window with Mel and chats with a couple of the guys sitting at the counter, nursing their coffee. Cab and Maggie, already in their jackets and standing beside the front door, tell him to come on. Finally

Becca Sue comes to the counter and digs Jameson's bill out of her uniform pocket.

"I'm sorry. Can't believe I didn't leave this at your table." She hands it to him, then steps toward the kids and waves. "Good to see you two. I'll be looking for you later, Mags." As she turns around, Jameson has stepped away from the counter and is standing in front of her.

He puts both hands on her shoulders and kisses her. Hard. Then leans his forehead against hers. "I'll be looking for you later, too." One of his hands holds the back of her head now, and when he kisses her a second time, he holds onto her longer. "Later," he says as he releases her.

Becca Sue takes a deep breath and jumps as Mel yells her name.

"If you're through putting on a show for the customers, maybe you'd like to consider taking them their food!"

"You were surprised Uncle J kissed you, weren't you?" Maggie asks me as we walk down the far aisle in the South Georgia Shoppes.

"Yeah. Guess I was."

"I wasn't. He likes you. He talks about you all the time."

Stepping away from her, I ask, "Did you know my old teacher, Mrs. Fulbright, has a shop here? There on the right." She follows me to a display of purses and scarves with writing on them. "Guess these are quotes from books. Cool."

She examines the writing. "We had to read some of these books. They're kind of boring."

"Really? Makes you wonder how they got to be classics, don't it?" I elbow her, and we laugh together.

"Because they speak to universal truths," Mrs. Fulbright says from behind one of the shelves.

"Oh, hi. Didn't see you there. Look, I brought Maggie."

"Hello, Margaret. You didn't enjoy Jane Austen? Or Dickens? Oh, excuse me. Those are for later grades. You're a freshman, right?"

"Yes, ma'am," Maggie says. "We did Edgar Allan Poe last year, though. We had a sub that read him to us around Halloween. It was spooky, but I liked it. And then we did Dickens' *Tale of Two Cities* this past fall. I'm in honors lit." She's not the shy girl she was last summer, I can tell you that.

"Becca Sue, you read a lot in high school as I remember. Nothing noteworthy, but you did always seem to have a book."

"But I wasn't in honors lit, for sure. I like, you know, romances and stuff." While I'm talking, Mrs. Fulbright stares at us and then she moves to a shelf of books at the back.

She is holding a book when she comes back to the front where me and Maggie are. "Here, Becca Sue. Try this. *Pride and Prejudice* by Jane Austen. It will be difficult to understand at first, but I want you to stick with it to the end. When you finish, bring it back to me and I'll give you your choice of the scarves there."

Maggie turns to the scarves and picks up a soft yellow one with blue writing on it. "These are from books, right?"

"Yes, famous lines from literature. That one is from *Jane Eyre*. A book I believe you'd both enjoy. Now, I have to get back to work. Take this," she finishes as she pushes the soft-covered book towards me.

"Okay, thanks." I turn to leave, and when Maggie also turns, I roll my eyes at her and give her a goofy smile. Which she doesn't return. When we get to the big front doors, we stop to look out at the soft day. The air is mild and the sun fills the air with hazy yellow light. There's no breeze, and everything seems to be smudged, like a chalk drawing.

"It's getting late," Maggie says. "Glad it's not as cold today. You ready to go?"

"I am. It's been a long day. Who's picking you up?" I ask.

She looks sideways at me. "You're taking me home, I figured. It's kinda on your way."

I catch my breath. "Oh, I don't think so. To the house? Honey..."

Maggie turns to face me. "What's wrong? Nobody cares if you are at the house. So you lived there with Dad. So what? You don't even have to get out of the car." She huffs at me, then walks out into the parking lot and towards the diner.

Caleb's house. Caleb's mother's house. Everyone here acts like Caleb didn't matter. Like he's been gone forever. But last January he was here. He lived in that house. He ate at the diner. He was real, and I don't want to remember. I can't go to that house. "Mags, wait." I follow her as she walks to the other side of the diner. By time I get around the side, she's sitting in my car, her door open.

"See what happens when you don't lock your doors." She grinning, but it's not funny.

"Mags, I don't want to go there. I can't. Please understand."

She jerks the door, and my hand falls away from it. She slams it and waits with her arms crossed. Okay. I'll just pull up and drop her off. She doesn't say anything until I start the car.

"You got the book from Mrs. Fulbright?" she asks.

"Yes. It's in my pocketbook. Have you read it?"

"No. Think I read something else by her, but I don't know." She's quiet as she stares out the window. The air is peach and blue and white and settles close to the empty fields of reddish-brown dirt. Her voice is heavy when she says, "You know, you and me are the only ones that miss Daddy."

So many words come to my head, but they aren't true and she'll know it. So my only response is to say nothing. She responds the same way.

Finally, at the end of a mile of white fencing, we turn underneath the tall signpost for Mason Farms. My stomach decides to stay out on the main road, but my heart is very much along for the ride. I think they can hear it pounding up in the house.

The big white house with black shutters and a wide front porch. The porch where Mrs. Mason found us wrapped up in her white feather comforter and then found out we were married. The car slows to a crawl because my feet have turned to stone. There are the windows to our rooms, our suite, where I stayed like a good little girl until we moved into our house behind the big one. And I was only there until I was kicked out for Audrey, and for Caleb's baby she was carrying. And then, standing on that porch, there's the reason *I* never had Caleb's baby—Mrs. Mason.

"Grandmother's home. She's been in Atlanta since last week. I think it was Atlanta. Come say 'hi'—"

"No. Go, Maggie. I have to leave. Please."

She opens the car door and gets out. She tries to lean in and say something to me, but I put the car in drive and pull off. The door doesn't latch, but I reach across and pull it closed. At the white fence I barely stop to look for traffic before pulling out. Stupid of me, because me dying on the highway in front of her house would just make Mrs. Mason's day.

25

"They've been in there a long time," Pearl whispers to Ruth. "What do you think they are talking about?"

Ruth shakes her head, lips pressed firmly together. Then suddenly she's yelling. "Phillips Baets King, don't take off those pants! If you want to go outside you have to stay dressed! For God's sake, Pearl, take that cup away from Emerson. There's still coffee in it!"

Pearl reaches for the coffee cup, grabbing it just before the toddler dumps it onto the floor. She then scoops up the girl and asks her where her boots are. Emerson doesn't answer, but her grandmother points toward the back porch.

"They're out there, both pairs. Would you mind getting them?" Ruth grabs her grandson and puts him on the couch beside her. "Leave your pants up and let me put on your socks if you want to go see the doggies." Struggling with him, she apologizes to her friend when Pearl comes back into the room with two pairs of shiny rain boots. "Pearl, I'm so sorry for yelling at you like that. These two are about more than I can handle."

Pearl sits down with Emerson on her lap and pulls the boots onto her tiny feet. "You're excused. Seems like since the idea of Bradley and Olivia going off together didn't work, their mother shouldn't have just left for a vacation. I'm exhausted just watching you. Bradley should be out here helping you instead of being holed up in Eason's office with Mimi and Drummond."

"There," Ruth says as she sets Phillips down with both boots, pants, and pull-up in place. "Now, let's get your coats and we'll go on our walk."

As Pearl heads toward the front door, she pauses beside Eason's office. Ruth notices and announces, "Come on, Auntie Pearl. Let's go see your babies."

Pearl shakes her head as she stares at her friend. Finally she walks past her and out the front door. "I know you don't want me to know what's going on. You being so secretive isn't helping, you know? Makes me even more curious. I thought we were friends."

Ruth sighs and closes the front door behind her. "Pearl, please just leave it alone. I have too much on my plate to deal with all that right now." She pauses to zip up her jacket then shouts, "Phillips, don't go into the road! Pearl, please catch him."

Ruth walks into the grass to the left and takes her granddaughter's hand. "Come on, let's catch up to your brother." As she leads the little girl back in front of the house she watches Pearl and Phillips examine something beside the road. Probably road kill. She sighs again and says quietly to herself, "Sorry, Pearl, but the longer you go without hearing, the better." More loudly, she speaks to her granddaughter as she releases her hand, "Go catch Brother!"

Pearl hears her and turns to watch as Emerson waddles and runs past her. "Those big boots are brilliant," she says to Ruth. "They can't really maneuver in them. Slows them down so we might be able to keep up." At the sandy drive leading to Becca Sue's house, the twins jump in a puddle, and the ladies slow their walking to let them play.

Ruth and Pearl look through the woods at the house, and Ruth asks, "Wonder why they're not working? You'd think with having to live with Drummond and Mimi, Becca Sue would be in an even bigger hurry to move out."

"Not from what I hear," Pearl says with a lilt in her voice.

"Didn't you find it odd that Becca Sue left so very early Sunday morning? According to Carlos, there was a fire in Becca Sue's fireplace after the party Saturday."

Ruth turns away from her friend, jams her hands into her coat pockets, and shivers. "I wondered if everyone knew about it." She sighs. "It's chilly. C'mon, kids, let's go see the doggies." She removes her hands and holds them out for the children to grasp.

"Oh, Ruth! The kids are fine. Aren't you at all curious about Becca Sue and Drummond?" Pearl demands.

Ruth turns around, pulling the kids with her. "Becca Sue and Drummond?"

"Yes! Carlos saw him follow her to her cabin Saturday leaving the party. As much as I disapproved of her being with Magnus, at least *he* wasn't married." Pearl walks past Ruth. "Auntie Pearl has hot chocolate at her house and the doggies are there. It's cold out here."

They all pick up their pace, with the kids repeating "Doggie! Doggie! Doggie!" Pearl looks back and laughs. "Why, Ruth, look at you. See, a little fresh air has made you all smiles!"

"Yep. Guess that's all I needed. Some fresh air." She adds in a happy mutter, "And a little mistaken gossip."

26

"Is this becoming a habit? Where's Cab?" Becca Sue asks Maggie and Jameson as she places fresh silverware on their table.

Jameson holds his coffee cup out for her to fill it. "We dropped him off early at school. He had an FFA meeting."

Becca Sue puts a fist on her hip and pulls her chin back. "FFA? Since when did a Mason boy deign to consider himself a Future Farmer of America? The Mason boys I knew would've rather died."

Jameson clears his throat and tilts toward the end of the table where Becca Sue stands laughing. "Well... we were obviously wrong."

Maggie interjects. "But how could you *not* be in FFA? Mason *Farms*, hello?"

"Your grandmother would've burnt down the school, so it truly was in the best interest of everyone," Becca Sue explains. "What can I get you?"

"Um, pancakes today and one piece of sausage," Maggie says as she hands her menu to Becca Sue. She then adds, "Grandmother wondered why you didn't come in last night. She said you should stop by."

"*Your* grandmother? Your Grandmother Mason said I should stop by?" When Jameson tries to give her his order, Becca Sue just holds out her palm to him. "Maggie, are you making that up?"

Her green eyes never looking away, the girl says, "No. She really said that. She's, well... kind of different."

Becca Sue looks at Jameson, and he nods, then shrugs. "She told me the same thing. Maybe Caleb's death is finally hitting her." Cutting his eyes toward his niece, he says, "We can talk about it later. I need to get Maggie to school." He picks up his menu and stretches it towards Becca Sue. "I'll have the number one again, and whatever eggs it comes with will be fine."

Becca Sue takes his menu and rolls her eyes. "This morning has been much better. Over easy, right?"

"Whatever you bring me, I'll love," he calls as she leaves the table.

"You look awful happy," Pepper says from her seat at the counter. "How's your daddy doing?"

"Thanks for asking," Becca Sue says. "He's doing better. Momma's goin' a little stir crazy, that trailer does get small."

On Becca Sue's next trip to the counter, Pepper asks her another question, "So, how are things with Jameson? He looks mighty happy, too."

Becca Sue balances a plate on her arm and picks up another plate with a bowl of grits, but takes a look at the booth with Jameson and Maggie. "He and Maggie always get along well."

She sways around the end of the counter with her load of food and dishes. As she's close to Pepper, Pepper says in a low voice. "Is it being with his niece now, or being with you in the front seat of his big SUV last night that's got him so happy?"

Becca Sue's momentum stutters and the plates wobble, but she rights herself and takes them to the table. The wrong table. Flustered, she picks up the plates and puts them on the right table, where the man winks at her. Mel shouts her name and she hurries past Pepper again, her face growing redder every minute. With Maggie and Jameson's plates in her hands, she tries to ignore Pepper's giggle when she goes by.

"Here you go! I believe it's all right." She sets the dishes down and rushes away from the table. Back at the counter she looks to see if she has any more orders up, then turns and bends close to Pepper. "How do you know that?"

Pepper shuts her big, blue eyes and shakes her head. "No sirree, I don't give out details unless I *get* details. Let's have lunch in my office over at the Shops. Schedule says your lunch break is ten-thirty, so I'll see you then. Bring me a veggie plate with mac and cheese, collards, sweet potato casserole, and lima beans."

I drop off Jameson's check and make sure when he and Maggie leave I'm very, very busy at the rear of the diner. No repeat of yesterday's kiss is happening. No way. Every inch of my skin burns thinking everyone knows about last night in his car. His big, warm, new-smelling car. Okay, maybe not every inch of my skin burns, just the parts he touched. Granted, that's pretty much all of it.

That book Mrs. Fulbright gave me? It took some time to get into it, like she said, but it's so good! Who knew olden times in England were so much like times these days in Georgia? Who you're supposed to marry. Who you're not supposed to marry. Mommas and daddies and everybody getting into your business. Who knew?

After dropping Maggie off at home, all I wanted to do was go home and get warm. I had a bowl of Irene's leftover soup and fell slap asleep on the couch before the evening news was even on. It was just barely dark. So when I woke up after an hour sleeping, I decided to read. And I decided to keep reading even when Jameson kept texting me to meet up somewhere.

I was well into that English Lizzie's story when guess who texted he was outside? So, of course, I went out. Just for a minute. Like I said, the car was so warm and big and new-smelling. Those seats kind of lay back, and well, he had this nice music on. The soft lights from the dash were almost like candlelight, and well, it was really nice.

But how in the world does Pepper know?

And who else knows? Mel keeps shaking his head, but I don't know if that's because of my poor waitressing or my poor choices last night. And that guy that winked at me this morning? Was it just a wink, or was it a *wink*? Finally it's ten-thirty, and I can get some answers. I add a couple squares of cornbread to the bag carrying our takeout veggie plates and head over next door.

Pepper's office is right as I go in the big doors, which are closed today as it's raining a bit. Her office door is cracked, so I stick my head in.

"Hey there. Ready for lunch?" Her office doesn't look anything like the office over in the diner. That one is cluttered and small with a metal desk and old chairs. The decorations are just calendars with pictures of softball and baseball teams wearing Piney Diner T-shirts in a variety of colors.

Pepper's office, first of all, has the thickest carpet I've ever seen anywhere. The carpet is white, and the furniture is not much darker. It doesn't look like Piney. At all. "Are you sure you want to eat in here? It's awful clean-looking."

"Of course," she says from behind her desk. I can see her crossed legs and high heels because her desk is really more like a big table. She motions for me to set the food on her desk. It's empty except for her laptop, with anything that looks like work stacked in the fabric-covered boxes behind her. It smells good in here, too, then I see the candles lit around the room.

"This is really nice, Pepper. I hope I don't drip anything."

"Oh, no worries! It's all IKEA. Don't you love that place? Bruce says we should just buy one since I shop there so much. Wouldn't that be fun? So—just say 'thank you.'"

Okay. So I say, "Thank you for lunch."

"No, silly. Lunch is part of the perks of working at the diner. I meant for Jameson last night. Just say 'thank you' for me sending him to you. He was mooning something fierce about you not answering his texts. Harry showed him how to use Find Your Friends on his phone, so we knew you were at your folks. I told him to get over there. Make something happen!" She takes a big bite of sweet potato casserole. "Law, I love this stuff. Bruce wanted to change the diner's menu, says it's not healthy. I told him no way. When he's here, I can't eat all the good stuff, so I load up during the week. Oh, bless you, you brought cornbread, too."

"Harry? Who's Harry? And how does he know about my phone?"

"You met him. Bartender at El Dorado's. Apparently Mason Farms still has your phone on their account."

"Jameson was at El Dorado's with you?"

"With all of us, Carol and Jessie and the guys. That's why we wanted you to come. It's such fun. Tonight is church night, so we won't be there and then tomorrow we'll all be at Buck and Carol's for their dinner party. But Friday night we'll all be there. Do you sing? That's karaoke night." She looks down at the Styrofoam container. "Shoot, I'm talking too much, and my food is getting cold. Besides, I want to hear about last night. Give me details!"

"Well, honestly, I don't know." I lay my cornbread down in my to-go box. "Do you have some water here? I didn't bring drinks."

With her mouth full, she points at the cabinet behind me. I find a little refrigerator there and sit two bottles on the desk. I open mine and take a long, slow drink. I haven't had much time to think about last night. Pepper waits, and that surprises me. Maybe she is a good listener after all. Okay, I'll give it a go.

"We didn't have sex."

Yep, she's as surprised as I am. She looks down at her plate and takes her time spearing lima beans. Chewing, she stares at me. "Really? Although, now that I think about it, he didn't actually say you had sex. He didn't really say much of nothing."

"When did he report back to you?"

She draws in a breath and grimaces. "Last night. He came back to the bar. Some of us were kind of... waiting."

"What did he say?" *This is Piney. This is Piney. This is Piney.* My mantra is keeping me from getting too angry.

We both eat a few bites while she thinks. "Really, nothing. Just grinned a lot. Guess we just assumed... I mean, everyone remembers you and Caleb, so..." She shrugs. "But it's probably good you didn't let him, you know. Like, it was hard to overcome my reputation as a stick in the mud when I came back. So, you holding Jameson Mason off will help everyone think differently of you. Good thinking."

Closing up my container, I stand. "Guess I better get back to work."

She closes hers, too, and stands. She takes it to the refrigerator. "I'll save the rest of mine for later. Now, don't you work too hard," she advises as I open the office door and leave.

I can hear the rain as I approach the outside doors. I step into the overhang and wait for a minute to see if it will lighten up. Leaning against the cold stone wall, I think back to last night. If only it had been me thinking of my reputation that stopped us from having sex.

If only.

Wonder where Magnus went off to after knocking on the steamed-up car window last night? By the time I got my clothes back on, he was gone. Jameson didn't see Magnus' face, so he's doesn't know who interrupted us. And now Magnus won't answer my calls.

But the question lingers at the back of my mind. What in the world was Magnus doing in Piney?

27

"Sometimes you just can't keep people apart," Miss Bell says with a long sigh. She's wrapped in a navy blanket on the Kings' screened porch. There's a small heater pointed in her direction so she won't feel the chill of the drizzly day.

"Why don't we go inside?" Ruth offers again. "I don't want you to catch a chill. Bad enough you walking over here in the rain."

"Honey, don't worry about me. Listening to the rain on a porch roof is one of life's greatest pleasures. Life's too short to miss a chance. Are *you* warm enough, honey?"

"I'm fine. I was sitting out here before you rang the bell. Porch rain is one of my favorites, too. So soothing. Sorry you missed seeing the twins, but Bradley took them into Jacksonville to one of those big toddler play places. Those two are something else. About to wear their Nana out."

"Children are sweet, but they are a lot of work. Even when they're grown." Miss Bell shifts in her chair. "Ruth, I didn't come over here just to listen to the rain, but to get your opinion on this investment Drummond is hell-bent on joining in with Eason and Bradley. What do you think?"

Ruth holds up a hand. "Wait, before we get into that, you said something about not being able to keep some people apart. Who were you talking about?"

"Becca Sue and that Magnus." Miss Bell clicks her tongue against her teeth and shakes her head. "He wasn't back but a couple days and they were already back together. I tried, but, well, sometimes you just can't keep people apart."

Ruth sits up. "Magnus and Becca Sue? When did they get back together? I thought she was up in Georgia with her parents."

"Before she left. That night after the party. I knew she left without talking to me because she was feeling guilty, and I was *hoping* it wasn't anything to do with *him*." She shrugs and then laughs. "Drummond and Mimi were so serious, like they were telling me something new when they said Magnus and Becca Sue spent the night together in the cabin. Oh, poor Drummond. Maybe having Drummond around has also stirred up my memories of being fiercely in love and ignoring everything else. Just like Becca Sue." She closes her eyes for a moment, and when she opens them, they are shiny with tears.

"Oh, Virginia, are you okay?" Ruth asks. "Can I get you anything?"

"You're sweet. I'm all right, but can I tell you something? Something I've never told anyone?"

"Of course." Ruth settles back into the chair.

The older woman pulls the blue blanket up closer and inhales deeply. "Mr. Bell was married when he and I became involved. Married to Drummond's mother." The words rush out and then Miss Bell releases a long breath. "There. Finally said it." She winces. "Hope you're not too shocked. We were together for so long that I don't even think about it anymore. Then Drummond showing up, and seeing how Becca Sue and Magnus are... well, just got me to remembering."

"I'm not shocked. You are such a good soul. Sometimes these things just happen," Ruth says.

"Maybe I'm a good soul now, but I was not early in my life. Ruth, I stole him from his wife and family. When I saw him, I knew he was supposed to be mine. I was nineteen. He did business with my father and uncle. I did some bookkeeping for them, and they asked if I'd help Drummond, Drummond Senior, out with his books. Right off, I saw his company was growing. His home was large and right downtown. It's hard to say, but I decided it was supposed to be mine, too. How could I have been so awful?" Tears are now running down her face.

Ruth takes in a breath as if to say something, but then just lets it die.

"And, yes, I'm crying now, but I didn't cry a single tear for his wife or son back then. Even with these tears, I'm ashamed to say I would do it again. I loved him so much. His wife had to move back to Wisconsin to be near family. She took their son with her. See, I was going to fill that big house with so many children, he'd never have to even think about him or her again."

"But you never had children, right?" Ruth says sadly.

"No. No, we never were able. And in my youthful arrogance, I didn't allow Drummond Junior to come stay with us ever." She sticks one hand out from under the blanket and waves it. "Out of sight, out of mind."

"He was Mr. Bell's son. He could have easily overridden you."

"Yes, he could've. We'll never know why he didn't. My Drummond was so in love with me and we were so very happy that by time we realized we weren't going to have children, well..."

The rain pings on the roof and runs down the screens. A soft rumble comes from the heater. Miss Bell sniffles, and Ruth hands her a Kleenex from the box on the side table.

"Thank you for letting me talk, Ruth. I'm really good at ignoring things until I'm forced to look at them. Having Drummond and Mimi stay in my house is forcing me to look at myself. I get aggravated at him, but how else would he have turned out? Having his father and me dump him like that." She says louder, "Oh, his father paid for everything, of course. Drummond went to the best schools and had everything he needed. But that's not enough for a boy, is it?"

"What about his mother?"

The older woman laughs. "Oh, the witch of Wisconsin? That was what I called her."

"Oh, now, Miss Bell, I doubt that. Just doesn't sound like you."

"Please believe me, I was an awful young woman. As I grew up and matured, I learned not only how to behave, but why it's a good thing to be a good person. I could've become a bitter person, but Mr. Bell started going to church and, of course, I went with him. Lots of lonely hours for me to fill. But I never made any amends with Drummond or his mother. Mr. Bell did, some. But I just closed the door on it. Until now."

Ruth lays her blanket aside. "So sorry to interrupt, but I *have* to go to the bathroom. Can I bring you back a cup of tea or coffee?"

"A cup of tea would be wonderful. And Ruth, never mind my questions about the investment. I owe it to Drummond to trust him. And I *do* trust his judgments. He's done very well for himself and has become a successful man, despite my interference in his life. Whatever he decides will be fine."

Ruth smiles and nods, pausing before going inside the house.

Miss Bell breathes deep and lets it out. "Feels good to get it all out and start trusting people. If Becca Sue and Magnus love each other, who am I to interfere? And I am going to trust Drummond. After all, he *is* his daddy's son. I will trust him and be happy for this time with him."

"Eason, nobody knows!" Ruth whispers loudly as her husband enters their bedroom. She's propped up in bed holding the video monitor from the room where the twins are sleeping.

"Well, they will soon. Tonight's meeting was more than we bargained for." He takes off his tie and unbuttons the sleeves of his dress shirt. "Somehow people know, and they came out of the woodwork. Some for and some against, but all loud." He walks into their bathroom and shuts the door.

There is a knock on their bedroom door, and Ruth says, "Come in."

Bradley sticks his head in the door. "Hi Mom. How'd things go with the kids tonight?"

She holds up the monitor. "Just fine. They're sleeping like angels. I can keep the monitor tonight, let you get some sleep. Dad said the meeting was loud?"

He leans on the doorjamb. "Yeah, and if you're okay with it, I'm going to go get a beer with some of the folks I met there."

"Who? Do we know them?"

"Think so. The newspaper lady, Ashleigh or Ansley. She was at the party. And her husband, Carlos from the restaurant. So it's okay with you? Kids are okay?"

She shrugs. "Fine with me. Just behave and don't mention Becca Sue. She and Ashleigh are good friends."

He grins and agrees. "Whatever you say. Thanks, Mom."

Shortly after he closes the door, the bathroom door opens. "Where's Bradley going?"

"Out with Ashleigh and Carlos, but never mind that and never mind your meeting. Nobody knows it was Bradley with Becca Sue after the party!" Hey eyes are bright as she laughs. "Pearl thinks she was with Drummond, and Mrs. Bell thinks she was with Magnus! Isn't that wonderful?"

Eason gets into bed. "I guess it's good. Less drama right now wouldn't be a bad thing. Okay if I read a bit?"

"Sure," she says. "Wonder how people get things so wrong? Becca Sue being with Magnus is understandable, but Drummond? Pearl was very sure of herself, of course."

Eason lays his book on his lap. "Pearl is always very sure of herself. I'm dreading when she finds out what's going on. Everything from the meeting will be in the paper on Friday. Maybe we should talk to her and George and let them know first."

Ruth turns off her bedside lamp and settles down on her side, facing away from her husband. "There's no 'we' in this. You and your son can tell her. She's not been a huge fan of the idea of Backwater from the beginning. Telling Pearl Manningham she's going to live across the street from a marijuana dispensary? I'll bow out of that conversation, thank you."

Eason sighs and lifts his book. "You are a wise woman, Ruth King."

28

"No way! Marijuana?" Becca Sue says into the phone. "Ashleigh, how can that happen? Wonder if Roger knows?"

"Good question. Can you give me his phone number?"

"No. I'll call him and give him *your* number. If he wants to talk to the press, he can call you. Just a minute." She holds the phone away from her. "Daddy, I'm done with my shower, so you can get in the bathroom." Stepping into the kitchen, her hair wet and wearing only a towel, she says, "Lord, you'd never know the man just had heart surgery the way he was banging on the bathroom door when I was in the shower."

Ashleigh sighs. "Hard living back at home, isn't it? Okay on Mr. Worth, but be sure and tell him it's not just plain old marijuana. It's medical marijuana. You have to have a prescription from a real doctor, and you have to be on some checklist. Law just passed in Florida last November, so everyone's trying to figure it all out. I was up on the computer most of all night researching for my article. Or should I say, 'articles.' I'm up to three different angles already. Bradley King is pretty impressive with what all he knows. He was real helpful last night."

Becca Sue sits down at the kitchen table, holding her towel around her. "Bradley King?"

"Yeah, Ruth and Eason's son. You met him at the party. Apparently that's why he's here, to get this business started. He's been involved in the same thing up in the Northeast. And with his dad being a retired doctor, he thinks it's perfect for Backwater. Another rule is that a prescribing doctor can't be involved in the ownership. I think that's what it means. It's a lot to think about, isn't it?"

When Becca Sue doesn't answer, Ashleigh asks, "You still there?"

"Oh, yeah. So, you're hanging out with Bradley King?"

"I don't know that you'd call it hanging out. After the meeting, he and Carlos and I went to the Down Under for a couple beers. Seems like a nice guy. Why?"

"No reason, just wondering. Hey, Daddy's out of the bathroom, and I've got to get ready for this thing tonight."

"Okay, so you'll be home this weekend, right? Do you have to go back on Sunday or you gonna wait until Monday morning?"

Becca Sue puffs out her cheeks, pauses, then answers as she stands up, adjusting her towel with her free hand. "Umm, maybe I'll just stay here. No sense in all that driving, you know."

Now it's Ashleigh who's silent.

Becca Sue doesn't try to draw her out. Instead, she ends the conversation with "Okay, gotta go. Bye."

Ashleigh says, "Bye," but her friend has already hung up.

She shakes her head. "I knew it. They're sucking her in. Wait 'til Magnus gets there. Hopefully that'll help." She laughs and looks down at the little gray and white kitten at her feet. "Times do change. I'm counting on your daddy to get your mommy back down here." She laughs. "Me, Magnus's newest fan, who'd have thought?"

"You look beautiful," Jameson says when I meet him on the front deck of the trailer. He leans over to kiss me, but I pull back.

"It's cold, let's get in the car." I open the passenger door before he can do it for me, but he takes hold of the door to close it and steps closer.

He lays his hand on my thigh and pets my leg. "This skirt's nice, and I love the boots." He growls and raises his eyebrows in a funny leer, then he tilts his head and looks sweet at me. "Everything okay?"

I reach out my hand to touch the side of his face. He takes it in the hand not rubbing my thigh and kisses my palm. When he pulls on my hand, I naturally lean toward him and we kiss. I feel his hand leave my thigh and land gently on my stomach and his other hand moves to the back of my head. It's a long kiss, and when he pulls away, he's grinning. "That's more like it." He closes my door and walks around to get in the driver's seat.

He starts the car, puts on his seatbelt, and then, backing up, he says, "Missed seeing you last night at church, but I'm so glad Mother finally got to talk to you."

I lick my lips and ask, "Is she okay? You said she'd changed, but she was almost, almost *nice*."

"That new young pastor—she hated him when he came— was really good to her when Caleb died. Then she started going to his Bible study on Wednesday nights. Sometimes I think it's the start of dementia. Sometimes I think maybe it's something more."

"Like a God thing?" *That was what his mother attributed it to, but really?*

He shrugs. "Maybe, who knows? I would've warned you if I'd known you were going to church with Pepper last night."

"I didn't plan on it, but Pepper makes it hard to say no. It was nice. People, well..." My words fade into silence.

He makes the turn onto the highway, then looks at me. "What? People were rude? Mean?"

When I shake my head, my loose hair swings around my face. "No, they were nice. Really nice." I smile to reassure him.

He glances back at the empty highway. "I like your braid,

but your hair down looks pretty. The sweater makes it look redder."

"Really?" I look down at my soft gray sweater. Another outfit picked out by Ashleigh. This one from the mall, not Target, for the rehearsal dinner before her wedding. "Thanks, I guess redder is okay."

"It's very okay. So, Mother said you weren't sure about Saturday. That you're planning on going to Backwater for the weekend."

I gaze out at the familiar scenery, empty cotton fields out Jameson's window and deepening shadows in the pecan grove outside of mine. The evenly planted trunks are solid and the bare branches interlace as far as I can see, but I know the grove ends at the creek over the hill. All so familiar.

My stomach growls, more from nerves than hunger and I lay my hand on it, where Jameson's hand laid just a bit earlier. Looking down, the view is more unfamiliar than the one out my window. *My* flat stomach. *My* leather boots. *My* straight hair falling to my chest. *My* string of pearls. *My* cashmere sweater. On my way to a dinner party with Carol and Jessie and their husbands.

"Yes," I say, lifting my head to look straight ahead. "I was planning on going back, but I changed my mind."

I take a deep breath, then turn towards him with a smile. "Tell your mother I would be delighted to come to her birthday party."

Ashleigh was right. Boots are really in. Carol and Jessie both have on boots. Carol is wearing hers with tight white pants and a long sweater. Which is not quite long enough. When she bends over or stretches you can see where, well, where you're not supposed to see. Those pants are really tight, but I think they must stretch, so she can bend and move. Jessie has a skirt on, but it's not as long as mine. It's really cute on her, and I wish I'd worn clothes like that when I was heavier.

I know Buck, Carol's husband. He was in Caleb's grade, and he and Caleb were good friends. Matter of fact, Carol and Caleb dated in high school. Caleb was eight years older than me, and Carol is four years older than me. They were the prom king and queen, which was unheard of since she was just a freshman, but well, you know how things are in a small town. Her father *was* the mayor.

So it's pretty crazy that Caleb's gone, and I'm here with his brother, his old flame, and his best friend. Pretty crazy.

"Lasagna is ready. Everyone find a seat," Carol says as she comes into the living room. "Buck, open two bottles of red wine. Everyone drinks red with Italian food."

"Isn't she pretty?" Jessie says as she comes up to where I'm looking at the pictures on the bookshelves. "She's six and just as smart as a whip." She drops her voice to a whisper. "Carol didn't want any kids, but Buck would only marry her if she had at least one. He always thought she'd want more after they had one." Jessie shakes her head, her voice stays low. "But no, sirree. Belle is it."

"Is she here?" I ask. House seems awful quiet.

"Oh, no. She's at her grandparents. Carol and Buck bought this house from her parents, and then her parents moved across the lake to a new house they built. They all go back and forth on their golf carts." She laughs as she steers me toward the dining room. "Wish we had grandparents living that close. Martin's from the other side of Atlanta, and his parents live there. His brother and sister live there so his parents are too busy taking care of those grandkids to bother much with ours."

In the dining room, she studies the table and keeps talking. "My father got a promotion and they moved to Ohio. Can you believe it? They seem to love it, but I've told Martin if the bank ever wants him to move, he can just tell them no. I can't even begin to imagine living someplace new. Besides, my kids would die somewhere else. They love Piney. Let's sit here. I don't care if Carol wants it boy-girl." She giggles and squeezes my arm. "I want to hear all about that place you started in Florida."

Pepper's voice rings out as she enters the room carrying a basket of bread. "Bruce, you sit there on the other side of Becca Sue. I'm going to plop myself down over there between these two good-looking boys."

Jameson winks at me from across the long table. I smile back. The dining room is at the back of the house, and the windows must look out toward the lake. However, they're covered by heavy curtains in a dark red and navy blue floral pattern. The wallpaper is a coordinating pattern, and the bottom half of the wall is painted dark blue. Everything in the house looks very planned. Very pretty, but very planned.

As we bow our heads and Buck says grace, I try to come to terms with where I am and who I'm with. Lake Crest was, and still is, *the* neighborhood to live in. The houses surrounding the lake are all big. Except now that I'm in one, they're nowhere near as big as the houses in Backwater. And it feels kind of old, out of date. Maybe it's that for the first time I'm going to own my own house, so I'm paying attention. I don't like this style. It feels cluttered. Stuffy. Me judging a Lake Crest house makes me giggle, and I look up to see Buck is still praying. Quickly I bow my head again and concentrate on hearing his 'amen.'

Dinner is actually fun. Jessie tells stories about her kids. She and Martin have four, which is hard to believe. Pepper can talk about anything and everything, and she does. Jameson talks all about Backwater, making it sounds like a place in a movie—and I honestly don't think he's exaggerating. Bruce, Martin, and I don't talk much at all. Carol talks mostly about the food. Apparently she's really into cooking.

And Buck? Well, Buck makes comments and tells jokes that I don't really get. No one seems to get them, really. But he was drinking quite a bit. He played football at Georgia Southern, and he told some stories about that. He and Caleb were football stars in Piney and best friends, like I said. When he talks about Caleb it feels like he's staring at me. But I think I'm just sensitive. Buck was there for some times with Caleb I'd rather forget.

We finish dinner and go back to the living room. Just as we get there, the doorbell rings. Buck answers and lets out a big laugh. Then he turns to the rest of us as he pulls the door open wide. "Look here, the neighbors say we're making too much noise! Sent the president of the Neighborhood Watch Association to tell us to knock it off. Come on in, Wayne, glad you could stop by. I think you know everyone."

The tall, broad-shouldered man looks the same as ever, except his thick hair is completely white. His eyes scan the room and he nods, then they land on me and he focuses. "Hello, Rebecca. I heard you were in town."

All I can do is swallow. And then swallow again.

It's strange when you are thirty years old and your grandfather speaks to you for the first time.

29

Ashleigh, kitten cuddled in her arms, opens the front door, and early morning sunshine floods her living room. "Come in," she says to Magnus. He opens the screen door and steps inside.

"There he is," he says reaching to rub the kitten's head. "He behave for you?"

"He's been a doll baby. I'm going to miss him," she says in baby talk as she nuzzles the kitten. "Here you go," she says placing him in Magnus' large hands. "I'll get his things. We, well, my mother, might have bought him a few more toys. Think the woman needs a grandbaby."

Magnus follows her farther into the small house. "Things have been busy here, haven't they?"

Ashleigh looks back to roll her eyes at him as she collects kitten toys. "I hear you pulled out as an investor in the dispensary business. Conscience get the better of you?"

He laughs. "Me with a troublesome conscience? Not so much. Matter of fact, I'm already looking into some other same type deals." Seeing her inner reporter brighten up and focus on him, he shakes his head. "Not here. No story of inter-neighborhood competition. Projects I'm interested in aren't even in Florida."

"So, why pull out?" Ashleigh holds the bag of toys just out of his reach and stares at him.

Magnus stares back. "None of your business," he finally

says, adding a smirk. "But thanks for watching the cat. Hoping to get him back to his owner soon. She still coming home this weekend?" He reaches and grabs the bag of toys.

"Ugh," Ashleigh says, turning away from him and picking up her coffee cup. "Oh, did you want some coffee?" When he shakes his head, she takes a sip. "No, she's not coming home this weekend. They're going to suck her in if you, or someone, doesn't do something. What did she have to say when you saw her?"

"Not much." He grimaces and then grins. "You're good."

She shrugs with a grin. "Okay, so now you've told me you talked to her. So, what happened?"

"Nope, that's all. No comment on anything else, madam newspaper writer." He tips his head at her. "Me and Mr. No-Name here are going to take our leave. Paper comes out today, right?"

"Yes, and I do have some people to track down for reaction. Let me know if you decide you have anything to share. You can even be off the record." They both laugh, and he pushes on the screen door. Halfway out, he stops and turns to her.

"You may be right. What you said about Becca Sue." He stops and clears his throat, but his voice is even scratchier. "After all this... she may run right back to Piney."

"I couldn't tell if he was sad, or mad, or just didn't care," Ashleigh says to Carlos. "And you know what? Becca Sue didn't even mention him coming up there. Not a word. Not one."

Carlos shrugs and gets up from their table at Sybil's. "Need more coffee?"

"No, I just wanted to stop by and tell you Magnus picked up the kitten and see if you'd heard anything about the article yet."

"Sybil called, and she's irate. Says it will damage the reputation of Backwater. That it'll bring in an 'unacceptable clientele.' That's her words. Said she's coming back for the public meetings."

"How did she hear about it? Don't believe the *Island Times* has New York delivery."

"She didn't say. Listen, I have to get back to work, but see you at two? Our regular Friday date?" He comes to stand beside her chair.

She stands up into his arms. "Yes. I left a bottle of wine in the fridge. You bringing something from here? Or I can pick up something from the grocery."

He wrinkles his nose and then kisses her. "You're so cute. Thanks for offering, but I'll bring something from here. Maybe eventually I'll wean you off that prepackaged grocery store stuff."

"Not a chance. Then again, if I don't have to wear myself out going to the grocery store, I'll have more energy for our date." They kiss again, longer, then she pulls away. "Get back to work and keep your ears open."

"Yes, ma'am! See you at two. Be on time. I have to be back here by three. We are fully reserved tonight."

Ashleigh pulls her coat closed and leaves the restaurant by the front door. She's only halfway down the sidewalk before she's untied the belt and shrugged the coat off her shoulders. "It's warm in the sun," she says as she lifts her head to the light and closes her eyes.

The new row of condos across the street catches her eye. She's surprised to see that some of them are occupied. She muses out loud, "Roger Worth sure gets things done. That reminds me." She strides to her car, throws her coat into the passenger seat, and then settles into the driver's seat with her phone in her hand.

"Hey," Becca Sue answers.

"Oh, didn't think I'd catch you. Planned on leaving a voicemail. Don't you work the breakfast shift?"

"Yeah, this is my break. Getting busy with folks here for the weekend. You have no idea how strange it is to think of people coming to Piney for the weekend. So, what's going on?"

"Um, okay, first, did you reach out to Roger Worth? Is he going to call me?"

"Oh, shoot. I forgot. I'll text him right now. He needs to know what's happening anyway. Paper comes out today, right?"

"Yes. Thanks. And second, you didn't tell me about Magnus' visit."

"Oh. So you talked to Magnus?"

"Yes. Tell me what happened."

Becca Sue is quiet, and then she yells to the side of the phone. "Okay, I'm coming." Into the phone she says, "I've got to get back. Talk to you later. Bye."

Ashleigh looks at her phone, presses her lips together, and shakes her head. "Girl, you are just itching for a surprise visit." Laying down the phone, she sighs. "With this story breaking, I just can't get away. Guess I'll have to depend on Magnus."

Drummond stops in the living room as he pulls on his jacket. "Virginia, you sure you don't want to come? After all, it's going to be *your* golf cart."

"No, the sunshine looks warm, but I know it's cold out there. All that running around yesterday wore me out." The small woman stiffens her shoulders and draws a deep breath, then speaks firmly. "And you don't need me there. I trust your judgment."

"We'll bring home lunch. What would you like?" Mimi asks as she steps around the couch.

"Oh, something chicken. A sandwich or, no, chicken strips. You're so sweet to think of me." She pulls the plush blanket up around her chest and lifts the remote. "I'm going to watch that baking show while you're gone."

Mimi helps her tuck in the blanket then bends to kiss the older woman's cheek. "We'll be home soon."

The TV chimes that it's coming on, and Mimi joins her husband at the entrance to the front hallway. Miss Bell calls out, "Drummond? Please use my card to pay for lunch. This is turning out rather convenient having you on the account, even with all the rigmarole the bank put us through yesterday." She leans up and to the side to see him. "Thank you for taking care of all this. I am getting excited about seeing the golf cart."

Drummond steps to her and touches her shoulder over the back of the couch. "We're family. We're all each other has. Enjoy your show and we'll be home soon."

To the voices of the British TV hosts, Drummond and Mimi leave out the front door.

Once the heavy front door is closed and they are in the car, Mimi asks, "Are we actually going to buy a golf cart?"

Her husband cuts his eyes at her and scoffs. "That's what I said we were going to do, isn't it?"

She huffs and folds her arms across her thin chest. "Seems to me we should be more worried about putting together our investment package for Bradley and Eason King than getting a new plaything for Virginia. But I'm sure you think you know best."

"Of course I know best." As he backs down the driveway he adds, "When you get through pouting, find a dealership with this car on its lot."

"This car? Our car?"

"Yes. Same make, year, and color."

"But why would we want to change for the exact one? Why not get something newer?"

He sighs and pulls out onto the paved highway. "No need for anyone to know we've turned in our leased car, right? But those payments are killing us. You heard Virginia. She trusts my judgment, and in my judgment paying lease payments when you have cash to outright buy a car isn't wise."

Mimi's mouth falls open. "Cash?"

Her husband's only answer is a smile. After a moment, she

joins him. "Oh, so when you said everything went well at the bank yesterday, you meant *really* well."

He shrugs. "Just doing my duty as the loving son. Besides, it's my father's money. He never did get to buy me a nice car."

30

Hearing Ashleigh's voice kind of makes me homesick for Backwater. It's a mite too easy to forget all that back there. Feels almost like a movie I watched. Last night, hearing Jameson tell everyone about it at the dinner party, just didn't seem to fit with Piney. Or me.

I push out the back door of the diner to get a breath of fresh air. My break is almost over. It's a bright, sunshiny morning, but the air is still chilly. Especially with it being so hot in the restaurant kitchen.

Looking past the highway I can see miles of brown dirt. Empty fields just waiting for spring planting. Part of growing up in a farming area is you tend to know who owns what land. Especially when the owner is related to you and you officially met him for the first time just last night.

Wayne Cousins. My daddy's daddy is a big deal in Piney. He disowned Daddy when he married my momma. Irene, Daddy's step-momma, had raised Daddy. She worked and worked to get her two men talking again. She had no such drive to get me and Momma into her husband's good graces. So that's how it is I've never talked to him. Until last night. Small towns are only as small as people want them to be.

Coming back into the kitchen, I warm back up as I scurry to get back out to the counter area. I feel more in the routine by now and quickly catch up with my tables. Picking up the check from a table near the front windows I see Momma stomping up the front steps. Uh-oh.

"Hey Momma," I say as I meet her just inside the front door.

"Don't you 'hey Momma' me. So, you're best buddies with Wayne Cousins now?"

"No, Momma. He was just there, and we talked for just, I don't know, like, two minutes."

Momma puts her hands on her tiny hips and tips her head at me. "Sugar. That man can't be trusted. Maybe you need to just go on back to Florida now. I can make do with things for your daddy."

I whirl away from her and start taking used plates from customers at the nearest table. Momma scoots around me and is waiting when I get to the counter with my armload of dirty dishes.

"Momma, move." I nudge her away from the rinse station with my hip. She moves to let me get next to the sink, then sidles up right next to me.

"I heard he offered you one of his rental properties. Sugar, he don't give nothing without strings. Why do you think we still live in that trailer?"

"I know, I know. I've got to work. We'll talk tonight, okay?" I whisper to her. "I promise, Momma. I won't do anything without talking to you. Promise."

She closes her eyes and then nods. "Okay. Tonight. Don't do anything until then." She grabs my arm and keeps me next to her for a moment. Then as she maneuvers away, she looks at me. "Remember, Piney don't change."

One of the waitresses is passing, and she laughs. "You can say that again, Brenda. Piney don't change."

Momma laughs with her, and they both walk back out of the counter area. Looking at the sink full of gray water and dishes, I echo their words in my head. "Piney don't change." Pulling out my order pad and lifting my chin, I answer quietly, "But maybe I do."

"Wait 'til Jameson Mason sees you in this!" Pepper exclaims as she jumps up from her seat in the dressing room. Pepper had assumed (correctly) that I didn't have anything appropriate to wear to Mrs. Mason's birthday party tomorrow.

"It's so soft," I say, running my hands down my hips. The plum sweater dress fits close to my body, but it's so light it doesn't feel tight.

Pepper walks around me, nodding her head and chirping. "So classy. Sexy, but in a mother's birthday party kind of way. Pumps. Nude pumps. And those pearls you wore the other night. Are those yours?"

"The pearls? Ashleigh gave them to us girls in her wedding party. So, yes. They *are* mine."

She bats at me. "Don't get snippy, young lady. Thought maybe you borrowed them to wear up here to show off."

"Told you I'm not like that. I don't care what people in Piney think."

She looks at the mirror and meets my eyes there. "Of course you don't. Your eyes did *not* light up like a Christmas tree when your granddaddy hugged you last night. You did *not* examine Carol's house, compare it to those ritzy places Jameson told us about in Florida, and find it wanting. You did *not* jump like a little girl when I said I was taking you shopping this afternoon. Nope, you are just so above all this."

"I didn't say I'm above it, I just don't..."

Pepper shoos me back into the dressing room. "You just don't think about it like I do. Completely understand, but you *are* buying that dress and you are going to knock their socks off tomorrow. Now let's get going. Karaoke awaits. And here."

As I pull the dress over my head, she hands a black shirt and bra over the dressing room door. "These are a gift from me for you to wear tonight. I took off the tags, so you don't have a choice. Wearing those, no one will care if you can sing or not."

Of course, Pepper was right. The shirt and bra fit right well. And as we walked through El Dorado's crowded gravel parking lot, they did give me a jolt of confidence. When we entered, people actually called out to us and we got hugs from pretty much every table as we made our way to *our* table. It was the same crowd as last night, but instead of being at Pepper's afternoon table beside the front windows, we were seated around a long table next to the karaoke stage, where a large mirrored ball added to the atmosphere and I laughed to think I might actually get up there.

Looking down, I see Jameson can't keep his eyes off me. Only took a couple margaritas and two tequila shots, but here I am, up on stage singing ABBA's "Dancing Queen."

As I come off the stage, Jameson meets me at the stairs and pulls me to him. Our long kiss gets more applause than my song, from not only our table but several around us.

"Come on, we're going to the bathroom," Jessie says as she grabs my arm and pulls me away, leaving Jameson complaining loudly. She shushes him and says, "We'll bring her right back. Just cool down, boy!"

The harsh light in the bathroom makes me squint, and the shrill chattering is abrasive. I stumble into a stall. It feels good to sit down.

Pepper says from the stall next to me, "Jameson is all hot to trot, girl. You better finally nail that down tonight. Can't keep him waiting forever."

Carol exclaims (from out beside the sink, I think), "What? You're not sleeping with him? What about that weekend in Tifton? Y'all were in the same hotel room, right?"

"It's complicated," I say, pushing out of the stall. As I wash my hands, I glance up in the big mirror and can see Carol and Jessie rolling eyes at each other.

When Jessie sees me catch them, she drops her eyes. Then looking back up she smiles and says, "But no worries, you don't have any competition. Not any that matters, that is."

Pepper steps to the mirror. "Shut up, Jessie. We've got us a true love match here. She's got Jameson right where she wants him. Right, sugar? But you do need to seal this deal. Don't want someone else stealing your man." She winks at me in the mirror and I nod as I laugh.

At the table there's another round of margaritas waiting on us. Pepper laughs as she hugs Bruce from behind. "Looks like there's some guys here wanting to get lucky tonight!" She whoops as Bruce pulls her into his lap.

I hesitate before I sit down and look around me. We are the center table. As I scan those around us, I see appreciative nods by the men (might be the new shirt and bra) and little waves from the women. Many whom I've known for years without ever getting one of those little waves.

But then, I have to be honest. Where would they have waved at me? Caleb and I never, not once in all ten years, went out like this. When we were dating, we stuck to riverbanks and his mother's front porch. After we got married we stayed at the house. No, me and the kids stayed at the house. All the time. He, well, he didn't. After we got divorced, well, we couldn't be seen out in public 'cause Audrey's daddy would not have like that one bit. Not with that big wedding he was paying for. So we were back to riverbanks and his truck. Like the night he died.

Caleb is dead. I look across the table to find Jameson staring at me. Jameson, not Caleb.

Walking around the table, I'm sure to nod and wave and be friendly. Jameson Mason is sitting at the center table with me. Right out in public. When I get to my seat, I don't sit in it. I lift up my fresh margarita and take a long drink. There's whooping and laughing, but I ignore it and lean down to Jameson's ear. As I whisper and kiss and whisper some more, he scoots his chair away from the table.

"Here's where we take our leave, folks," he says as he stands up. Of course that leads to more whoops and laughter.

Pepper catches my eye and winks. As we pass her, she

reaches out to touch my hand. "You've done real good, girl. You have a good night. A real good night."

31

"What do you mean she went back to Boston?" Ruth snaps at her son.

"Mother, you know as much as I do. Olivia called this morning to say I'd get the divorce papers today and said she'd flown back Wednesday night to finalize things. Then apparently she went back to Tybee. She'll be here Sunday." He drops a FedEx mailer onto the coffee table and then sits down on the couch beside his mother. "So, I'm assuming these are the papers." He sighs, then chews on his bottom lip.

"I'm sorry," Ruth says patting his leg along and taking a couple deep breaths. "No matter how bad things are, it's still a rough road. Sad for the kids, but at least they're too young to really understand."

Bradley smiles. "Yeah, that's true. I just don't get what the hurry is. We don't have living arrangements worked out yet. We were going to talk about things, work out the details of what happens now *before* we signed the final papers. All the other financial stuff is cut and dry thanks to her family's pre-nup. Even the shared custody agreement." He picks up the cardboard envelope. "Think I'll take these in Dad's office and look at them while the twins are still napping." He stands and walks across the living room. "Where is Dad?"

Ruth waves her hand in the other direction. "Kids wore him out this morning. He's laying down in our room. Office is all yours."

"Dad's taking a nap?" He turns to look at his mother, but she's already up and walking away from him into the kitchen.

She says over her shoulder, "You better hurry. You know Phillips and Emerson will be up soon. I'm going to start dinner. Spaghetti tonight!"

Bradley looks down at the envelope in his hand, then steps into his father's office and closes the door.

Olivia Baets King stands on the deck at Tybee Island, Georgia, looking out to the ocean. Her dark hair whips around to cover the front of her face, so she uses one hand to pull it back and holds it pinned against her neck. Her winter-white coat is belted around her, but her legs and feet are bare. She smiles when she feels a tugging at the back of the coat's belt.

"Who is it?" she asks. "What if I don't have anything on under my coat?" Her smile grows as she pretends to struggle. Then she turns around into the arms untying her belt. As the belt falls away, the view verifies her claim of having nothing on underneath.

"Then we better get you inside," Magnus mumbles into her hair as it whips in the wind. His hands move inside the coat. "Hope I'm the man you're out here waiting on like that." He grins and says, "Man, am I glad you called me Sunday night. It was a very unexpected pleasure."

"I'm glad you answered my phone call." She bats her eyes. "Was that all that was an unexpected pleasure this week?""

He smiles as he moves her toward the doors and says, "Not even close. Don't think your mother-in-law planned for me and you to share the love nest she rented. But I sure enjoyed myself and am extremely glad to be back here. So are we celebrating things going well on your trip back to New York? Papers signed?"

Olivia stops and puts her hands on his chest. "Actually, we are celebrating. Bradley should've gotten them today."

"Good, can't chance any other man having some kind of claim on my future children." He pushes against her hands to kiss her neck, but she pulls back.

"And you? The hillbilly is all out of your system?"

"Hell, yes." He frowns and looks toward the ocean waves for a moment, "She'll probably end up back in that podunk town."

Olivia pulls close to him and he turns back to look down at her. She tips her head up. "Probably. Besides, if she's stupid enough to let you get away, she's too stupid to keep you interested. I plan on keeping you very interested." She meets his lowering lips and as they kiss, he pushes open the glass door.

Warmth spills from inside, as they enter the darkening house. Olivia pulls away towards the kitchen. "I brought champagne so we can toast to getting everything we want. To starting the life we deserve. Leaving our mistakes behind."

Magnus closes the door, but remains there, staring out.

Champagne in hand, Olivia comes back to him. "Darling, don't get moody on me now. We have very expensive champagne to share. After all, remember that once I get pregnant I won't be able to drink. Come on."

Magnus takes a deep breath, then turns. "Exactly," he says, following her up the open staircase. "Here's to getting everything we want."

32

"Surprised me that Jameson moved into our old suite and out of our old house," I say, as uninterested as I can, to Maggie. We are sitting on her bed while the caterer and florist and everybody in central Georgia that has anything to do with throwing a big ol' bash scurries around downstairs. Maggie asked me to come early so we could chat. The party starts at noon.

Maggie and I hung out a couple times this week after she got out of school. Mainly walking around the Shoppes. She and Jameson also came for breakfast every morning at the diner, but as the weekend got closer, I had less time to chat. However, I did get their orders completely right on both Thursday and Friday.

"Yeah, Grandmother had lots of remodeling done after Dad died. Before that the whole wing still looked like it did when me and Cab were little. My room still had that pink lamb wallpaper. Remember it?"

"Yeah, and Cab's was all Atlanta Braves, right? I hadn't thought about those rooms in a long time. So it's all Jameson's now? Our old house is just sitting empty?"

"Yep." Maggie stands up and feels the curlers in her hair. "Think they're dry? I hope this works."

"It should give you some volume." I stand up and feel the curlers, too. "Yeah, here let me take one out. Oh, there ya go. That's nice. Just a little bounce." She's looking at herself in the mirror as I unwind the curlers. I'm amazed at the maturity and confidence she's gained.

She sees me watching her and grins. "Why do you keep asking about Uncle J?"

I grin back. "I'm asking about the house. Both houses. I *did* live here, you know."

"Has Uncle J asked you to come look at his rooms?"

I tug one of the curls. "You, ma'am, are just plain rude. Let the curls hang for a bit before you brush it. And, no, I've not seen the suite since I left it over a year ago."

She goes to the bedroom door, listens, then looks back at me. "Grandmother's calling me. She wanted me to help her put out the pictures. Stay here and I'll be back. Gotta tell you about a guy from school. He's coming to the party today." She wiggles her eyebrows at me and disappears down the hall.

Her windows face the front, and I look down on all the commotion along the drive. There was a lot of commotion out there the night I left for the last time, too. It was the annual Mason Christmas party. Like the years before, I figured I'd stay up in the suite. Put the kids to bed when it was time. We always moved into the suite for parties so the kids could come upstairs after making a quick appearance. When I first moved in, they were so little, I was more like a nanny. Most years it was an adults-only Christmas party, so there was no talk of me going because someone had to stay with the kids. Plus, my grandfather would, of course, be at the party, and that would make things awkward, right?

But the last couple years I was here, the kids were invited to the party and they didn't need me to put them to bed. However, me going to that last party never entered anybody's mind, especially since by that time Caleb and I weren't publicly together.

Until Audrey found out I still lived in the house. They were announcing their engagement at the party, and she felt I might cause a scene. Now, I'm the least likely person to cause a scene in all God's green earth, but you know how pregnant women can be. So, Audrey caused a scene and demanded I not be there. Honestly? I think Caleb and his mother had forgotten I still lived there. Which might've been my fault because, see, that's what I was hoping for.

Anyway, as all the flowers and glasses and food were being brought in, me and my stuff were going out. To Momma and Daddy's trailer.

Since that day I don't think I've thought one minute about our old suite.

Until last night.

"Hey, Becca Sue," Cab says as he knocks on Maggie's bedroom door.

"Cab. Come on in. I'm just waiting on Maggie. You look nice."

He's got on dark pants and a white dress shirt, and he looks at himself in Maggie's mirror as he comes in the room. "Thanks. Hey listen," he says turning toward me and the front windows. "Has Grandmother said anything about me and the farm? Or anything?"

"No. She and I only talked a minute at church Wednesday night, and today I got here early to be with Maggie. Haven't even seen your grandmother. Why?"

He shuffles back and forth a bit. He's taller than he was last summer, but it's more than that making him look older. He's cracking his knuckles, and his hands are strong, muscled, like a man's hands. "You've seen the Shoppes, right? You know Pepper." He takes a deep breath, and his words jump out. He talks low and smooth like his daddy did, but I can still hear his nervousness. "She wants us to open a Mason Farms stand there, and I really want to do it. Like your Backwater stuff. I... uh... I think it would go real well. Can you talk to Grandmother? Please."

"Oh, honey, I would, but she's not going to listen to me."

"I don't know, she's changed. Seriously." He sits down on the corner of his sister's bed. "Since Daddy died. Anyway, if you get a chance, will you?"

Reaching over to smooth the fabric of his shirt on his shoulder, I nod and say, "Of course."

He grins. "Thanks. Did you know Mags and I are flying to London tonight? Spending our winter break there with Mom."

"Yeah, Maggie told me. I'm excited for you two."

"Whole Worth clan is going to be there. Remember last summer when they came to Florida?" He laughs as he stands up.

I grin. "Yes, I remember their visit to Florida well. You take care of your sister and don't let those cousins of yours make her feel bad."

"Yes, ma'am. Although Maggie's grown up a lot and having Grandfather Worth on her side doesn't hurt. He sure does think a lot of you, and he's made sure Grandmother Mason knows."

Before he walks to the door, I reach up to hug him and whisper in his ear. "You do your daddy proud. Your daddy and your mom. All of us, actually."

He hugs me back and laughs again. "Boy, sure didn't look that way last summer, did it?"

We walk out into the hallway and then take a couple steps to the right. There the walls become a railing on one side and a two-story window above the front door on the other. The hallway turns into a staircase that descends in a sweeping curve down to the foyer. It has a twin staircase on the other side of the open room. That staircase leads down from Jameson's suite, and as Cab and I watch all the downstairs activity, Jameson starts down it.

"Uncle J!" Cab says above the noise below. Jameson looks up, waves, and then hesitates before waving to me also.

"You coming?" Cab asks as he steps onto the top step.

"No, I'll wait for Maggie. She should be back up soon."

He lopes down the stairs, and I dash back into Maggie's room and close the door. A few minutes pass, and there's a knock on the door. I know it's not Maggie. "Come in," I say, then leap up off the bed like it's on fire.

"You're here early," Jameson says as he closes the door behind him. "I've been calling you."

I shrug and fiddle with the things on Maggie's dresser.

"Phone is in my purse in the car. Maggie wanted me to come early."

We neither one move or say anything. I'm not looking at him, so I'm not sure what he's looking at, but I think it's me. When I feel him moving closer, I look up. He reaches to touch my hair, but I move just enough to not be in arm's reach.

He chuckles. "Becca, it was just a fight. Not our first fight, we've done plenty of that. But our first lover's quarrel."

I snap my head around to look at him. "Don't say that. We are *not* lovers. Remember?"

He gives me some space and sighs. "I don't want to make love to you in my car. I want it to be special."

"Okay, fine. But why did you not tell me you were living in mine and Caleb's suite?"

"I told you last night, I didn't think you'd care."

I drop down to sit on the edge of the bed. "And I don't really care about that. But, where did you think we were going to go last night after you nixed the car *and* your mother's house? Back to my parent's trailer? I just don't understand what's going on in your mind. I thought you wanted..."

He sits down next to me and reaches to hold my hand. "You just get me so excited I guess I forget to think." He squeezes my hand. "Sugar, it's about time for the party and I'm needed down there." He reaches into his suit pocket and pulls out a box. "I know it's Mother's party, but here's something for you."

I open the box to find a beautiful, multi-strand pearl bracelet.

He lifts it out and says, "Look, it does match your necklace." He bends his head to look into my eyes. "Can I put it on you?"

I nod, and he slips it onto my wrist, then connects the delicate clasp. "Your dress is as beautiful as Pepper said. Took my breath away when I saw you standing on the landing just now." He puts his hand into my hair and leans into me. As we kiss, we ease back until we are laying on the bed, then he sits up and laughs. "See? You make me forget my mother's own party!"

I sit up as he stands and then goes to the door. "See you downstairs soon, okay?" He opens the door and moves out of the way as Maggie comes in.

"Finally!" she says with a big smile. "People are starting to arrive, and I still haven't brushed out my hair. Didn't know if I'd ever get into my own room!" She pushes at her uncle. "Go on. Grandmother wants you. We'll be down soon. I won't keep your lady up here too long!"

He rolls his eyes at his niece, smiles at me, and walks off down the hall. Maggie goes into her bathroom, and I take a moment to look at the bracelet. It is beautiful, and it does match my necklace. *Did me and Pepper talk about my dress last night during karaoke and dinner? Or mention me wearing the pearls? No, now that I think about it, we didn't. So he and Pepper have talked since then. Just seems weird how involved Pepper is in us, me and Jameson. Why does she care so much? And does it bother me he's living in his mother's house? In our old suite?*

I stand up and take a couple deep breaths, but my stomach is churning wildly. *Am I really Jameson Mason's lady, like Maggie said? Am I really going downstairs to a Mason party as an invited guest?*

Maggie flings open her bathroom door. "Ready? Your grandfather is here already and asking for you." She checks her hair one more time and then turns to look back at me. "You okay?"

"No." I shake my head and manage to say, "Go on. I'll be right there," as I dash into the bathroom and slam the door.

A pearl necklace clanking against the side of the commode is about as classy as it sounds.

33

"I'm trying some new flavors for my biscones," Miss Bell says to Mimi as she enters the warm, fragrant kitchen. "I can hardly wait until we reopen the market next month."

"February?" Mimi asks as she pours a cup of coffee. "Won't it still be cold?" She sits at the kitchen table beside a plate of hot pastries.

"Chilly, but not cold. Those are maple flavored. I didn't feel like cooking any bacon, but they'd be delicious with slices of bacon on them. They'd be a big seller, I'm sure. I have citrus biscones in the oven now. Smell that? Orange and lemon. Going to try lime next."

Mimi yawns and stretches. "Where's Drummond? He got up early."

Miss Bell motions with her hand toward the garage door. "He took the golf cart for a spin. I'm waiting until it gets a little warmer to go for a ride. But thinking about the market, the golf cart will make things much easier." She looks up and smiles. "You two are sure making my life easier. I'll hate to see you go home." She stares at the younger, pajama-clad woman, willing her to expand on the idea of them going home.

Mimi stops mid-stretch and pauses. Then she shakes her head and says, "Dear Virginia, you've made your home so open to us, and we are falling in love with Backwater more every day. Maybe we'll stay longer than we planned. It's good for

Drummond to be near family. He no longer has any in Wisconsin, you know."

"But don't you need to get back for work, and..." Miss Bell's question is met with a big shrug and smile, so she turns toward to her oven. "This batch looks done." The oven buzzer sounds as she prepares to open the door. "Yep, right on time." Busy with her baking, she turns her back to her daughter-in-law and mumbles, "Going to be crowded."

"What?" Mimi asks. "Is everything okay?"

"Yes, I mean, I think it is." The older woman speaks louder. "The house will just be crowded when Becca Sue comes back."

"Hmmm, but her cabin will be done soon, right?"

"Oh! You're staying until her cabin is done?" Miss Bell's eyes are open wide and staring at Mimi. "That could be months!"

Mimi comes to put her arm around her host. "Isn't it good we all get along so well? I'm going to get dressed and see if I can track Drummond down." She pats Miss Bell's back and then leaves the kitchen with a flourish. "Have fun baking!"

Her smile turns into a snarl as she walks down the hall. "The old woman is right. Her house *will* be crowded if that girl comes back. We've got to make sure she knows just how unwelcome she is here."

Magnus pulls into his garage, turns off the car, then just sits as the big door closes behind him. "I'm too old to stay up that late," he says as he opens the door. Taking a deep breath, he pulls himself out and stretches before stiffly walking inside. He grins as he punches the alarm code because of what he hears on the other side of the door. When he opens it, a tiny ball of gray and white is poking around and meowing up at him.

"I know, I know, you were lonely. But it was only one night. Told you I'd be home early this morning." He picks up the kitten and takes him into the living room, where he collaps-es onto one of the couches. "You missed me? You miss your mommy, don't you? Well, she's coming home today."

Magnus drops his head back and closes his eyes. The kitten paws at his chest and purrs as he pushes his head into Mag-nus's massaging hand. Suddenly Magnus sits up. "Nope, not falling asleep. I need a shower and to see when your mommy will be here."

He pulls his phone from his pocket and scrolls through his unanswered texts to Becca Sue. The last one was sent just be-fore he left Tybee Island, a couple hours ago. "She's going to have to talk to me today," he mumbles. He looks up a number and punches it in.

"Hey, Ashleigh. Hope it's not too early, but do you know when Becca Sue is getting in today?"

"Becca Sue? She's not. Old Lady Mason is having a big birthday party, so she stayed. Haven't you talked to her? What's going on?" Ashleigh's voice goes from sleepy to upset. "Magnus, they are sucking her in. I just figured you were up there, and that's why I hadn't heard from her. You said you were driving up north when we kept the kitten. Where were you? And you were gone again last night."

His mouth hanging open, he just shakes his head, then fi-nally says, "Listen, I've gotta go." He hangs up the phone and throws it onto the couch. He holds the kitten in front of his face. "You miss your mommy? Fine, let's go see your mom-my."

Ashleigh lets her phone fall on her chest.

"Told you not to answer it," Carlos says as he snuggles clos-er to her. "But since we're awake..."

She turns to look at him. "How did I get so lucky to find you?" She moves down in the covers to be closer to her husband. "Cell phones are nice, but I hate when I know someone is purposefully ignoring you. You know she has her phone with her. You know she's seen my calls and texts."

"Mmmm. Yeah." Carlos mumbles as he pays more attention to his wife than her talking. When she doesn't say anything for a while, he stops kissing her shoulder and looks at her. "Aw, honey, are you crying?" He moves to hold her.

She sniffles and wipes her nose with the palm of her hand. "Becca Sue deserves to be as happy as I am, and I promise, if I thought being in Piney would make her happy, I'd give her up. Gladly. Or like I've told you, if she's meant to be with Magnus, then I'll be fine with that."

He brushes her hair away from her face. "Well, maybe she's doing good there. Maybe things are going so good, she's too busy to talk."

Ashleigh closes her eyes and sighs. "No, that's not how women work. When things are going well for a woman, she wants to tell her friends. Especially if it's with a guy. Not like men, when you get a thing going with a girl, you go dark. She's not talking to me because she knows I'll figure out what she doesn't want to actually know, but should. And that just makes me so sad, because she's going to end up in a mess back in that place."

Carlos groans as Ashleigh struggles to sit up. "You're getting up?"

She takes his face between her hands. "Yes." But then she laughs when he gives her puppy eyes. "Okay, maybe not right this minute." She slides down into his arms. "After, we can talk about a road trip I have in mind."

He mumbles, "*After,* we can talk about anything you want."

34

"I can't think what to tell you, sugar," Rick says to Becca Sue. "Your momma is dead set on you going back to Florida right this minute."

"I know." Becca Sue kicks at the dead leaves along the side of the road. She'd put on a pair of her mother's boots, but was still wearing her dress from the party under her coat. Rick had been set to take his daily prescribed walk just as she got home, so she'd joined him. "I'm just not sure Momma can be unbiased about anything here."

"You might be right about that. Not that she don't have her reasons. Good reasons. Dad never gave her the time of day." He pauses for a minute and takes some deep breaths.

"You okay?" Becca Sue moves closer and slides her arm under his.

"Oh, yeah, just takes time. I been walking down to the end here, then turning around to come back. Well, *trying* to get all the way to the end." He grins. "Never felt so helpless. So out of shape." He starts walking again. "So Dad's taken to talking to you. That makes me happy. How was the party?"

"It was beautiful, of course. No expense spared. Wayne, he wants me to call him Grandad—can you believe that? Well, he acted like nothing had ever been wrong. Even stranger? Nobody acted like there'd ever been anything wrong. I'm sure when they all went home they talked about us, but at the party? Not one word. Kind of felt like I was crazy."

"That's how it is. If Wayne Cousins said you can grow ice cream, folks here'd be plowing under their cotton tomorrow."

Becca Sue motions with her head at the house they are walking past. "Do you ever regret standing up to him? I mean, you were supposed to have a house like that. Like all your school buddies."

"Nah, I hate that I've hurt you and your momma and that you didn't get to live like that. But I couldn't give an inch and neither would he. Then in my anger I made every one of his predictions about me come true. Dropped out of school, lived hand-to-mouth, killed myself working out in the heat and cold. Basically, the exact opposite of him."

"He wants to give me a house."

"Your momma told me."

"But I have a house being built in Backwater."

"Yeah, you do."

They walk in silence, and as they near the end of the lane, Rick slows down. "Let's rest a bit here. I usually lean on this fence." The brightness of the day has melted into the softness of color and smell. Quiet all around adds to the softness, with only the occasional caws of crows in the tops of the trees.

The road ends at a forest, and Becca Sue looks off towards it.

"I know all this so well," she says. "There's a path there that goes down to the creek and the Woodhull's pasture with the little pond. And the willow with the low branches where I would hide my treasures." She laughs. "I loved reading down there. No one ever bothered me."

"Including your momma and me, right?"

"I didn't say that. I liked being alone."

He pushes away from the fence and starts on to the end of the road. "Not right of us, the fact that we didn't hide from you that we didn't plan on having kids. Guess it made us feel less guilty for not looking after you. We didn't do much right."

Becca Sue leans her shoulder lightly against his. "Don't worry. I didn't expect much." She looks at him and grins. "I did okay, right?"

"Girl, you did more than okay." As they reach the end of the blacktop, he stops and turns. "See, made it all the way, thanks to you." He reaches out his arm for her to twine hers in and looks at his daughter. "You know, if you decide to stay here, I think it'll be okay. Besides, I hear Jameson Mason is sweet on you."

She holds out her wrist with the pearl bracelet on it. "Look what he gave me."

"Now that's pretty." He shakes his head. "Masons. Talk about mixed-up folks, but Jameson seems okay, I think. Hear the old lady's got religion."

Becca Sue shrugs and sighs. "That's what she says. She sure acts different towards me, but..."

"But you don't trust it, right?"

"Right. It's kind of confusing with her and Wayne and everybody acting so nice."

"Maybe they ain't acting. There's some good in most everyone. Maybe the new you brings it out better. Your momma doesn't really give folks a second chance. Or even a first chance if she thinks you might look sideways at her. Couldn't be blamed if you were a little standoffish."

"Oh, so now *I'm* standoffish!" She laughs and pulls her father close. She lays her head on his shoulder as they walk on.

"Looks like we got company," Rick says as they come around the last curve toward the trailer. "New York plates."

Becca Sue clutches her father's arm tighter. "Oh, no."

Rick hangs on as she strides up the steps onto the deck. She opens the door and is greeted by a sight she never imagined—Magnus Llord sitting on the flowered sofa in her parent's trailer.

He looks up and smirks. "I brought you your damn cat."

"Would you want to know?" Jessie asks in a low voice across the table.

Carol shakes her head. "Why are you whispering? The kids can't hear us over the TV and the noise they're making. I can hardly hear myself. We should've gone to my house. Belle went home with my parents after the Masons' party."

Jessie rolls her eyes at her friend. "Because I'd have to pay a babysitter. I got the morning at the salon with Martin watching them and Martin gets golfing this afternoon. When you have only one, you can take her to a nice party. Four? Not so much. And three hours of babysitting with four kids adds up to a pretty penny."

A squawk from the sunken den at the back of the house causes Jessie's head to snap up, then she yells, "Henry, put that down!" One of her toddlers waddles towards her, and her voice softens as she coos, "Sweetie, come here. You didn't get a good nap did you?" As she scoops her into her lap, she yells again, "Henry, if I have to get up, you *are* getting a spanking. You hear me?" She kisses the red curls tucked under her chin and settles the youngest of her four into her.

Carol tightens her mouth and breathes through her nose as the child snuffles and burrows into her soft mommy, while Jessie soothes her with words and soft pats. She tips her head and shrugs. "See, this is why a sitter is such a pain. Imogene should still be napping, but the sitter just let her fall asleep on the couch and of course the older kids woke her. Want some more?" she says as Carol finishes her glass of wine.

"No, thank you. I need to go on, I guess." Carol moves up to sit on the edge of her dining room chair, but doesn't stand up.

"Why? Another glass of wine and the kids seem better behaved. I promise." Jessie laughs as she finishes her last sip. "You know Buck won't be off the golf course for a while and Pepper is totally preoccupied with the Shoppes on Saturday afternoons."

"Maybe I'll go down there and take a look around. I haven't been to the Shoppes since before Christmas." Looking down and smiling, she says, "She's fallen asleep. They are sweet when they are sleeping. Okay, maybe a little bit more." She stands and walks around the corner into the large kitchen, returning with a bottle of white wine. Pouring a half glass for herself, she pours a full glass for her best friend, then sits back down.

After a sip, Jessie asks again, "So, would you want to know?"

Carol takes a deep breath, then a drink of wine. "I don't know. Haven't thought about it."

"I'd want to know. I think I *would* know. Martin is so straightforward, he's not a very good liar. Some people are just really good at keeping secrets. You are. Me, not so much." She grimaces at her friend.

"Which I have learned well in the thirty years we've been friends. But that makes you much less complicated, right? That's why we fit so well together." Carol laughs and leans back in her chair.

Carol meets her gaze and then smiles as she lifts her wine glass, tips it towards her friend, and finishes it. "Wait 'til Pepper hears they didn't do it last night either. She'll have Jameson Mason's head on a platter for dinner tonight." Smoothing her navy knit dress, she stands up.

Jessie grins. "Are you going to tell Pepper?"

"Didn't I mention I was going to stop by the Shoppes?" She leans down to kiss her friend's cheek and smooth the baby's damp curls. "Thanks for the wine. I'll call you and let you know what Pepper has to say." She tucks her flat purse underneath her arm. "Don't get up. I'll let myself out." Her navy heels match her outfit perfectly, and they make a wonderful sound as she picks her way around toys and books across first the hardwood floors and then the kitchen tiles.

Jessie watches her friend and sighs as Carol steps out of view. Kissing her daughter's head, she rocks a bit and sighs again as she hears her kitchen door open and close. Lips pressed against her daughter's curls she mumbles, "Seriously, Becca Sue should know better."

After backing down the driveway, Carol drives past her own house as she leaves the Lake Crest subdivision. She tells the car to call her mother. "Hi. Everything okay with Belle?"

"Of course. She and Papa are watching golf. Are you home?"

"No, I'm going to run by the Shoppes. Belle has clothes for church over there so she's good staying the night, right?"

"Sure. You and Buck going to have a date night?"

Carol smiles. "Sure, Mom."

"Oh, wonderful. You are both so busy you need to take time for you as a couple."

"Yes. I know. I've got to go. Tell Belle I'll see her at church." Carol pushes the end button, waits a minute in the silence of only the car sounds, then picks up her phone and presses a button on it. When her call is answered, she cuts off the hello saying, "Seven o'clock. Look for my car." She hangs up, sticks her phone back into her purse, and turns on the music as she talks under it. "Sure, Mom. A date night, whatever you say. First, let's see what Pepper has to say about her Jameson project."

35

"Welcome to Italian night at Sybil's," the young lady greets George and Pearl as they enter the small restaurant.

"We're meeting some friends," Pearl explains. "That's probably our table there, we like to get here early to get George's chair situated."

"Yes, ma'am. King party?"

George answers by driving his chair in that direction. Pearl hangs back. "Yes, that's us. Can you tell me if my *dear* friend Sybil is here tonight?"

"I'm not sure. I'm new," the teenager says. "Do you want to talk to Carlos?"

"Maybe later." Pearl hurries to her husband who is already situated at the table. "Don't think Sybil is here. The girl wasn't sure, she looked at me like, 'Hmmm, I've heard the name Sybil somewhere...'" Pearl matches her mocking with rolling eyes. "Wonder if she even knows the name of the restaurant?"

She's barely seated when noise at the door gets her attention. She waves at the Kings, Esme and Patrick, and Marie and Harold Thompson. There's air kisses and quick hugs as everyone finds their seats.

Harold holds out his long arms to the table. "So glad to be back together after the holidays. Every year we are more and more anxious to get back here, and this year is even more

185

exciting. We need champagne to toast your new venture, Eason!"

Eason nods and smiles tightly. "Yes, in a bit. There are still some kinks to work out and some minds to change." He sighs. "Hopefully."

Pearl leans forward and says in a low voice, "I don't think Sybil is here."

Ruth catches her breath. "Oh, thank goodness. She left some scathing phone messages for Eason."

Esme says, "Not scathing enough if you're still going through with it."

"But Patrick said..." Eason starts.

Esme smacks her partner's chest with the back of her hand. "He does not speak for me. I pay all the bills and let him do my talking? Not in this lifetime. Eason and Ruth, let me tell you, this drug thing is a mistake. A huge mistake." She shakes her head a bit, then takes a deep breath. "But I am not here to discuss that. I'm here because what would 'Italian Night' be without the resident full-blooded Italian? Now, where is our waiter?"

"Here I am," a young man standing behind her says as he leans forward. "Just waiting for a break in the conversation. Hi y'all, I'm Chigger, and I'll be your waiter tonight."

George scoffs, "What's your name? Chigger. You're named after a bug?"

The waiter leans his head forward laughing and blond hair falls around his face. He lifts his head and pushes the hair back. "Sorry 'bout that. Everybody calls me Chigger, but I was supposed to use my real name, John. So, I'm John, and I'll be your server."

He lifts up a list and stumbles through only the first two lines before Esme puts her hand up and says, "Stop!"

"Stop reading. You are destroying not only the Italian language, but also English. Give me the card, I'll read it to everyone." She jerks the card out of Chigger's hands, and he shrugs. He listens as she tells everyone what the set menu for the evening is. She hands the card back. "Someone else can order the wine. And, please, don't let *Chigger* read anything off the wine list."

"Chigger," Marie says as the boy leaves their table, then she laughs a bit. "Can't believe Sybil hired him." She clears her throat then lifts her head higher. "And might as well say, while I do appreciate the financial windfall the dispensary will be, and I do believe I'm not understating the case at all when I say 'windfall,' I don't want it in my community. In all my studies, and you all know studying investment opportunities is my forte, I believe there is simply not enough long-term data to make this kind of decision. We all know, if it gets approved, it will be almost impossible to remove at a later date if the experience turns sour. I'm officially a NIMBY. Not In My Back Yard."

Harold harrumphs. "We disagree, along gender lines apparently, much like Patrick and Esme. It will just be another business in our community. A well-regulated medical facility. Exactly the type of business Backwater is all about."

Eason cuts his eyes to the side to see if his wife is going to join the female chorus, but she tucks her head and lifts her glass of water to take a drink. He then speaks up, "Pearl, as unusual as this sounds, we don't know your opinion."

Pearl tries a little laugh and then looks around. "Oh, here's the wine."

As the wine is served on one side of the table, small plates of antipasto are placed on the other. Chigger clears his throat and announces, "Don't worry. This isn't all y'all's meal. Although I reckon you could put some of that meat and cheese pieces on hunks of the bread there. Make a right nice little sandwich." He steps back and waves. "Y'all enjoy!"

As they meet eyes, they all start laughing. George spears an olive and pops it in his mouth. "I guess as much as I've complained through the years about pretentious, smug, better-than-you waiters, I better just eat me a little sandwich and shut up! But first..." He lifts his glass of wine and the rest of the table follows suit. "To good friends."

As glasses are clinked, Eason studies Pearl. She eats with

her hand never far from her mouth or plate. She doesn't make eye contact and doesn't seem to be following any of the conversations around the table. He's as startled as her when Marie calls out Pearl's name.

"Pearl, you didn't tell us where you stand. Are you on the ladies' side in the matter?"

George reaches over and covers his wife's hand with his own. "I'll answer for her—"

"No!" Esme reacts. "She's a grown woman. She can have her own opinion. We don't need men to speak for us. Tell us, Pearl. We *know* you have an opinion. You *always* have an opinion."

Pearls mouth drops open, but nothing comes out.

Then George speaks up. "I've used medical marijuana for years. Began shortly after the accident. There, you happy to know our little secret, Esme?" He reverses his chair away from the table and throws his napkin onto his appetizer plate. "Tell Chigger we had to leave. C'mon, Pearl."

She's up and following him before the rest of the table has processed what they've just discovered. Calls for them to come back fall on deaf ears, and as Ruth hurries to the door, the rest of the table settles back down.

Ruth shakes her head as she comes back to the table. "They say they're fine, and they'll talk to us tomorrow."

Their thoughts are broken when Chigger, swinging his blonde hair back says, "Hey, y'all are gonna love the soup. It's got some fancy name, but it's really just dumplings. D'ya hear there's going to be a pot store here real soon? Give y'all something to talk about while I go get your soup."

Bradley pushes the double stroller past stores and restaurants with beach themes and wooden pirates. One even has a koi pond, but the fish aren't visible in the chilly water. "We can see the fish in the summer, guys," he says to Emerson and Phillips who are stretched forward, looking down into the concrete pond. They sit back as he turns to continue walking. "Ready for ice cream?"

Inside the corner store, he moves to the end so he won't stop traffic with the big stroller. He places their order, pays and then maneuvers to go back outside where tables are open. He parks the stroller in front of the window next door, where the store is closed already, and then pulls over an unused chair from a nearby table. Just as he gets settled and ready to eat his cup of ice cream, a woman comes up to him.

"Hey, having some ice cream?"

He doesn't really look up at her, just nods and continues eating.

"Bradley? It's me, Ashleigh," she says and causes him to actually look.

"Oh, Ashleigh!" He jumps up to give her a one-armed hug. "Sorry, just, well, with the twins, a lot of women, I mean people, come up to talk."

She laughs. "No, I think you were right the first time. I'm sure *women* would find y'all irresistible. Oh my, they are sure enjoying their ice cream."

He grimaces at the mess the two are making of themselves and the stroller. "Guess I should've taken them out of the stroller or at least put on bibs. It sounded easy when Mom suggested I take them out for ice cream. I'm finding out nothing is easy with twins by yourself."

Ashleigh pulls over another empty chair and sits. "Haven't seen you since we went out for a beer that night after the meeting. Is your wife back in town?"

"Ah, tomorrow," he says as he retakes his seat. "Still up at the beach."

"Then y'all staying here while the whole marijuana thing works itself out?"

"Maybe, I don't really know." He eats a spoonful of ice cream. "I didn't mention it before, but... we're getting a divorce. No, wait. We got a divorce. Just signed the papers."

"Oh, I'm sorry. I didn't know."

He nods as he takes the small napkin in his hand and tries to wipe up ice cream off of his children's faces. Ashleigh stands and says with a laugh, "I'll go get you some more napkins. Don't think just one is going to do it."

She returns with a handful of napkins and a cup of water. "Here, a little water might help."

"Thanks, although I guess me cleaning them is useless until they're through." He sits back and picks up his cup of ice cream. "It's nice being able to be outside in January. Still seems strange, though. You were raised here, right?"

"Yep. Lived here all my life. Well, except for college. I think I would die up north because I think *this* is cold. I was just wondering about the kids being out here in the weather!" She jumps up. "I'll leave you three to enjoy your ice cream and what you think is warm weather, but I'm freezing. Hope things work out with, well, everything. I know Ruth and Eason would love having you nearby. Me and Carlos, too. There aren't many folks around Backwater our age. You met Becca Sue at the party, right? She'll be back soon, I hope."

"Uh, yeah, I met her. Yeah." He looks up at her. "Can I ask what people are saying about things? You know, the dispensary?"

She folds her hands inside her arms and hugs herself as she shrugs. "Mixed reactions. Guess it's just such a new concept that those not entrenched on one side or the other really don't know what to think."

"Sounds about right." He starts wetting napkins and cleaning the kids. "Thanks for the water and napkins. Guess I've got a lot to learn if I'm going to have the kids half the time, don't I?"

"I don't know. You look like you're doing pretty well. Well, see you later," Ashley says as she unfolds her arms and waves at the kids. "And good luck with everything tomorrow."

As she turns and walks past the lights of the ice cream shop, Bradley asks himself, "Tomorrow?" Then he remembers. "Oh, Olivia. Yeah, tomorrow."

36

The trailer got real small, real quick. "Oh, hey, kitty," I say, dropping Daddy's arm and rushing across the room to scoop up the tiny thing perched on Magnus' knee. Momma is sitting next to Magnus, so I whirl around to sit on a stool at the bar that separates the living room from the kitchen. Daddy still stands in the door.

"Lord's sake, Rick, close that door!" Momma yells as she snuggles up to Magnus. For warmth, obviously.

Daddy just shakes his head and turns to close the door. With his back still turned, he shrugs off his coat while Magnus struggles up from the sagging couch and Momma.

"Good to see you're doing well," he says as he steps away from the couch to shake Daddy's hand.

Daddy only nods, then sits in the chair across from the couch. Magnus examines his seating options and decides to stand.

"I thought of a name," I practically shout. When they all look at me, I hold up the kitten. "Squirrel. All the squirrels in the woods here reminded me of him since he's gray and white. Isn't that a cute name?"

Momma looks up at Magnus and pats the couch. "Hon, sit back down. We can visit for a bit."

He looks from me to her and then shakes his head. "Thanks, but no. I need to get on the road. Just felt like Becca Sue must be missing the cat. Squirrel, whatever." He steps towards me.

"Everything he needs is there in that bag. I left his litter box on the deck." His words trail off as he points towards the front door. We all look at the door, but no one says anything for a bit.

Daddy gets up. "Good to see you again, Magnus. I'm tuckered out. Going to bed," he explains as he walks past us all and down the hall where we hear a door close.

"Rick don't do awkward situations," Momma explains.

Apparently *she* does, because she settles back into the couch and picks up her drink. "Becca Sue, offer our guest something to drink."

"No, no, thank you," Magnus says. When he looks like he wants to say something, I jump up and shove Squirrel into his hands. "I'm getting me a beer. You sure you don't want one?"

"Yeah, I'm sure. But I would like to talk to you for a minute."

I turn around and look at him, then at Momma. She flicks on the TV with the remote to show she's staying. Staring at the screen she says, "Why don't you two just go on back to Florida? Talk there. She needs to go back home."

Magnus scowls and looks from Momma back to me. He moves closer and whispers, "Are you leaving here? What about Mr. Jameson Mason? Looked to me like he was making a pretty solid pitch for you to stay up here from what I saw *last* time I was here."

Slamming the refrigerator door, I twist around and stick my chin out at him. "Oh, when you were playing peeping tom? Looking in the car windows? And where did you go? You just disappeared."

"Well, it took some time for you to get your clothes back on, didn't it?" He looks around and shakes his head. Lowering his voice again, he smirks and says, "I don't know why I thought you'd be any different than your parents. Screwing that jerk down in Backwater then scurrying up here the very next day to jump in Mr. Mason's big, fancy car and do him! I'm not even sure I should leave the kitten with you."

I reach through the bar opening and grab for my kitten.

Magnus keeps him just out of arm's reach. "It's all fine and dandy when you sleep with every woman in Backwater, but it's different for me?"

Magnus pulls out of my reach. "So it's true? You really did sleep with that jerk?" His mouth falls open and he stares at me.

Swallowing, I realize he didn't actually know. "I don't know what you're talking about," I mumble.

He backs away and drops the kitten onto the couch beside Momma. Pulling his coat off the rack, he leaves, closing the door quietly behind him.

Hmmm, apparently people know about me and Bradley King. This time when I open the refrigerator I really do pull out a bottle of beer and open it. I kick off Momma's big boots I'd pulled on for mine and Daddy's walk, then sit on the couch with Momma and Squirrel.

Momma reaches toward me with her drink and tips it for me to click with my bottle. Then I take a long drink and place my kitten on my lap.

Momma pats my leg, much like she did Magnus'. "Baby girl, you know the number one fact about secrets?"

"No."

She sighs. "They don't work."

Night has completely fallen when I walk back outside of the trailer. This time I'm wearing my own shoes and my heavier jacket. But I still don't know if I'm going any further than this deck. I lean on the side railing looking down into the dark woods. There's some light from a half moon, but nothing in the woods for it to reflect on, so it falls in gray shadows.

Momma finally quit watching TV and drowsing on the couch to go to bed about fifteen minutes ago. That's when I decided to look at all the messages that had been causing my phone to vibrate in my pocket for the last two hours.

Pepper and Carol were bugging me to come down to El Dorado. They wanted to know where I was.

Then Jameson chimed in when he showed up, thinking I'd be there.

Ashleigh's bugging me about what I'm doing tomorrow. She must know about Bradley and me because she mentioned running into him downtown with his kids. *Oh my God, I not only slept with a married man, but one that has kids!* I bet Ashleigh wants to tell me off and then will never speak to me again. Carlos has pretty strong standards and now Ashleigh wants to have babies, so she'll be on Bradley's wife's side, of course. Why would she want to be my friend, anyway?

There are no calls or texts from Magnus. When his mouth dropped open, standing there petting Squirrel, he looked so sad. I wipe away the tears that spill over onto my cheeks and bite my lip. Crying over hurting Magnus Llord? Guess I didn't think it was really possible to hurt him.

All my life I've heard that thing about burnt bridges, but this is the first time I feel like I lit the match myself. I don't answer any of the texts. From anybody.

I pull my phone out again and look at the time. Hard to believe it's only eight-thirty. Early, plus I don't have to go into the diner tomorrow. My phone buzzes, and its Jameson asking if I'm coming. So I text "yes" real quick, tuck my phone in my pocket, and jog down the steps to my car.

Walking into El Dorado feels like stepping into a big, loud hug. Jameson stands up and waves me to the seat beside him, and as I swerve through the tables, I don't find myself surprised folks are talking to me. Even more surprising is that I want to talk to them. Some I've known most my life, but many are people I've waited on at the diner. By the time I get to our table, I'm laughing and warm.

Jameson wraps me up in a tight hug, and I can see he's been drinking quite a bit. It's funny because he usually doesn't remind me of Caleb at all, but tonight his face is so relaxed and his smile is bigger. I shake my head because Caleb doesn't belong here. If Caleb were here, I wouldn't be, that's for sure. I'd be at the hunting lodge waiting for him to finish up. A flush of heat that has nothing to do with me still having my coat on, rolls over me, it's anger How dare he treat me that way!

I pull back from our hug and twist my head around to kiss Jameson hard, right there in front of everyone. It's a long kiss, and when we break it off, we get a round of applause. Jameson drops into his seat and grins at me. Shrugging off my coat, I chatter with the ladies. It's the same group as usual except Jessie and Martin aren't here. Pepper and Carol are at the end of the table where my chair sits.

"It's about time you got down here," Pepper shouts over the music. "Band's going on break in a bit. Wasn't Mrs. Mason's party fun? You looked amazing. Everyone said so. Glad you're still wearing that dress."

Carol leans back in her seat, and I see she also still has on her navy dress and heels from the party. "Where's Jessie and Martin?" I ask as I slide into my chair.

"Jessie didn't want to get a sitter tonight since they had one this afternoon," Carol says with a shrug.

"That's it!" Pepper shouts as she jumps up. "Slow song. Let's all dance. Come on!"

I'm taking a sip of my margarita so I don't immediately get up, but the rest of the table does. Bruce and Buck and Jameson get up as fast as Carol and Pepper, and I'm the only one still sitting.

Jameson grabs my arm. "Come on. Your drink will be here when we get back."

The dance floor is on two levels beside the band. Jameson has my hand and he follows Pepper and Bruce up to the top level, which is only two steps above the floor, but feels like everyone can see us. I try to stay on the bottom level, but he pulls my hand up.

He holds me, and I realize it's the first time we've ever danced. It feels nice, but it's hard to relax when it feels like everyone is looking at us.

"You were wonderful today at the party," he whispers into my ear. "Mother was so impressed with you, she's now one of your biggest fans. Didn't stop singing your praises all afternoon." He leans to the side to look at me. "Did you enjoy the party? Glad you're not still mad at me."

"Well, guess I can't be mad about where you live." I smile up at him and admit, "Guess I was just disappointed in not getting to be alone with you last night. I actually did enjoy the party, once I got over my nerves. It was really strange to be there and not upstairs waiting for the kids."

The confused look on his face tells me he doesn't know what I'm talking about. Why would he have noticed I wasn't invited to family parties? I hug him close to me, settling my chin into his neck, and sigh. Then I ask, "So Cab and Maggie are headed to London with the Worths?"

"Yep. House will be quiet with them gone. Mother's glad I'm not still out in the guesthouse. She gets so lonely."

I'm glad he can't see my face because Mrs. Mason being lonely is not something I think is possible. Sure, she's been nice to me recently, but I watched her at the party and she is far from a helpless, lonely old lady. "But the guesthouse would've been nice the other night," I say close in his ear.

He chuckles and kisses my neck as he holds me close. With his lips at my ear, he whispers, "Becca Sue it felt so right to have you there today. Mother, the kids, your family and our friends, it all works when we're together. I get so tired of thinking and worrying. You are very good for me, Becca Sue. Everyone says so."

He squeezes me and holds me as the song comes to an end. The floor begins to clear, and he's still holding me. I push, and he releases me. Turning, I see our friends aren't leaving the dance floor. When I smile at them, Pepper motions for me to turn back around.

So I turn around and Jameson Mason is down on one knee holding up a diamond ring. I catch my breath and reach out a hand, palm out, towards him. *What in the world? This can't be happening. Is this a joke?*

He smiles up at me and says it.

"Becca Sue, will you marry me?"

37

"George? Is that you?" Magnus calls softly as he crunches across the pine bark border between his yard and the Manninghams'.

"Yes. Magnus? What are you doing out there, creeping around in the shrubbery?"

"Working out the kinks from too much driving today." He opens the door to the dark screened porch. The only light come through the doors and windows from inside the softly lit house. "Mind if I join you for a bit?"

"Not at all. Help yourself to a drink," he says as he waves toward the bar in the corner. "Pearl was beside herself wondering where you went when you'd just come home this morning."

Magnus chuckles as he jiggles his glass to let the ice melt in his drink. "Poor Pearl. I should've printed her an itinerary. Where is she?"

"Too cold out here for her, but I think the little heater keeps the chill off just fine. Of course, you and I grew up in northern New York State. We know what cold really is." He sighs and takes a sip of his own drink. "Also, I told the others at dinner tonight about me using medical marijuana. Pearl needed to lay down when we got home."

"Why? Were folks upset? Wasn't Eason there? Surely he'd be delighted to find out. It helps his cause."

"I didn't handle it too well. Esme was running her mouth,

and I jumped right into it. Marie Thompson was on a soapbox as well. It was turning into a men versus women thing, and Pearl got caught in it. You know she's always been afraid of people finding out. Thinks it will hurt my book sales. She won't even let me tell the kids. You and my doctor are the only ones that know."

Magnus speaks into the dark. "Until now."

"Until now." The electric heater whirs and the ice in their glasses clinks as they watch the moon reflect in the lake.

"You never did say where you drove today," George says. "All those driving kinks you were working out."

"Took that cat up to Becca Sue."

"Thought so."

Magnus turns to his friend. "You did? Why?"

"Maybe it's a writer's word, but it fits here. You're *smitten* with that girl. Not saying it's love, but she has your attention. Also, I can't say if it's long-term, but she's definitely in your head."

"Not anymore." Magnus shakes his head, then says again, "Not anymore. I don't have time to waste. All the money in the world and no one to spend it on. Becca Sue let me down. You don't know what she did before she left here. She..."

Both men's heads swing towards the door when it opens.

"Oh, Magnus. I didn't know you were out here," Pearl says as she stays in the doorway, clutching her robe around her. "I wanted to make sure George didn't fall asleep out here and freeze to death. Where've you been today?"

"Took a little drive." He drains his glass, then sits it on the table as he stands up. "That drink was all I needed to put me right to sleep," he says as he walks to the door. "Have a good night." He walks through the wet grass and back through the shrubs. He goes faster than he came.

Pearl tsks. "Hope you got more out of him than I did. Where was he today?"

George turns his chair towards his wife and the interior door. "Can you turn off the heater? I'm ready to crawl into bed." As he rolls past her, she pats his shoulder. He stops and reaches out to hold her hand. "I'm lucky to have you. Sorry about tonight. At the restaurant."

She bends down to kiss his cheek. "I just worry about... well, about everything. But we are lucky to have each other. Poor Magnus. Did you tell him about Becca Sue and that awful Drummond Bell?"

"No. But I think he knows," George says as he rolls on into the house.

Pearl steps out on the porch and hurries to turn off the heater. She picks up both glasses and looks out. There are no lights on across lake, and with a shiver she dashes back into the house.

From his porch next door, Magnus is staring out at the dark houses across the lake, too. As he turns to walk back into his softly lit living room, he takes a deep breath and says out loud, "Truest thing said all day, 'I don't have time to waste.'" He locks the door behind him and walks through the high-vaulted rooms and down the hall.

"Besides, imagine taking children to visit their grandparents in that trailer," he says at his bedroom door. He pulls his phone from his pocket when it rings. "Olivia. I was just thinking about you."

"You already in bed?" Carlos asks as he walks into their bedroom. "Come have something to eat with me."

Ashleigh pats the bed beside her. "Bring a sandwich in here. It's too cold out there."

"But I need a shower. The restaurant was really busy tonight. New staff were a pain, but we made it out of there alive." He leans against the doorjamb. "Starving, but alive."

His wife pushes the bedcovers down and struggles out from underneath them. "Make you a deal. I'll fix you a sandwich while you take a shower. Meet you back here in ten." She pulls on a hooded sweatshirt over her long-sleeved night gown and then slides her feet into thick, wool-lined slippers.

Carlos is all smiles by time she gets to the doorway. "You are too cute, wife." He folds her into his arms. "See you in ten minutes, and we can get you out of all those cumbersome clothes and back in bed where you belong."

As she moves past him, he begins shedding clothes at the door to their one tiny bathroom. "Still wanting to go on a road trip tomorrow?"

She turns around and nods. "Yeah, more than ever. Becca Sue has been on my mind. She hasn't answered my calls or texts tonight."

He turns on the shower and yells over it. "Well, you'll get to see her tomorrow. Find out what's going on."

Ashleigh fills her arms with meat, cheese, and other fixings out of the refrigerator. As she starts assembling a sandwich, she folds a piece of cheese and puts it in her mouth. Then talking to herself while she chews, she mutters, "She probably just went to bed early. Lord knows nothing happens in Piney, Georgia."

Within minutes, the bread is toasted, slathered with mayonnaise and heaped with ham and cheese. She's bored and Carlos is still in the shower, so she scrolls through Facebook. What she sees at the top of her newsfeed freezes her in place.

The water shuts off in the bathroom.

"What's going on right now," Carlos calls out, "is that I'm going eat and then give you some sweet, sweet lovin'." When she doesn't respond, he defends himself. "Okay, I know that was cheesy, but I don't care. I stand by what I said."

"Where are you? Thought you were meeting me in bed." Her husband comes around the corner into the kitchen wrapped in a towel. For once, not distracting Ashleigh. "I'm missing a wife," he calls out with a laugh, but he stops when he sees Ashleigh standing beside the counter staring at her phone.

Ashleigh lays the phone down, her face frozen in shock.

"Your sandwich is done, but uh, you're not going to believe what happened."

He strides toward her. "Are you okay? What's wrong?"

She blinks away the tears in her shiny eyes and picks up the phone, turning the screen towards him. "It's on Facebook. Becca Sue is engaged."

38

Jessie slides into the church pew next to Carol, causing Carol's eyebrows to flatten. "This isn't where you sit," Carol says. "You know my parents always sit with us."

Her friend smiles real big and slaps at her hand. "Oh, silly, I just wanted to say good morning and give you a hug." Jessie wraps her arms around her, and in Carol's ear, she says, "Why didn't you tell me Jameson was going to propose last night? You know I would've come if I'd known." She pulls back and perches on the edge of the pew. Her smile is just as big as before, but hard, like those wax lips given away at Halloween.

Carol shrugs her red, wool-jacketed shoulder. "What makes you think I knew in advance?"

"Please. Are you saying you didn't?"

Another shrug is all Jessie gets. She huffs. "You could've at least texted me last night, or even this morning. Pepper is just using you, you know that, right? She's playing everyone."

"Miss Jessie, are you going to sit here?" a soft voice says from behind her. Jessie stands and turns, looking down at Belle. "No, sweet girl. Just needed to ask your momma a question. Don't you look pretty?"

Jessie joins Martin two pews back, where he is reading his bulletin and ignoring the knockdown drag-out fight that two of their kids are involved in. She grabs the brawlers' upper arms in a death grip, pulls them apart, and sits between them.

When Martin looks up, he grins and winks. She ignores the quieting sanctuary and pulls her phone out of her purse.

"Mom, I thought we weren't allowed to have phones out in church," her oldest says.

"This is an emergency," she spits as she opens Facebook. She flips through the pictures Pepper tagged everybody and their brother in of all the festivities last night at El Dorado. She finds the one she wants and pulls up the comments. Pepper had responded to a comment about it being a surprise with: "It was a surprise for Becca Sue, but the rest of us were in on it all afternoon!"

"Honey, stand up!" Martin whispers. Jessie looks up to see she's the only one still sitting.

She jumps up and her oldest, Henry, giggles. "Mom got in trouble."

She grabs his upper arm again and snarls through gritted teeth, "Shut up before I show you what trouble is. Now sing." Jessie drops her son's arm and places her hand across her eyes. "They knew I'd tell her if I knew he was going to propose, and now it's too late." She lifts her head to look at the lyrics on the screen, but she can't block the cherry-red suit from her line of sight. She closes her eyes, glad she knows this song by heart, and sighs. "It's too late now, but it's really none of my business."

"I hear congratulations are in order," Brenda Cousins says as she walks into the trailer's living room and sits in the chair across from her daughter's stretched-out body on the couch.

Becca Sue pulls open one eye. "What? Why are you waking me up? I don't work today."

"Just wanted to see the ring. Of course, I saw the pictures of it on Facebook, but since it's right here in living color..." She pauses and waits for her words to sink in.

And they do.

"Facebook!?" her daughter squawks. "It's on Facebook?"

Brenda stands up. "Coffee's done. Want a cup?"

Becca Sue doesn't answer. She's propped up on one elbow and searching the depths of the couch for her phone. By time she's found it, opened it, and scanned over the pictures, her mother is sitting a cup of coffee on the table beside the couch.

Brenda reaches for her daughter's left hand. "There it is," she says as she holds Becca Sue's hand still in the morning light. "Hmm, it actually looks bigger on Facebook."

"Of course we'll have to wait for Cab and Maggie to return from England," Mrs. Mason says as she stirs her coffee. The long sleeve of her robe threatens to droop in her cup, so she watches it. Lifting her spoon, she also lifts her eyes to her son. "Right? You want Maggie and Cab there, or are you planning to elope? Eloping might be a good idea. I'd pay for a wonderful trip somewhere for you both. My wedding gift."

Jameson stretches his eyes and shrugs. "Hadn't thought that far ahead. We got engaged, can't everyone give us a little time now? I mean, I'm not sure Becca Sue wants a wedding to happen that fast."

"Of course she does," his mother says as she sips her coffee and looks at the datebook open in front of her. "If you don't elope sooner, Valentine's Day will be perfect." She sits back and looks toward the kitchen, muttering, "How long does it take to toast a croissant? Are you eating or going for a run first?"

"Mother, Valentine's Day is in two weeks. That's crazy."

The older woman leans into the stream of sunlight crossing the table, and it amplifies her wrinkles as she lets her face droop. "Son, I've done so many things I regret, and one is not enjoying Cab and Maggie when they were little. I want to have your children running around here, laughing and making this old place a real home. And don't I have a lot to make up for with Becca Sue? You agree, don't you? You aren't getting any younger. People will start to wonder if you even *want* to get married. You already broke off one engagement." She sighs and leans back. "Son, I know you don't like to hear this, but we have to think about what people might say."

"I understand that, but...two weeks?"

"Ah, here's my croissant." She speaks to the tall, thin man carrying the plate towards them. "Tom, you worked with the caterers from the party yesterday. How do you think they'd do with an impromptu party in, say, two weeks? Do you think they could handle it?"

"Absolutely, ma'am. They did an excellent job, and I'd recommend them for any function. You're not having another birthday party, are you?" He chuckles as he places her plate on the table.

"No. A wedding. A Valentine's wedding for Jameson and Becca Sue."

Tom's eyebrows jump, then he nods first at his boss then at Jameson. "Congratulations to you both. Especially you, sir." He nods again and then turns toward the kitchen.

As she lifts the pastry for her first bite, Mrs. Mason concludes, "See? Everything is fine. We both know Becca Sue doesn't like to plan things like this. Let her focus on finding a dress with her little friends. Pepper did a wonderful job helping her find that dress she wore yesterday. I'm sure Pepper will be happy to take her shopping for whatever she needs. Now, let me eat my breakfast and you enjoy your run. I need to get dressed for church."

Jameson walks towards the stairs to his rooms. He turns when his mother calls his name. "Yes?"

"Be sure and invite Becca Sue for Sunday dinner this afternoon. Without the children it will be quite lonely, don't you think? We can discuss wedding plans and get things moving."

"Okay. Um, I'm going to drive myself to church. I'll see you there."

Upstairs, behind the closed door to his suite, he leans against the door and closes his eyes. "Two weeks. Yeah, that will be good. Need to just get things on track and it'll all work out. It's time to get things settled."

Jameson gets out of his car and scans the church parking lot for his fiancé. Jessie comes toward him waving.

"Hey, there. Congratulations are in order, I hear!" she says as she gets to him. She takes his arm, then leans in to kiss his cheek. "Sorry we weren't there last night. It was a full day for the kids, and we didn't want to get another babysitter. So, how are you?"

Jameson nods and smiles. "Overwhelmed? Happy? Have you seen Becca Sue?"

"No, we were at early service and then Sunday School. Listen, are you sure about *everything*? Don't let other people force you into something you aren't ready to do. You know?"

"There he is!" Carol says loudly as she strides down the sidewalk. "There's the groom. Good morning, Jameson."

He waves at her, but turns his head back to Jessie. "No one is forcing me to do anything. God knows I need a little push sometimes. Decisions don't appear to be my strong suit. Besides, it's time I grow up, and everyone loves Becca Sue now." He turns and reaches to give Carol a hug. "Good morning to you, and I can't thank you enough for planning all that last night."

"Oh, it wasn't me. Mostly Pepper. She is rather tenacious when she gets an idea." Just as she finishes speaking, the church bells ring.

Jameson looks up. "I better get inside. Mother will be looking for me." He waves at them and jogs down the sidewalk.

Jessie turns to Carol, grasping her forearm. "Carol, you really think this is going to all be okay?"

"Don't grab me," she says as she pulls away. "We really don't need your negativity. If you really cared for Jameson, if you were really his friend, you'd be more helpful. I have to go. Don't you have some *family* thing to see to?" Carol marches back down the sidewalk, high heels clipping in the brisk, sunny air.

Jessie looks in the opposite direction, where her minivan is literally rocking from her kids bouncing around. Martin is in the driver's seat, punching the buttons on the radio, looking for the Atlanta Falcons' pregame show, she assumes. As she gets closer to her van and hears the kids singing songs from Sunday School at the top of their lungs, she can't help but smile and says to herself, "Becca Sue is going to have to take care of her own problems, Lord knows I've got my hands full."

Opening her door, she climbs into her seat and adds to the noise, "Who's ready for chili and football?"

39

"Well, that was a disaster," Becca Sue says as she gets in the back seat of Ashleigh and Carlos' car in Mrs. Mason's circular driveway. "So now you've met the crowd."

Carlos grimaces in the rearview mirror and Ashleigh chews on her lips while she takes several deep breaths through her nose, calming herself, or at least trying to.

"Thanks for coming in and meeting everyone," Becca Sue continues. "You want to go see the Shoppes? Did y'all eat lunch on your way here? I sure didn't eat much here, so I'm kind of hungry. But if you're not hungry, no problem."

Ashleigh turns in the seat. "If you're hungry, then we'll go get some food. Unlike *some* people, we actually *care* about your opinion."

Becca Sue leans back in her seat and sighs. "They care. They just get carried away."

Ashleigh opens her mouth in outrage, but Carlos interrupts as he takes his right hand off the steering wheel and lays it on his wife's thigh. "So, remind me who all those people were?"

"Well, you know Jameson. The older lady at the head of the table is his mother, Mrs. Mason. Then there was Pepper and Bruce Johnson, she's the little blonde and her husband was beside her. They own the Shoppes and the diner. Carol, the one in the red suit, I've known her since I was born. She's a few years older than me, but she has always kind of run the town. She actually dated Caleb when they were in high school. Isn't that crazy? And her husband Buck was one of Caleb's best friends. Then the real surprise was my grandfather and step-grandmother being there. He was the one with all the silver hair. My step-grandmother Irene works for Mason Farms."

Calmly, Ashleigh asks, "So everyone thinks a Valentine's wedding is a good idea?"

"Apparently. Jameson told me about it when he picked me up for Sunday dinner. Must've just missed y'all getting to Momma and Daddy's. What a nice surprise! What are y'all doing up here?"

Ashleigh can't help herself. "I saw your engagement on Facebook and thought I'd better see what in the Sam Hill was going on up here. Have you—"

Carlos pats her knee as her volume increases, and he interrupts again. "Which way do I turn here?"

"Is El Dorado okay with y'all? Not many other places open on Sunday afternoon. Diner closed at three. Turn left here, then go straight about a mile. Yeah, can't believe it was on Facebook last night."

"After meeting Pepper, I'm amazed you're only engaged. Shocked she didn't throw you in the trunk of her car and haul you to a wedding chapel in the middle of the night. What in the world—"

Carlos speaks loudly toward the rearview mirror, "Then turn right up here back into town?"

"Yep," Becca Sue says from the back seat. "You know, Pepper's just like that. Makes things happen. Like the Shoppes — and have I told you about her? She came from nothin'. I mean, I was well-to-do compared to her family. She's real smart, went to college and everything. She's been a good friend. You'll like her when you get to know her, I think."

"Here we are," Carlos says as they pull in the gravel parking lot.

They hurry into the front door as the sunshine has turned into clouds and wind, where they all stop to breathe in the warm air and spicy smells.

Ashleigh looks around. "So this is where it happened? Where you said 'yes'?"

Becca Sue scrunches up her eyebrows, and the rest of her face follows. "Funny, but I don't remember actually saying 'yes.'"

Daylight is going to come early. *Shoot, I have to be up way before daylight.* I roll over and check that the alarm is set for four-fifteen—again. Funny how when you've got to get up early you waste so much sleeping time making sure you'll be sure to get up early. Tilting my phone, I use the light to look at my ring—again.

Mrs. Caleb Maso—no, Mrs. Jameson Mason. Can't let that slip out. It's understandable, though, isn't it? Ashleigh even asked, several times, how the last quickie marriage to a Mason worked out for me. She sees it as all bad, but it wasn't. But I guess I'm the only one that thinks that. Thank goodness she calmed down before she and Carlos left. She is my best friend.

And sometimes Jameson seems more like Caleb. Like today, he wasn't the one doing all the talking like he usually is. He and I just kept our mouths shut and let the rest of them plan everything. Jameson is usually in the middle of stuff like that.

And he even told me I can keep the cabin in Backwater for when we want to get away. Or, wait, did he say when I want to get away? But of course he'd come with me. Right?

It will be nice to be with Maggie and Cab all the time. Yeah, we can go down to Backwater in the summer. Guess I need to let Mr. Worth know what's going on. Although... I grab my phone again and pull up Facebook. *Oh, so Maggie did see the engagement stuff.* Her string of OMG's makes me laugh. *She's so dramatic. Guess she's told her grandfather.*

WISH YOU WERE HERE

Yep, an email from him. I drop the hand holding my phone. *Should I look at it? No. I have to get to sleep. All this can wait for tomorrow.* Laying my phone facedown, I roll over to face the back of the couch.

Stupid couch. Shockingly, Mrs. Mason said maybe I should go ahead and move in. She's real excited about the wedding. Jameson, bless his heart, is so traditional he said now that we're engaged we should just wait until we're married. Seems kind of strange, but I don't really know how to do things right.

Maybe I should get an etiquette book.

212

40

"I suppose it's better than her ending up with Magnus," Miss Bell says as lifts her spoon from the cup of soup. "Look at this fog. It's like we're in our own little world sitting here by the windows. I can't even see the beach or the waves. I'm so glad you suggested going out for lunch, Ashleigh. With the market closed for winter, I don't see enough of you. Tell me, how is married life treating you?"

Ashleigh smiles and takes a deep breath. "Is it bragging to say I never thought I could be this happy? We just fit so well together, it's like we've always known each other."

"That's how it should be. Mr. Bell and I were like that. Silly us being worried about her and Magnus! She and Jameson were meant to be, and like them, Mr. Bell and I didn't have a smooth road to our marriage. For that, I owe my stepson Drummond my support. I understand your questions about him and Mimi, but he truly *is* my only family."

"Of course, and I didn't mean to pry. I just worry about you since Becca Sue isn't here. Besides, Drummond and Mimi will be heading back home to Minnesota or Michigan or wherever soon, right?"

"Wisconsin. And I'm not sure." She looks down into her soup, only stirring it, not taking a bite. She looks up with a smile. "But tell me what Becca Sue thinks about being a Mason again? The engagement pictures looked like such fun. She has a lot of friends there, doesn't she?"

"Not sure they're exactly her friends." Ashleigh frowns. "Something just doesn't feel right. It's too rushed for my taste."

The older lady laughs out loud. "Too fast for you? This time last year you didn't even know a man named Carlos Ricci existed, and now you're married to him. You didn't even know him six months before you said 'I do.' Becca Sue has known Jameson her whole life."

Ashleigh opens her mouth to argue, then grins. "That's true. Guess I'm just going to miss her."

"We both will. But you have Carlos now, and I have Drummond and Mimi. Besides, she'll only be a couple hours away. If she'd ended up with Magnus, who knows when we'd get to see her? You know, maybe I shouldn't say anything, but..."

"What? What shouldn't you say?" Ashleigh leans closer.

Mrs. Bell lifts the napkin off her lap and pats her lips, then leans forward, too. "Becca Sue and Magnus. They were, well, together, the night before she went to Piney. After the party? Had a fire and everything down in her cabin. I was afraid that meant they were getting back together. That's why the news of her engagement to Jameson doesn't bother me."

Ashleigh pulls back. "Magnus? No, it was..." She stops and closes her mouth.

"It wasn't Magnus? Well, of course it was. Who else could it be?" The waitress comes to the table with the check. Mrs. Bell reaches for it. "I'll take that. You drove."

As Mrs. Bell gathers her money, Ashleigh steers the conversation to the reopening of the market, her hopes of having a baby, and the fog. Anything but Becca Sue and Magnus or Becca Sue and Drummond.

"Let's step outside," Ashleigh says to her husband as she comes into the kitchen at Sybil's. "Won't take a minute." She walks through the dining area and out the back doors. "Oh, y'all are putting up the outdoor tables? Already?"

The young man named Chigger turns toward her, wet sponge in his hand. "Yep, this week is supposed to be mild, and the boss says people might want to sit out here before dinner. Guess them northerners are used to cold weather. You lookin' for Carlos?"

"I found him. He's coming out here in a minute." She walks off the patio and down towards the lake. As she reaches the edge, she hears the door open and close and Carlos speaking to Chigger on his way to her.

Soon, a pair of strong arms wraps around her and a kiss finds its way to her temple. "You didn't want to stay on the patio and chat with Chigger?" Carlos asks with a laugh.

She nuzzles his neck. "No. That boy could talk the hind leg off a mule. How's he doing as a waiter? Can't imagine him actually serving food between stories."

"He's doing all right. We all know we have to push him along, but he's so friendly and the customers really like him. Well, most of them." He pulls back so he can see her face. "So? Did you find anything out about Drummond and Mimi?"

"Not really, although they are from Wisconsin, so that should make my web searching a bit easier. Wonder if he uses his mother's maiden name? It's just hard to imagine there not being more out there about him if he's this big business man. Although I'm also guessing that he's one of the partners with the Kings in the medical marijuana shop. Maybe I should just come out and ask Bradley. But that feels like taking advantage of a friend."

"That's true. Nothing like taking a little old lady out for lunch to pump her for information on her stepson," he says, wide-eyed.

She pulls an arm away and playfully slaps at him. "Hey, I wanted to visit with her! I didn't pump her, just asked friendly questions. But I did find out something interesting. She thinks it was Magnus with Becca Sue the night before she hightailed it to Piney. I almost blurted out that it was Drummond. Luckily, the waitress showed up right at that moment."

"Why does she think it was Magnus?"

Ashleigh shrugs. "Think she just assumed. Part of me wishes she knew it was Drummond so that maybe she wouldn't be so trusting of him, but he is her only family. Maybe we need to give him a second chance. After all, Becca Sue was there, too, and it was her house. Not like he took advantage of her."

"I need to get back inside," Carlos says as he steps back. "Are you feeling better about Becca Sue and Jameson?"

"I never had any problem with the two of them. It's all the pushy friends and pushy mother and her grandfather I have a problem with. She never spoke to the man until a week ago, and now he's helping plan her wedding. Why the hurry?"

"You know, that Pepper reminded me of my oldest sister," Carlos admits. "Not happy unless she's running everything around her. Remember our wedding? I told you when Marianna got here she'd try to take over. Maybe Pepper's like that. You know, Becca Sue kind of likes people that tell her what to do..."

As his words drift off, Ashleigh pulls away from his side. "Are you saying that's why she likes me?"

Carlos shrugs and folds his arms against his chest.

Before Ashleigh can say anything, Chigger makes it clear he's been listening when he speaks up.

"Some folks just like to have someone lay out the options for them. It's not being bossy, it's seeing the big picture and having the ability to lay it out for folks. It's a gift, Miss Ashleigh." He nods and plunges his big sponge back down into his bucket of soapy water.

Carlos grins. "Yeah, it's a gift, Miss Ashleigh."

His wife punches his arm and tries to keep her grin inside as she leans to kiss him. "Shut up and get back to work."

She leaves him talking to Chigger and walks around the side of the restaurant. "I am not like that Pepper and Mrs. Mason," she says to herself. "I honestly have Becca Sue's best interests at heart." But almost immediately she adds, "But how do I know that? Maybe they *do* know what's best."

41

"But I thought Olivia was coming home last night?" Ruth says to her son as he brushes Emerson's soft hair into a tiny ponytail.

Holding an elastic band between his teeth, he mumbles, "I thought so, too."

"But where's she staying? She can't still be at the house we rented. It had a new booking starting today. Did she say where she was going?"

"No, Mom. Emerson! Hold still. Where's Phillips?"

Ruth groans as she pushes up from the end of the bed she's sitting on. "Who knows? That boy is too fast for me. Phillips?" she yells as she leaves the bedroom.

Bradley releases his daughter and falls back onto the bed. "I have too much work to do to babysit." He covers his eyes with his arm, blocking out the early afternoon sunlight.

"Can't actually babysit your own kids," his father says from the doorway. "But you and Olivia do need to get on the same page. Where do you *think* she is?"

Without sitting up, Bradley shrugs. "You don't understand, Dad. People raised with staff don't worry about taking care of kids or being where they need to be. Well, at least Olivia doesn't. Me not knowing where she is IS normal. We have nannies, which for some inexplicable reason, she didn't bring on this trip." He sits up. "That what I need to do. Hire a nanny. Can't keep imposing on you and mom."

"Son, you need to find your wife. You need to slow down and talk about things with her. The kids are not just a problem to solve." A shriek from the living room makes both men's heads turn, and Eason says, "But they are wearing your mother out, and you and I do have a lot of work to do."

Bradley picks up his phone. "Ashleigh will know someone, I bet. I don't have her number." He stands up. "I'll take the kids on a walk over to the restaurant and talk to Carlos. You make mom sit out on the porch and have a glass of wine. It's too pretty of a day for us all to be inside."

"Days like today make me anxious to get the market going," Mrs. Bell says to her stepson as they sit on the wide porch behind her house.

Her porch isn't screened in like most of the others around the lake. It's a wide, flat surface of gray tiles bordered with smooth, white marbled stones. Below that carved border is a step to the thick lawn, green even in January. "Wait until you and Mimi see the market. You'll fall in love with it, too. People from all over, so many interesting things to buy. And of course my biscones are very popular. It won't be the same without Becca Sue." She falls silent for a moment. "You and Mimi will still be here for the market, won't you?"

"Will you even be able to reopen without Becca Sue?" Drummond asks. "Seems like she ran it. We know it's too much for you."

"Oh, everyone pitches in." She waits for him to answer her question, but he only stands and walks to the end of the porch.

He points to the empty lot next door. "This lot, where the market is held, that's your lot, right?"

"Yes. Your father bought both lots so we'd have some privacy. If he'd only known how it would be used!" She laughs out loud.

"It's a fine piece of property. Worth a pretty penny with all the improvements here in Backwater, I'd imagine. The other empty lots are selling rather well, I hear."

"They are? I hadn't realized," she says quietly.

He turns to look at her. "Maybe you should consider selling?"

"But our market—"

Drummond throws his hands up. "Virginia, do you honestly think you'll be able to pull it off without Becca Sue? Besides, you know how Father felt about getting all the information possible about any financial matter, so I'll check in with a realtor. There's a realtor opening an office in those condos beside the medical marijuana shop. Maybe I'll walk over there now, it's so nice out." He walks back inside before she can comment.

Her shoulders slump, and she shakes her head. "He's probably right. I am too old to do this all by myself."

42

"I haven't seen Jameson all week. Just Sunday for dinner at his mother's," Becca Sue complains to Tina, the pregnant waitress she usually work afternoons with.

"Maybe he's busy getting things done so he can take time off for your honeymoon. Y'all are going on a honeymoon, aren't you?" Tina is situated at the end of a booth, her swollen ankles sticking out in front of her. When her table at the front lifts a hand, she struggles to get up.

"No, stay there. I'll get it," Becca Sue says as she jumps away from the counter she'd been leaning on. She gets the customer's extra mayo and refills drinks at that table and one of hers. "Hard to believe I like being busy more than this place being empty like now. Time goes so fast in the mornings," she says as she comes back to lean on the counter again.

"I hear your momma is going to be back here to work tomorrow," Tina says, her head tilted towards the floor.

"Tomorrow? She didn't tell me. I mean, Daddy is doing good, but she didn't mention it." Becca Sue looks around. "So this is my last day?"

Tina shrugs. "That's what I hear. Don't think Pepper was happy either."

"Why wouldn't Pepper be happy? I'm not really a good waitress."

The dark-haired girl nods for Becca Sue to come closer, so she perches on the edge of the booth across from her coworker. "Pepper and your momma don't get along at all. Bruce won't let her fire your momma, but Pepper's tried a bunch of times."

Becca Sue whispers back, "Tried to fire *my* momma? Why?"

"Told you. They don't get along. Pepper likes things done her way and, well, so does Brenda. You know that."

"True, but Pepper knows I'm not going to stay working here."

Tina pauses and raises her eyebrows, then adds, "Does she? Has she hired anyone for when I'm off having the baby?"

"No, but... I'm not, I mean, she doesn't think..." When the front door flies opens, Becca Sue jumps to her feet. "Pepper! Hey there. Things as slow over at the Shoppes as they are here?"

Pepper gives a dramatic eye roll. "Lord, yes. Thought you'd want to know the wedding dresses are in for you to try on. Let's plan on going tomorrow. I'm taking the morning off. Guess your mother will be back to work, so no reason for you be here." She stops in front of Tina and leans down to pat her stomach. "Unless this sweet thing decides to make an early appearance. Good to know Becca Sue's around, isn't it, Tina?"

Becca Sue's mouth drops open as she stares at Tina. Tina just nods and shrugs a bit as Pepper dashes around them.

"Anyone you want to bring with us when you try on the wedding dresses?" Pepper asks from the office. "Guess your mom is out since she'll be here working, but I don't know that she's exactly into this kind of thing, right?"

"No, Momma wouldn't be interested," Becca Sue says as she pats Tina's arm and goes to collect the checks from two tables. As she comes back to ring them into the register, she winks and smiles at Tina. "So, Pepper. Guess today is my last day?"

Pepper comes out of the office, her high-heeled boots clacking on the linoleum. "Well, I did want to talk to you about that." She leans against the counter, her tight jeans making her hips look even smaller.

Tina struggles up from her seat. "Here, I'll take their receipts back to them so y'all can talk." As she takes the tickets from Becca Sue, both women roll their eyes.

Pepper waits for the short girl to waddle away and whispers, "I just can't see myself ever doing that, being pregnant. Thank God Bruce already has kids from his first marriage. That was one of his more endearing qualities when I met him."

"I didn't realize he had children," Becca Sue says.

"Oh, yes, they're cute, but they take up so much time. He has them when he's up in Atlanta, then we have the weekends free down here." She leans closer and smirks. "That's why I rarely go to Atlanta with him. Know what I mean? Come back here where we can talk."

Becca Sue follows Pepper to the door of the office where Pepper stops, lets her pass, and closes the door before turning to face her. "Bruce being in Atlanta is part of what I want to talk about. When he's not here, things don't run as smoothly. I'm sure you've noticed that. And I can't keep running back and forth to oversee things here and keep an eye on things at the Shoppes." She reaches out and grabs Becca Sue's hand. "We want to make you manager here! How great is that?"

Becca Sue is at a loss for words or reaction. "What?"

"People need a boss, and I need someone I trust. You and me. How fun will that be?" She shakes Becca Sue's hand side to side in excitement and then reaches up to hug her. "Best part? You get to be your momma's boss!"

A laugh bursts out of Becca Sue. "Boss my momma? Yeah, that dog won't hunt, no way, no how."

Pepper flings a hand out. "Oh, don't worry about that. I was kinda joking, but you *will* be making more than her. Not that she has to know." She picks up a folder from the desk. "Here, fill out these papers to get you on the payroll. I've got to get back to the Shoppes." She opens the door, and they both walk out to the counter. The petite blonde doesn't stop. "Good talk, Becca Sue. See you at church tonight."

Becca Sue is left nodding, holding the folder, and watching Pepper strut out the front door.

Tina looks at her and grins as she points to the folder.

"Told ya, didn't I? And don't worry, being the newest hire isn't that bad, even though you will probably get the worst shifts at first. I sure won't miss having to come in to start the coffee every day." She flicks a towel at Becca Sue. "At least you already know the ropes!"

"Tina? I'm going to make a quick call, okay?" Becca Sue says as she pulls her phone out of her purse under the counter and walks toward the back of the empty restaurant. There, a door opens onto a small stoop. The surprisingly warm afternoon causes her to pause, and she smiles looking out at dirt and gravel parking lot bordering a waiting field. "Hey Ashleigh, what ya up to?"

Her friend laughs. "You wouldn't believe me if I told you! I'm a nanny now! Still a reporter, but also taking care of Bradley's twins so Ruth can get some rest and he can get some work done. What about you?"

"Oh, just getting ready to leave work. But I was wondering if you want to come up tomorrow morning for me to try on wedding dresses. Although it is up towards Atlanta, so farther for you to travel."

"Shoot, hon, I'd love to, but I'm watching the kids tomorrow, too." To the side she says, "Thank you, Emerson." Ashleigh chuckles. "She just gave me a rock. Lord, they are cute. And I'm good with them. I really am. We're taking a walk, and we're at the cabin's driveway. It is such a beautiful day here. We don't even need jackets. Azaleas are budding all in the woods around your place. If it stays warm, they'll bloom early."

Becca Sue walks down the steps. "I haven't thought about the cabin in forever. The builders were waiting on me to give them the go-ahead on things. Guess they gave up waiting on me, huh?"

"Well, there's no one working there. Lots of work going on everywhere else, though. You won't recognize it here at all. But, never mind, sorry, back to wedding dresses. Hate that I can't be there. Um, it sounds like you're doing the whole rigmarole? Fancy dress and everything?"

Becca Sue laughs. "Apparently. Pepper has it under control. Y'all are coming, right?"

"Wouldn't miss it! Carlos has the day off. I mean, if you're sure you want to rush into it all..."

"Yeah, it is happening fast..."

"You're in love with him, right? Jameson?"

"Of course." Becca Sue digs the toe of her tennis shoe into the stoop. "Listen, I better get back to work since it's almost time for me to get off! I'll send you some pictures of the dresses. It'll be just like you're there. Have fun with the kids."

Becca Sue hangs up and sighs as she looks at the wide open fields before her. For as far as she can see, there is dirt and an occasional line of trees at a field's edge. A light breeze brings the smell of the dirt and clean air to her and she breathes deep. So familiar and comfortable.

"Better get inside so I can clock out," she says out loud as she turns back to the building. "After all, can't have the boss not following the rules."

43

"Listen, I can't meet you for lunch. Sorry, but something's come up at work," Jameson says as I answer my phone.

"Jameson, I haven't seen you all week," I protest. "I thought you'd be at church last night." I put my car back in park instead of pulling out of the diner lot where I'd left my car for dress shopping with Pepper. "I picked out my dress this morning," I sing-song to him.

"You did? Guess you can't tell me about it, can you?"

"Nope. But seriously, I do need to talk to you."

"Talk. I'm driving, so we can chat now."

"Where are you driving to?"

"Just out to a, a client out of town."

"Why weren't you at church last night? Did you know they're planning this big wedding shower for us on Sunday afternoon?"

"Do I have to come? Or is it a lady thing?"

"I think it's for everyone. They're doing lunch. Can we have dinner tonight?"

"Of course. Mother serves at six."

"I meant just the two of us." I pick at my fingernails and then remember Pepper smacking my hands this morning. She said I'd have to get false nails applied for them to look good by Valentine's Day.

"Sorry, but I promised Mother I'd be there. Listen, I'm getting another call. See you at dinner, okay?"

He's gone before I can say okay. Or *not* okay. Carol, Jessie, and Pepper were having lunch at the Salad Shack, and they'd expected me to join them until I told them I was having lunch with Jameson. I could join them now. My stomach rumbles, and I know I don't want a salad. Or lunch with the ladies. Turning the car off, I get out and walk into the diner.

"Well, la-di-da, look who's all dressed up to go dress shopping," Momma says as she stops and looks me up and down. "Did you find one?"

"Yep, you want to see a picture? Hey Tina." Tina sneers at me, then stomps past without even a smile. I step to the side and whisper at Momma. "What's wrong with her?"

"She's miffed that she was passed over for the manager spot. Seems someone with much more restaurant experience than her was given the job. Even though she's worked here for three years and has that degree from the junior college in restaurant management."

"Oh, um..."

"Yes, we know it's you. Guess it's true that it's all in who you know. Let me see your dress so I can get back to work. Don't want the big boss lady to get the wrong impression."

Holding out my phone, I show her the picture. "Hmmm, looks familiar, doesn't it?"

"Familiar?" I look over her shoulder.

"Tight, low-cut, picture it in green. A shiny green," she says as she hands me back my phone.

As Tina walks past, I reach out to touch her arm. "Tina, I didn't know anything about, well, anything. I haven't said yes."

"Whatever," she says, jerking away from my touch.

They both walk away to their tables, and I turn towards the back. Hanging on a rack is a pair of old jeans and a flannel shirt I left here last week to use for cleaning. Taking them into the bathroom I change out of my gray dress pants, boots, and long gray sweater. I fold them up and tuck them under my arm before I realize I don't have any shoes to put on since

I wore my tennis shoes home with my uniform the day I left these clothes here.

I leave the bathroom barefoot and don't even stop to talk to Momma or Tina. I don't care what they think anyway. Tenderly picking my way through the parking lot gravel, I shove my nice clothes into the back and get in the driver's seat. It's another warm day so my feet aren't cold. My jeans and shirt are big and raggedy and I'm barefoot as I head to the Handee Burger drive-thru. Yep, this is more like it.

Eating, driving, and listening to old country songs really loud on the radio, the car takes me where I need to go. Just didn't realize how much I needed to come here.

Turning the radio off, I roll the window down before I turn the car off, too.

The Masons' hunting lodge.

Sounds more impressive than it really is. It's an old concrete building with an old, wooden front porch stretched from end to end. An assortment of rocking chairs and an old easy chair line the porch. Inside it's just two rooms, the kitchen to the right and the living room to the left. The living room has two couches that fold out into beds. I'm the only one parked here right now, but there's space for a couple campers, which is where Caleb told me the guys sleep when they're out here hunting.

Wonder if anyone hunted here last year? Caleb was the big hunter of the family. This was his place. I'm not sure Jameson could even find it. Mrs. Mason likes to talk about "the Hunting Lodge" like it's some fancy place out on "the Property." Caleb's daddy came out here some, but mostly they all left it to Caleb.

And me. But they didn't know that.

I get out of the car and, avoiding sticks and rocks, pick my way up to the porch. Strange I haven't been here in so long. If Caleb hadn't died, I would've been here all the time. Like I was when we broke up, well, when we pretended to break up. See, we only got divorced so he could marry Audrey, join all their families' properties, and be a daddy to their baby.

Taking my key out from under the loose window board, I

open the door and step inside. Musty but so familiar, the smell makes me take a deep, deep breath. And I start to cry. I sink onto the dark red couch, and the sound of the springs screeching makes me sob.

We'd made love right here on this couch the night he died. We didn't even fold out the bed because he said he couldn't stay the nights anymore. He would have to go home to Audrey every night. He'd promised his mother. I'd usually stay after he left because Momma and Daddy's trailer was just so crowded. I'd sit here and read. My box of old paperbacks is still beside the fireplace.

Everyone was happy. Caleb Mason was no longer married to no-count me, and I didn't have to hide away from his friends and family. The Piney universe was back in order. Except nobody knew about the hunting lodge. Our place.

I was finally going to be so happy.

"Your Daddy says you're on the road back to Florida," Momma says when I pick up my phone from the passenger seat and answer it. I now have shoes on, but am still wearing my old flannel shirt and jeans.

"He wasn't supposed to tell you until you came home from work. I'll be back Saturday."

"Tina went into early labor, and as the new manager, you need to be here. Pepper is meeting with some caterer and said for me to call you. You weren't answering earlier."

When I got back to the trailer from the hunting lodge, I'd left my phone in the car and dashed in to pack a bag. Just a quick trip to say hi to everyone in Backwater. "But I'm off tomorrow. I'll be back Saturday."

"Being boss means you don't always get your scheduled day off." Momma clips off her words, but I can hear her waiting.

"What?" I ask.

"Why would you want to be manager here? Tell Pepper Johnson to go scratch. It's a made-up job anyway. Think about it. You've been here last couple weeks, kitchen runs fine, out front runs fine. Right? Does Bruce actually *manage* anyone when he's here? You want to marry back into the Masons, then do it. But work here?"

My head hurts. I pull off the side of the highway onto the sandy shoulder. I'm still miles outside Tifton and far from the interstate. Stopping the car, I take a long breath and feel tears gathering. "Momma, I've got to go. Pepper's on the other line." I think I hear her say "Whatever" as she hangs up.

With a quick sniffle, I pull back on the tears and push the green button. "Hey there. What's up?"

"Your momma didn't call you?" Pepper demands.

"Yeah, she just got hold of me. You really need me to come back? I was going to Florida for the night. Listen, about the manager's job..."

Then the sniffles are on the other end of the phone. Real sniffles. Finally Pepper sighs and her breath stutters. Then she not only doesn't stutter, she doesn't take a breath. "Oh, honey, I know the job is beneath you, but I just *need* to have you close. You are the only one in this town that gets me. Carol and Jessie have always had everything, didn't have to fight for a blasted thing like me and you. I just thought it'd be fun us being together at work. Taking lunches together, hanging out on the weekends. Me and Bruce just bought land to build a new house, and I thought you and Jameson could build out there, too. But never mind. Never mind. Just ignore me and go on to Florida. You have lots of friends there. You don't need me like I need you. Guess I'll help out at the diner. And if I have to hire someone to replace Tina, then so be it. She probably won't even want to come back to work after the baby gets here."

"Replace her? You can't do that, she wants her job. She needs her job."

"Oh, silly, I can't really replace her. Don't think the law will let me. But, you know, hire someone to help out and then take it from there when, or if, she comes back. I better go. Caterer has some crazy idea about a mashed potato bar at the wedding. Have you ever heard of anything so tacky? Told him we want classy. All classy. Mrs. Mason said to spare no expense. So, have fun in Florida, and I'll see you Saturday. Don't you worry about things at the diner. Lord knows I'm going to be crazy busy with working at the diner *and* planning your wedding, but you know what they say, 'No rest for the weary.'" She sighs and I can hear the stuttering of her breath as she forces a smile into her words. "Love ya. Bye."

I look over my shoulder to see empty highway, then pull a U-turn. What would I even do in Backwater? Ashleigh is busy with her husband, the newspaper, and her new nanny gig. Miss Bell has Drummond and Mimi there now. And Magnus... no. Crazy girl. You're engaged. You can't stay with Magnus, even if he'd let you.

Smirking, I speak to the mirror. "And we all know he'd let me."

44

"You two go for a walk. Me, Wayne, and Irene have some business to discuss," Mrs. Mason says as she motions to the young man standing at the door to clear the dining table.

Becca Sue looks at Jameson as he pushes his chair back. "Wonderful idea, Mother."

Wayne comes around the table to pull his granddaughter's chair out. "Good to see you again, darlin'. Must say I'm glad to hear you'll be working so close with Pepper and Bruce Johnson. Good business people and the right kind of contacts. Not only here, but up in Atlanta, too. Give your granddaddy a hug and go take a walk with your beau. We will see you at the shower on Sunday." he says with a wink.

Irene speaks up, "Becca Sue, I've made an appointment for you at the spa out at the club next week. All-day treatment, just a little wedding gift from me to you. I checked with Pepper, and she said Wednesday would be the best day."

Mrs. Mason smiles at Becca Sue. "Men do like to see their ladies getting all fixed up. Isn't that right, Jameson?"

He scowls at his mother, but smooths his face quickly and shrugs. "Of course. But Becca Sue looks beautiful to me without any trip to a spa." He leans to kiss his fiancée, and she blushes as he also wraps his arm around her waist.

"Even better than a walk," Mrs. Mason says, "go up to your apartment and light a fire. You two need some alone time."

Wayne chuckles. Becca Sue leans in to her fiancé and says,

"That might be a good idea. I didn't really wear any shoes for walking." She'd changed back into her gray slacks, sweater, and gray suede boots after closing down the diner. She tugs at his hand, leaning toward the stairs, but he doesn't move.

Jameson stretches, dropping her hand, and then rubs his stomach. "I really need to walk off that dinner. I bet there's an old pair of tennis shoes or boots up in Maggie's closet you can wear."

The older people all stop moving away from the table to look at him. His mother twists up her mouth, turns, and stalks off towards her office. Wayne and Irene shrug at each other, then follow Mrs. Mason. Becca Sue waits for him to look at her, but he doesn't. He pulls his phone from his pocket and, looking at it, starts for the front door. "Supposed to be getting colder again, so you might want to grab a jacket from Maggie's room, too."

Becca Sue is left alone. When one of the kitchen help comes back into the room, she turns to go up the other staircase and says loudly, "A walk will be nice."

"Are we going to get that cold front that's moving into Georgia?" Miss Bell asks as Ruth gets in the back seat of the car Mimi is driving.

"I think so," Ruth says over the closing of her car door. "I'm going to cover my orange tree and hibiscus bushes when we get home from the commission meeting tonight."

Mimi begins backing back down the Eason's driveway as she exclaims, "Cold front! You don't even know what a real cold front is until you've lived in Wisconsin. This is like spring-time. We are picking up Pearl, correct?"

"Yes," her mother-in-law says. "George isn't going to the meeting. Says none of our presence will make one bit of difference, but I want to hear the discussion. I'm still so torn on what's best for Backwater."

Ruth leans forward. "I thought Becca Sue was coming home for the meeting. I didn't realize she was going to stay up there this whole time."

Mrs. Bell twists to look at her friend. "She cancelled. Something to do with that diner. I think she said she was going to be made manager, but that doesn't sound right, does it? Marrying Jameson Mason and managing a diner? I'm kind of worried about her."

Mimi laughs. "Oh, Virginia, you're such a worrier. I don't think you understand what it does to a young person to feel like they are constantly being worried over. Let Becca Sue live her life. I find it completely understandable that she's happier there, surrounded by family and her hometown. There's Pearl."

Pearl waves from the sidewalk, then steps back as the car pulls up beside her. She slides into the back seat beside Ruth. "Did you hear it's going to get cold again tonight? I curse that nurseryman who sold us those stupid lime and lemon trees. Awful figuring out what things will life and which will die. Not like back home where everything dies, and there's none of this constant worrying and pulling out blankets to make the yard look like a full washing machine exploded." She mutters, "I hate Florida."

"At least here your car batteries don't freeze. You ladies would never survive a winter in Wisconsin, I tell you. One year—"

Pearl interrupts the driver. "You talk about Wisconsin like it's the Yukon Territory! We've *all* lived up north. We *all* know this isn't as cold as Wisconsin. Speaking of which, when are you and Drummy going home?"

Ruth and Mrs. Bell keep their mouths shut, but their eyes are wide open. Mimi scowls. "*Forgive* me! Just trying to make conversation."

Pearl waits, then exchanges questioning looks with Ruth before finally asking, "So? When are you leaving?"

"Don't you think we should at least wait to hear what the county commissioners say tonight before we decide? And with Becca Sue not coming back, who do you propose takes care of Virginia? You've already got a husband in a wheelchair who's apparently stoned half the time, which would explain his unreadable books."

"He is not stoned. Ever! How dare you."

Mimi shrugs and looks in the rearview mirror. "Just what I hear. Oh, and what I've read online."

"His newest novel just had its fortieth straight week on the bestseller lists!" Pearl snaps. But then her face folds in, and she slumps back into the seat. "I've always worried about whatwould happen if people found out. I don't want to even go to this meeting tonight."

Ruth leans toward her friend and pats her arm. "Of course you do." Then she whispers, "Ignore her. She doesn't know what she's talking about."

Mrs. Bell squares her thin shoulders. "Mimi, that was very rude. But since we're talking about you leaving, you need to know I'm fine by myself with my friends nearby. I think you and Drummond should plan on leaving this weekend. I understand you're investing in the cannabis store and you may need to be down here more often, but I believe it would be best is you stayed in a hotel next time." She lets out a long breath of relief.

Mimi ignores Mrs. Bell, staring straight ahead as she turns into the parking lot outside the county offices. She finds a spot, parks, and opens her car door, but before she gets out, she turns to face her mother-in-law. "Family takes care of family. Get used to us being here, because we are not going back to Wisconsin. Our house there sold last week, and we closed on it this morning. The moving van will be here Monday morning. This weekend will be spent deciding which of your furniture will be going into storage and which will be sold. Or trashed, as old as some of it is." She shrugs again. "You aren't in any shape, physically or mentally, to take care of things yourself. You've been very wise getting Drummond and myself to help you. We are just lucky our duty to *you* coincides with *us* moving to Florida." She cuts her eyes to the stunned women in the backseat and adds, "You might've heard—Wisconsin is cold."

"What happened? I thought you were going to be here tonight?" Ashleigh says.

"Didn't you get my text?" Becca Sue asks as she rolls over on the couch, whispering in the dark of the trailer.

"Yeah I got it. 'I'm not coming.' That's it?"

"You're right. I meant to tell you more, but I was driving, then at the diner, then this weird dinner at Jameson's mother's." She sits up, pulling the quilt around her shoulders. "I'm sorry. I know I'm not a good friend."

"Shut up. I'll tell you if you're not a good friend. You have a lot going on. First I'll tell you about the meeting, and then you tell me about the weird dinner."

"Deal, oh, and the diner. Remind me to tell you about the diner."

Ashleigh takes a sip of her wine before beginning. "Marijuana commissaries got county approval. Permission granted same as a pharmacy. Procedures sound pretty strict and it's only for the edible variety, but still a huge decision. The room was full, but I did see the Backwater contingent. Drummond, Bradley, and Eason were up near the front. The ladies didn't even get into the main room. I could see them in the overflow room next door where there were speakers set up. Have you talked to Miss Bell lately? She didn't look so good."

"No." Becca Sue moans. "See? I'm *not* a good friend. I'll call her tomorrow. Promise. So, did they say anything about Backwater?"

"Not specifically, but I saw a couple of the commissioners going over some paperwork with Bradley. He looked pretty mad, too. He said he'd talk to me in the morning for my article. So, now, the weird dinner?"

"Oh. Well, I've barely seen Jameson this week. Then when we finally do see each other, it's at his mother's dinner table with my grandfather and Irene there, too. I know Irene works for Mrs. Mason, but it's just annoying they were there. Never spoke to my grandfather before, and now we're just one big happy family?"

Ashleigh sighs and agrees. "I bet that is weird."

"It is, but even weirder is after dinner Mrs. Mason encourages us to go up to his suite, light a fire, and have some alone time. I'm all for it, but Jameson wanted to go for a walk instead."

"And let me guess, when you got back he still didn't feel like the fire and so you left. Now you're on the couch alone wondering what's going on?"

Becca Sue gets up, still wrapped in the quilt and walks to the refrigerator. "Exactly. Just a minute, I'm getting some wine. Can't have you drinking alone."

"Do you think he's just getting cold feet since the engagement?"

She frowns as she pours. "Maybe. On our walk, though, it was just like always. We talked and joked, held hands and kissed some. It was pretty windy and cold, so we didn't linger anywhere long. But I did... well..."

"You *did* think you'd go upstairs when you got back to the house?"

Becca Sue takes a sip of wine, then heads back to the couch. She sits down with a heavy sigh. "Yes, I did, and now I feel like something is definitely wrong. But then my two big experiences with men are Caleb and Magnus, and they were both such hound dogs. Maybe I don't understand how real men, *good* men, work. Maybe I'm the problem."

"You? I don't think so. Carlos and I weren't having sex before we got married, but we still couldn't keep our hands off each other."

"But what if I'm like my folks? What if I'm, I don't know, over-sexed?"

Ashleigh bursts out laughing. "No, you are not over-sexed. You are normal. Talk to him about it. I bet he's got something crazy going on with work, or the wedding is freaking him out. It is kind of sudden. Postpone it, there's no hurry."

"Try saying that around here. Oh! Pepper and I picked out my dress. I'll send you a picture. Is that Carlos I hear in the background?"

Carlos leans toward the phone. "Hi Becca Sue."

"Hi, Carlos. Ashleigh, I'll let you go. I know you want to tell him about the meeting. Oh, but one minute. The diner. Pepper wants me to be the manager there."

"For good? Like a real job?"

"Yep. I guess it would give me something to do here."

"That's true, but do you want to do that?" Ashleigh giggles when Carlos smooches her shoulder as he settles beside her on the bed.

"Maybe. You go give your husband some attention, and we'll talk soon. I promise I'll be a better friend."

"Shush. You have a lot going on, but I do miss you."

"Miss you, too. Good night. Be good to that hardworking man!"

"Oh, I intend to! Bye."

Becca Sue hangs up and sips her wine, replaying the evening with Jameson. "He did look tired. And worried. I'm going to be his wife, I need to get him to talk." She sets the empty glass on the coffee table, silences her phone, and snuggles back down into her blankets. "Tomorrow is Friday, and we need a night out. Just the two of us."

45

I dreamed about Backwater last night.

Summer. The pool. My cabin. Backwater Market. My office. Everything was so clear, but when I try to think about it now, it seems fuzzy. How can a dream be clearer than real memory?

Matter of fact, Backwater all feels like it was some dream I had. My own office? How can that even be a thing? The Shoppes of Georgia are real. Backwater Market is something I made up. Right?

This trailer in the early morning light is real. My cabin in the woods? Surely just fantasy. My face is buried against the back of the couch as I listen to Momma fix coffee and talk softly with Daddy. He's starting a job for his father today. Momma is not happy about it. But with his heart problems he can't go back to working construction like he was.

Laying here listening to them it's like I never grew up. Like I'm still a kid, which is sometimes how I feel here. Even working at the diner. Momma's worked there so long it's a part of me.

And the Masons. Was there really a time when I didn't know them? Even on the outside, I was part of that circle, that family, but treated like a kid. Or, honestly, like an old crazy person.

True to its name, life in Piney is almost like laying down on a thick bed of pine needles. Smells heavenly, gives a cushion, but don't move much if you don't want to get poked. As long as I don't move much, I think I can be okay here.

All that crying at the hunting lodge seems to have done something to my heart. Didn't realize it, but it was like I was carrying around a big, old sore. I tried to keep from touching it so it wouldn't hurt, but it still wasn't healing. Matter of fact, it felt like it was getting worse, redder, hotter, more tender. But I didn't want to look at it. Then yesterday, I did.

I thought it might kill me right out. But no. Not at all.

Washed, paid attention to, and treated. Now wrapped up, my heart feels like it's getting whole. Mending. Getting stronger.

My leg is asleep, so I move a little and pull my arms out from under my pillow. My ring picks up some of the growing light. My engagement ring. Jameson. We had heat between us last summer. I think we did. No, I know we did. Because of Magnus, I tried to keep my feelings for Jameson under wraps. Yeah, we just need this rough patch to figure this out. That's what couples do, right?

"I see you're awake. Feels good to not have to go in for the early shift, don't it?" Momma says from her seat at the kitchen table.

Stretching, I push up to lean against the back of the couch facing them. "Good morning. Yeah, it feels good to sleep in. Did you hear anything from Tina? She have the baby?"

"No, but she's home on bedrest until it comes. So what time *does* the boss lady have to show up for work today?"

Daddy fusses. "Brenda. Give the girl a break. She got a promotion, why do you want to rag on Rebecca about it?"

Mama rolls her eyes at Daddy. "You back to calling her Rebecca? Guess I'll go back to calling her Susan."

"Lord love a duck!" I yell as I get up, shedding quilts as I pass them. "Stop it. You two have fought over my name since the day I was born. Call me whatever you want, I'm taking a shower."

The bathroom is clean, unlike when I left here last year, but it can't hold a candle to the bathroom in my old house, or the one I'd planned for the cabin. Backwater seems to be stuck in my head this morning.

"Oh, bet it's because I need to call Miss. Bell!" I suddenly say out loud.

Yes, that's it. Momma and Daddy should both be gone when I get out of the shower. I can have some coffee and call her. Just thinking of talking to Miss Bell makes me happier.

Miss Bell speaks in her sweet, concerned way when I answer my phone. "Is it okay to call you now, Becca Sue? When I got back from the bank, I saw I'd missed a call from you. Are you okay?"

"Yes, now is perfect. Just a minute." Looking at the young waitress and Momma, I point to my phone and close the diner's office door. "And I'm okay, just wanted to hear your voice and see how you are."

"Well, I'm not sure how I am." Her voice has a strange tremble to it. "Becca Sue, I seem to have invited Mimi and Drummond to move here permanently."

"I don't think so. But even if you did and you wish you hadn't, just un-invite them."

"I can't! They've sold their house, and their furniture is on its way here. They are confused as to how I could've forgotten I wanted them to move here, but then I've forgotten so many things lately..."

"You? You have a mind like a steel trap. How are you feeling? You haven't been sick, have you?" I move to sit down behind Bruce's—no, *my* desk.

"Well, yes. I have been under the weather. And Mimi and Drummond have helped so much. However, Mimi does have a mean streak, I'm discovering. She was right rude to Pearl and Ruth last night. I was glad when she decided not to come to the bank with me and Drummond this morning."

"Why did you need to go to the bank?"

"Oh, just a few more papers to sign. Don't yell at me, Becca Sue. Ruth is quite put out with me already because I'm letting Drummond take care of my finances. He has much more experience than me, and I, well, I owe it to him. All this would be his if I hadn't married his father."

"Miss Bell, are you sure that's wise? I'm not yelling, but... it's not like you forced Mr. Bell to marry you."

I'm horrified to hear her break down crying. Through her sobs, she tells me she *did* steal Mr. Bell and then wouldn't let his son live with them. It reminds me of how my heart felt yesterday. She sounds raw and wounded.

I try to soothe her over the phone, but just as I'm getting ready to call Ashleigh on Momma's phone so she'll go see Miss Bell, she clears her throat and says forcefully, "I know I'm acting out of guilt. I know that for a fact, because I am guilty. I don't deserve anything I have." She clears her throat again and with a bit more sweetness in her voice says, "You have things to do getting ready for your wedding, and I need to go help Mimi get ready for their furniture. I did want to let you know that I'll be sure and put your things in a box for you."

"Thanks, but are you *sure* about all this..." My words trail off.

She hesitates and then clears her throat again before speaking. "You're moving on with your life, right? Fixing past mistakes and making atonements? I need to do the same. I will see you at the wedding, if not sooner. I love you, Becca Sue." She hangs up, but not before I hear her start to cry again.

Does she really think that's what I'm doing? Fixing past mistakes and making atonements?

For crying out loud. I *knew* that Drummond and Mimi were no good! *I ought to get in my car and go down there right this minute!*

My shoulders slump. And do what? They are her family. She's not senile so I can't force her to get rid of them. Besides, she said herself they've been good to her while she's been sick. Meanwhile, have I even called her? No. What did I think would happen when she couldn't live there by herself anymore? Was I going to move in with her? My responsibilities are to my parents, and they needed me. And now I'm going to have a husband and—

"There you are!" Pepper says as she bursts into the small office and interrupts my thoughts. "I see the office fits you perfectly. You can decorate however you like. I already have some things put to the side for you over in the Shoppes." She takes a look around. "Bruce never would let me fix this up, but you know what great style I have. Just another fun project for you and me!" She stands at the door, one arm full of books and paper. "Come on, let's have some coffee. We've got to make some decisions."

I follow her to a table at the rear. Most of the other tables are full as the weekend is picking up. As she passes Momma, she says, "Brenda, get us two cups of coffee and a piece of that cinnamon bread to share."

Momma rolls her eyes at me, but I ignore her and slide into the chair across from Pepper. Pepper pays no attention to how hard Momma sits our coffee cups down or how the plate actually bounces a bit when it hits the table. I try to smile at Momma, but she won't look at me and then she's gone.

Pepper opens the first notebook. "Okay, we have exactly forty-five minutes to make all the decisions for the wedding, then it's out of our hands. I'm having lunch with Mrs. Mason and the caterer today and handing it all over to them. You don't need to come." She looks up at me, her blue eyes wide. "Unless you want to. Do you want to?"

"Um, no. I'm good. I may run down to Backwater and see—"

"Today? But you can't! There's the shower on Sunday and, well, if you must know, we have a little surprise set up for you and Jameson tonight at El Dorado. It is Friday, you know." She bites her lip and shakes her head. "You can't miss it. Can't! Besides, I told Bruce you'd take care of things here from now on. He's still up in Atlanta. You'll just have to take your little fun trip later."

She checks the time on her phone. "We now have only forty minutes. Okay, tablecloths. Here are your choices."

"That was the longest forty minutes of my life," I tell Ashleigh as I drive down the highway. "I honestly don't care. I just want to get married."

"I remember that feeling, but listen, you've got to hear this. Talked to Bradley this morning and he's fit to be tied. Drummond's dragging his feet getting his financial stuff in and so they might not get their license. I mean, I know you like the guy, but—"

"Like what guy? Bradley?" I smack the steering wheel. "I knew you'd find out. It was just one night. Just a thing, but I don't *like* him, I don't even know him."

"No. Drummond."

Silence fills the line as we both try to reconstruct what's just been said.

At the same time, we shout:

"You think I slept with Drummond Bell?"

"You didn't sleep with Drummond Bell?"

Another silence falls, and then we both laugh.

"Whew," Ashleigh says. "I'm so relieved. But Carlos saw him head off after you that night. And then you left town so fast."

"Yuck, no way! He's disgusting. I'm not proud of sleeping with Bradley King, but it's way better than with him."

"So... Bradley? Are you two a thing?"

"No! It just happened. It just... I don't want to talk about it."

"Well, you *are* talking about it at some point, but not now 'cause I have to go. This story is past due. Did you get a chance to talk to Jameson yet? Straighten things out?"

"No, and I'm not sure I ever will. This place is wedding crazy, and I can't get a minute alone with him. Just called him and he can't do lunch again today. Tonight is some wedding thing at El Dorado's. Maybe tomorrow. But go, get your article written."

"Sure thing. You can't imagine how relieved I am to find out you aren't fooling around with that creepy guy. Bye."

I agree and shudder as I hang up the phone, then toss it into the passenger seat where it lands beside the peanut butter and jelly sandwiches I made at the diner. One for me and one for Jameson. He'd texted earlier he was going to be in the office all day, so I thought I'd surprise him with a picnic. There's a nice bench outside his downtown office, after all. But when I got there, no one was in the office. Even his secretary was gone, leaving a cute little "out to lunch" sign on the front door. When I called, he said he'd been called out, but he couldn't talk, he'd call later.

When I hit a bump, I realize I'm headed down the dirt road to the hunting lodge again. As good a place for a picnic-for-one as any, I guess.

Creeping down the potholes in the clay road, I stop when I see cars through the trees. Well, really I just see shiny metal as the trees and bushes are thick on that side of the road. Then there's movement on the porch, which I can kind of see through the bushes on the other side, that catches my attention.

The easy chair is occupied. There's a woman sitting in it backwards... on top of someone else. Oh my! They're having sex. I put the car in reverse and creep back around the curve. When I'm well out of sight, I push the brake and stop.

Chuckling to myself, I take a deep breath and let it go. Kids using the lodge like Caleb and I did for so long. Guess that's to be expected. She looked young. High school, maybe. Really short black hair and a thin body. I saw a little of her face and, yeah, she was real young. As I look over my shoulder to continue backing down the road, I think about the guy. I couldn't see him at all. Well, that would've been interesting if I'd gone driving on up. Thank goodness I was going slow and saw the sunlight off the cars! How embarrassing would that've been?

46

"Thank you, Ashleigh!" Ruth exclaims, like the young woman at her front door is Jesus on Resurrection Day. "So sorry to have to call you, but Bradley and Eason are still off wherever they are. I'm supposed to have bunco here this afternoon, and just look at this place!"

Ashleigh squats down and braces for the toddler running at her. "Phillips! Hi there, buddy! No problem, Ruth. Got my article in, and I'm free the rest of the day." She stands and looks around the expansive room. "And your house doesn't look bad, just looks like you've got a couple toddlers on the loose. Want me to help pick up before I take the kids?"

"No, my housekeeper will be here soon. I told her I didn't care what it costs, I need her to come two times a week as long as the kids are here. Emerson, come get your jacket on!"

Ashleigh zips up the front of Phillips' jacket and asks, "How long do you think the twins will be here?"

Ruth exhales loudly through her nose and rests her fists on her hips, one clutching a pink, fuzzy jacket. "Wouldn't that be nice to know? These," she motions with her eyes downward, "haven't heard from their, you know, all week. God only knows where she is. And can Bradley take the time to find out? Nooo, he's too busy with, and I quote, 'the biggest business venture of my life.' Eason is just as bad. They stay holed up in his office until they go scurrying out of here to 'deal with things.' Meanwhile, I get left with—" She stops herself just in time and smiles. "Well, you know. You've been an absolute lifesaver."

She helps pull Emerson's jacket on as she looks out the front window. "Now, there's Cheryl. She's blocked you in, but that's okay, right? You're just going to take them for a walk and then play with them when you get back?"

"Exactly. Let's go for a walk!" Ashleigh exclaims as the kids jump and holler. Ruth moves to open the door for her house-keeper. There's a momentary traffic jam as the kids dash out.

"Hi, Miss Cheryl," Ashleigh says. "I'm taking the kids out from underfoot."

"Good to see you, hon. Was just out at your momma's house yesterday. Thanks for getting me set up with these folks out here. I didn't even know there were houses this nice way out here. And now Miss Ruth and that daughter-in-law of hers want me two days a week!" The older lady bends toward the kids. "Bye, you sweeties. Have a good walk."

At the end of the driveway, Ashleigh takes the kids' hands. "Let's walk down and see Becca Sue's cabin, okay? That's where we throw sticks in the lake."

The dark green of the water is still until the two find sticks to throw in. Low cloud cover makes the sky a consistent gray and holds in the humidity so that Ashleigh's holding both little jackets before long. The two jabber at her feet until they both suddenly stop.

"Mommy?" Emerson says.

"No, it's just some people over there across the lake," Ashleigh answers and then tries to distract them. "Here's a huge stick! It'll make a humongous splash." Phillips reaches for the stick, but then turns quickly to look out at the lake like his sister is. When a woman laughs somewhere on the other side, both kids perk up and face that way.

Both say "Mommy," then turn to Ashleigh and say it again. "No, sweeties, it's just a lady laughing. It's not Mommy." But Phillips starts walking away from her and back towards the road. Of course, his sister follows him.

"Okay, guess we're done throwing sticks." Back out on

the road they are quickly distracted by a frog, and Ashleigh breathes a sigh of relief. Under her breath, she mutters, "What kind of a mother would do this to her children? Doesn't she miss them?" Out loud, she asks, "Want to go see Carlos and have some hot chocolate?"

Phillips shouts, "Yep!" and they start walking on the road, enjoying the warm afternoon.

"See that girl? That one at the table by the bar with the short hair?" Becca Sue whispers into her friend's ear as she points with a nod. "Who is she? Is she even old enough to be in here? Highly doubt she's old enough to drink."

Carol snoops, then looks back at Becca Sue. "Well! Aren't *you* being judgmental? Why do you care if she's old enough to drink? There are kids in here with parents, so of course she's okay being here." She tsks and shakes her head. "I never thought of you as being such a prude."

Becca Sue turns away, too, and picks a chip out of the basket to dip in the communal bowl of salsa. "I'm not judging. Just wondering who she is. I don't really care, but I did see her earlier today."

Carol leans forward. "You did? Where?"

"Oh, um, at... never mind. Probably wasn't her," Becca Sue says quickly, then asks, "How's work going? Did you have fun at lunch with Pepper? Sorry I couldn't make it. Something came up." Becca Sue dips another chip and chews with her mouth closed, like she wishes her mouth had been closed earlier.

Carol sits back in her chair and shrugs. "It's all good. Nothing much going on at work. Pepper is really excited about the wedding plans. I bet you are, too."

"Did I hear my name taken in vain?" Pepper speaks up from across the table. She's wearing a short jean dress with dark blue cowboy boots and her hair down. She looks like a country singer and has already performed a couple karaoke songs.

Becca Sue says, "Just wedding stuff."

Carol adds, "She was just wondering who some of the people here are—"

"No, I wasn't," Becca Sue says as she bats a chip-laden hand at Carol. "Pepper, you are *so* much better than that girl up there now."

Pepper shrugs like that was an obvious statement. "Well, of course, she's an amateur. When are you going to get up there and sing? Maybe you and Jameson should do a duet! Yes! Give me that book, let me find a duet for them."

Becca Sue laughs and gets up from the table. "That is so not happening. Anyone want to go to the bathroom?"

"Me," Jessie says from the other end of the table.

"Might as well go, too," Carol says, sitting her glass back down. She pushes Buck's arm off her leg as she jumps up in an uncharacteristic leap.

"There's no hurry.," Becca Sue says with a question in her voice.

"Yeah, hon," Jessie drawls. "You don't usually move that fast. You must really have to go."

Carol takes a breath and smiles as she steps between Jessie and Becca Sue. "Yes, I guess I do."

Jessie waits for her to go by and then sticks her tongue out at her long-time friend, then winks at Becca Sue as she weaves her arm around the taller girl's arm. "Haven't seen you all week. How are things? Wedding plans coming together?"

As another singer starts, Becca Sue bends down to talk into Jessie's ear. "Okay, I guess. Planning is not really my thing. Pepper and Mrs. Mason have it under control." When she starts to bend back up, Jessie pulls on her arm.

"We need to talk. That is, if, well..."

"What? Just say it," Becca Sue says as she stops in her tracks.

Jessie twists her neck to look up at her friend. "If you get cold feet, call me. Okay?"

"Hey, y'all coming?" Carol walks back towards them, and Jessie pushes forward, in her direction.

"Yeah, it's crazy in here tonight. Becca Sue just wanted to know what the surprise is. Don't worry, I didn't tell her!" She pushes past and opens the bathroom door. "After you, ladies! Stalls for all!"

"Love the way tight jeans look, but it's such a hassle getting them buttoned up in these tiny stalls," Carol says from behind her door. "Lucky you, Jessie, wearing that long, full skirt. Plus, it lets you eat as many nacho chips as you want."

Becca Sue steps out of her stall with a chuckle. There at the mirror is the girl with the short, black hair from both the table beside the bar and the recliner at the hunting lodge.

"Hi," she says as she steps forward to wash her hands. The girl watches her in the mirror.

"I'm Riley," the girl says as she pulls a paper towel out of the dispenser.

"Oh, I'm Becca Sue." They both look at the stalls when Carol fumbles with her door latch and curses.

Riley laughs and rolls her eyes. "You work at the diner? Right?"

"Yeah, but just for a little, oh, wait, no I guess I'm there for good now. I think." Becca Sue shrugs.

They toss their paper towels into the trash can as Carol and Jessie come out of their stalls. Carol's chattering, and Jessie's smiling and watching. Riley runs her hand through her thick, dark hair, then shakes her head before walking out the door.

As the door closes behind her, Jessie makes eye contact with Becca Sue. "So, you met Riley."

"You know her?" Then Becca Sue looks at Carol. "Do *you* know her? She's the girl I asked you about."

"Oh, Riley?" Carol says as she smooths her usual calmness back over her words. She slowly answers, "Why, yes, I know Riley. I just didn't realize that's who you were asking about."

She dries her hands and then walks to the door, holding it open for Jessie and Becca Sue.

Becca Sue pauses before walking out the door. But hearing Carol and Jessie whispering behind her, she turns around. "What's going on?" The whispering stops and Becca Sue watches as Carol and Jessie's eyes rise to look over her shoulder. She follows their looks and sees Riley at their table. She turns back to her friends, still standing beside the bathroom door. "Who is she?"

Carol's mouth opens, but nothing comes out.

Jessie answers as she walks past Becca Sue. "Riley is Pepper's little sister."

47

"I didn't know you had a little sister" is my opening line the next morning, when I step into Pepper's office at the Shoppes.

She doesn't lift her head from her laptop screen as she says, "You didn't? How could you not know that?"

"Well, I, uh, she looks young. Guess we wouldn't have been in the same circles."

"Honey, you and I weren't in the same circles, if you recall. You were just trash, I was poor trash." Her eyes still never flicker my direction.

"But it seems like you would've mentioned her."

"Riley? Hardly. She's still poor and still trash." She looks up and pushes her chair back. "But did you have fun last night? Wasn't that great?"

The big surprise began with wedding karaoke. Before I even made it back to the table, Jameson and I were whisked up on stage to sing the duet, "Don't Go Breaking My Heart," then the guys from our table sang "I Want to Hold Your Hand" and the girls sang "Going to the Chapel." From there it was all love songs directed at me and Jameson, who were given a little table on the side of the stage. People kept buying us drinks and then, when we were feeling no pain and the restaurant was officially closed so kids and families had left, there was a lingerie shower. No sweet, white lounging robes – no, the kind of lingerie shower you'd expect late on a Friday night in a bar. It was tacky. It was raunchy.

"Yeah, that was pretty fun," I admit. "Embarrassing, but fun."

She laughs. "I bet Jameson is hurting this morning. You talk to him?"

"No, I was up early. I think we're doing lunch today. At least that's my plan. He's been so busy with work it's hard to nail him down."

Pepper has come out from behind the desk and stops near me. She reaches out and takes my hand. "Jameson just has a case of cold feet. Ignore him. Probably best if you don't spend much time together before next weekend or you'll have some big fight and call the whole thing off." She drops my hand and plants her fists on her hips. "Shoot, me and Bruce almost eloped because we kept arguing over the wedding. Me and Jameson's mother are trying to make things as easy as possible for you, okay?"

"You think that's it?"

"Yes. So quit worrying and enjoy your last week as a single lady. And just a little word to the wise, I hope you have clothes for warmer weather." She grins as she pushes me out the doorway. "Jameson is busy planning a spectacular honeymoon!"

"Oh, I hadn't even thought... where?"

She shakes her head. "Nope, I've said enough. Now, quit worrying and get to work. Bruce is waiting at the diner to go over things with you, Miss Manager."

I leave her office and walk into cold morning sunshine. The brightness makes me shield my eyes. Both parking lots are filling up and there's a log jam at the front door of the diner, so I walk around towards the back door.

A honeymoon? Why I hadn't thought of him planning that. Probably one reason he's been so awkward, trying to keep such a big secret. Wonder where we'll go. Then I freeze at the corner of the building, and I practically shout, "Wait! Pepper said somewhere warm. What if he thinks we're flying? I'm not flying. No way."

I pull my phone out of my pocket and stare at it. Carol? No, she won't tell me. Jessie said if I got cold feet to call her. I bet she knows if we're going to fly somewhere. "Jessie, its Becca Sue. The honeymoon. You asked about me getting cold feet, well, I got 'em. I've never flown. I don't want to fly."

"What? No, that's not what I was talking about. You've never flown? Really, it's not a big deal."

"But you said that about cold feet. What did you mean?"

A kid screams and Jessie shouts, "I'm on the phone!" Then says, "Sorry Becca Sue, I can't talk now, but I meant cold feet because of anything else. Mainly, don't let Carol railroad you into anything. Yes, she's my best friend, but she's bossy and likes to control things. She was bad enough on her own, but with Pepper here now? They think they are unstoppable." Then she mumbles, "And maybe they are." She draws in a deep breath. "Listen, Piney is a great little town. Most small towns are, but—oh, I don't know what I'm saying. Just pay attention to what all's going on. Piney is still Piney and always will be. Martin! Do you hear her screaming? I've got to go. Martin is still in bed with a hangover from last night. Must be nice, huh? Wish they'd let *me* stay in bed."

"Yeah, okay. Thanks. Have a good, well, bye," I mumble as Jessie hangs up with a shout at a kid or her husband or maybe just life.

I lean against the side of the building. Cars are now pulling into the back parking area around me. Piney is still Piney. Piney is still Piney. Piney is still Piney. The words run though my thoughts and seem to ground me. Like a stake that holds a tent down. I'm not just marrying Jameson. I'm marrying Jameson Mason, the Mason family, and Piney. I'm marrying Piney.

What in the world is wrong with me?

The morning floated by with the refrain Piney is still Piney echoing in my head. Through the session with the restaurant books with Bruce. Through coffee with Momma in the back booth once the breakfast crowd cleared. Through a walk in the busy Shoppes and another chat with Pepper. It's colder than ever by the time I get to my car and am finally alone. I don't wait for the car to get heated up before I pull out of the parking lot and onto the little road next to the diner. At the stop sign, I reach for my phone in my purse and I turn it off. Not just down, but off. I toss it back into my purse, turn the radio up, and make a right turn.

48

"I didn't know you were coming!" Ashleigh yells when she opens her front door to Becca Sue standing there. "What are you doing?"

"I needed to see you. And Miss Bell. And Backwater. Just for the night, I have to be at church for the big wedding shower tomorrow."

"We'll take what we can get. And I'm headed over to Backwater right now to watch the kids. You wanna come?" Ashleigh steps out onto the little concrete stoop. "I mean, like right now. I'm already kind of late."

"Um, of course. Should I just ride with you? I'll move my car."

"No worries, I'll drive around it. One of the blessings of not having a decent lawn." She grabs her friend's arm. "Where's your coat? It's freezing out here."

Becca Sue laughs. "Freezing is where I came from. This is downright balmy." She takes a deep breath. "It smells so Florida."

"Are those tears? Sweetie, what's wrong?"

Becca Sue pulls away and sniffs as she walks to the passenger door of Ashleigh's car. "No, I'm just tired." She whirls to look at her friend. "And so glad to see you. Now, let's go."

When they turn off the road into Backwater, Becca Sue's mindless chattering about the wedding details fades off. To her right is the house she moved into in the middle of the night, the night of Caleb's funeral. Then the huge empty lot, home of the Backwater Market. Miss Bell's house with Drummond and Mimi's big SUV and an even bigger storage pod warring for dominance over the drive.

"What's that for?" Becca Sue asks. "Miss Bell mentioned something about furniture, but I didn't know whether she was serious." She whips her head around to her friend. "Are they really moving in?"

Ashleigh looks grim. "Apparently so. Does Miss Bell know you're coming?"

She turns back to the window and shakes her head. "No. Guess I didn't think things out much."

Pulling into the Kings' driveway, Ashleigh apologizes. "You're staying the night, right? Sorry, but we don't have an extra bed, and our couch is really only a love seat. You're welcome to it, though."

"I'll figure something out." Becca Sue opens the car door and steps out. "Oh, do you think Bradley is here?"

"Doubt it, seems he's always meeting with lawyers and such, but I don't know."

"Doesn't really matter, I have to pee. Plus, I want to see Ruth and Eason."

The front door opens before they reach it, and Phillips comes running out. Ruth is right behind him. "Get back in here! It's too cold for you to be out here barefoot. Oh, Becca Sue!" Ruth opens her arms and then stops as she remembers the last time she saw the young woman –wrapped in a quilt on an early Sunday morning. "Oh. You're here."

Ashleigh grabs Phillips and walks past Ruth. "Doesn't Becca Sue look great? She had a long drive, though. Can she use your restroom? Hey there Emerson. Ready to play with Miss Ashleigh?"

"Of course," Ruth says quietly. "Come in, Becca Sue." She turns without a hug and leads Becca Sue inside. "Eason, look. Becca Sue is back."

The tall young woman follows them into the house, but stops just inside the door, her arms hugged around her waist.

Her hair is smoothed into a loose braid, and she unfolds her arms to tug on it as she explains. "Just for the night. I have to leave early in the morning."

"Like last time?" Bradley steps out of his father's office. "They saw, they know. They'll get over it. Good to see you again." He steps to her, leans, and gives her a quick hug. "You helping Ashleigh out with these two rug rats?" He moves into the living room area. "Hi, Ashleigh. You sure have been a life-saver."

Becca Sue stays by the door, watching Bradley and Ashleigh put coats and shoes on the children. Finally she blurts out, "I'm going to the bathroom," and she dashes down the short hall beside the office.

"Did I hear you say Becca Sue is here?" Eason says as he comes out of the office. "I was on the phone."

Ruth doesn't look up, but her lips get tighter. Bradley rolls his eyes. "Yes, she's in the restroom. So they'll meet with me this evening?"

His father sighs. "They say it's highly irregular, but they understand the urgency, so yes. But not at the bank. Here's his address, he wants you to come to his home. So," Eason looks down the hall at the still closed bathroom door. "She here to see you?"

"No, Dad. She's here with Ashleigh. I've told you, it was just a thing. I was as good as divorced," he whispers the last word. "And from what I hear she's not married, yet. Forget it. Now, I've got to go. Everyone good here?"

"Yes, "Ashleigh says. "So we're going to go on a little walk and then come back here, right?"

"If that's okay with you," Eason says. "Want to take my bride out for a nice dinner. She deserves a little wining and dining."

"And I may beat my parents back home. Depends how my meeting goes. Thanks, Ashleigh. Tell Becca Sue I said thanks, too." He leaves out the front door.

That door barely closes before the bathroom door opens. Becca Sue comes out, keeping her head down, says a quiet hello to Eason, and follows Ashleigh's directions on getting out the door with both kids while Ruth and Eason leave by the door into the garage.

Ruth slams her car door and settles herself into the passenger seat. Eason also gets in and starts the car. Ruth's lips are pressed hard together, then they snap open. "At least she has the decency to be embarrassed. Your son acts like some cross between Frank Sinatra and that basketball player that slept with all those women, that tall one?"

"Dear, they are all rather tall. But I think you mean Wilt Chamberlain."

"That's not him. But whatever. He's acting like a regular cad."

"Wilt Chamberlain?"

"Shut up. You know who I mean." She turns to look out the window. "I'm having two glasses of wine at dinner, and you better not say one thing."

"Well, that was awkward," Ashleigh says.

"So embarrassed. They all knew about me and Magnus last summer, and now with," she raises her eyebrows at the kids, "you know who."

"Well, to be honest, some of them might think it was Drummond, like me and Carlos thought."

"And that's better how?"

"Oh, I didn't say it was better, just different. Don't worry. In a week, hey, one week from today, you'll be married to Jameson and the very soul of propriety. It'll all be water under the bridge."

The kids automatically turn at the cabin lot's entrance. Ashleigh explains, "We always walk down there to throw sticks in the water, but we don't have to if you don't want to see the cabin."

"It's okay. I'd kind of like to see it. Dreamed about it the other night." Even in the quiet subdivision, walking into the property with the trees is like walking into a church. Many are still covered in leaves, and the undergrowth thick with huge palmettos and brambles. The soft air is hushed, and no breeze penetrates the seclusion. The sun is slanting down at the other end of the lake and lays in a shimmer of gold on the surface. "See, I wanted the living room windows and decks to face this way for the sunsets."

As the kids begin tossing sticks into the lake, the women are quiet.

Finally Becca Sue breaks the silence. "I went to the hunting lodge. Caleb's hunting lodge."

Ashleigh doesn't look at her friend or say anything. She waits.

"Caleb and I were there together the night he died. Everyone thought we were broken up, but we weren't. And we weren't going to break up, no one had to know. He was the first person to love me and he was all I wanted. He had a bigger life, and that was okay. They put expectations on him that I didn't. He could be himself with me. That hunting lodge was the only place on earth where I was good enough."

"No, that's not true." Ashleigh turns around, angry. "You are good enough. He was—"

"I know. I know he wasn't who I wanted him to be. I know now." She pauses, drinking in her almost-view. "Did you look at the picture of the wedding dress?"

Ashleigh hands a stick to Emerson. "What? Your dress? Yeah, I looked at it. Why?"

"Did it look familiar to you?"

Ashleigh sighs. "Honestly, I didn't look at it that close. Been a little busy, you know."

Becca Sue laughs. "Don't be mad. I'm just thinking out loud."

"I'm not mad at you. I'm mad at Caleb and, well, maybe I am kind of mad at you. Why do you let people do that to you?"

"Do what?"

"Use you! Oh, never mind. Emerson, Phillips, let's go finish our walk." As she takes their hands, Emerson turns back to the lake. "Mommy."

"Honey, come on. It's not Mommy." Ashleigh whispers to her friend, "Women's voices over the lake makes them think it their mother. They really miss her."

As they all walk back down the road, Becca Sue asks, "Where is she?"

Ashleigh shrugs. "I think back up north. I've actually wondered if she's punishing him for sleeping with you."

"How would she know?"

"Well, everyone else knows something happened."

"Great. So now I'm responsible for this mess, too. It'll be best for everyone if I just go back to Piney, get married, and never leave Mason Farms again."

"And drink. Don't forget the drinking that makes that kind of life possible." She whirls around to face her friend. Still whispering, she spits, "Remember how much you were drinking last summer? Just to make life palatable? You're going to need a lot more than that to stay under the same roof as Jameson and his mother. Oh, and working with *your* mother? Add in those high school mean girls? Oh, I'm not sure there's enough alcohol in all of Georgia!"

She turns back around and scurries after the kids who are nearing the road, leaving Becca Sue standing next to the cabin.

"This was a mistake. A big mistake," she mutters to herself. "Ashleigh, wait." She catches up and takes Emerson's other hand. "We're going to keep walking around the lake?"

"Car-os," Emerson says. "Car-os."

"Carlos," Ashleigh interprets. "We walk to Sybil's to see Carlos and get some hot chocolate. Hey, I'm sorry."

"Naw, I've thought the same thing. The drinking."

Ashleigh looks at her. "What?"

"Yeah, but it might not be that bad. I'd get to manage the diner, and Pepper is a lot of fun. It's kind of neat to be the center of attention in my hometown. Maybe it'll be different.

I was always on the edges, if even that. One thing I've realized is that Caleb liked me out of the way. I made that easy for him. I thought I was happy."

The large blonde laughs. "And who am I to talk? Moved right back to my hometown, got married, and settled down into a little house with no heat. Maybe I'm the one that needs to drink more."

Emerson pulls away from Becca Sue's hand and runs into the lawn beside them. Phillips follows her, and they dash between the houses. The women follow them and catch up quickly as the kids are standing looking into a screen porch—Magnus' screened porch, where two people are sitting.

As Becca Sue and Ashleigh reach the kids and begin to corral them back to the street, both children say "Mommy" and run toward the porch.

"Emerson! Phillips!" A tall, beautiful woman comes off the porch. "Come see Mommy!"

Ashleigh and Becca Sue stand with their mouths open. Then Ashleigh hustles to follow the children. Becca Sue takes her eyes off the reunion to look at the other person on the porch.

Magnus grins at her and tips his glass her direction. "Hi Becca Sue. You're home."

"Here, take my car," Carlos says, digging for his keys in the pocket underneath his chef's jacket. "It's getting dark and you don't need to be walking out there. Where is Becca Sue staying?"

Ashleigh closes her eyes and shakes her head. "Hell if I know. Maybe our love seat." She looks into the dining room where Emerson and Phillips are seated on one chair in the middle of their mother and Magnus. "This is weird, right? It's not just me."

"No. It's weird, and now she wants you to take the kids with you? She's not seen them in how long, and she's sending them off with the babysitter?"

"Well, thank God. How could I just leave them with her when Ruth, Eason, and their father have no idea where she is? And I think she's been there more than just today. But we'll talk later. You're busy. Looks like a good crowd tonight — and these are not all Backwater people." She kisses him even as he looks back at the kitchen and starts directing things there.

Becca Sue is standing in a corner near the front door, watching the table. She looks up as Ashleigh comes by, gives her a shot of raised eyebrows, and says, "Okay, let's get the twins."

Olivia has on a deep purple jumpsuit with a wide, burnt orange sash. It's flowy and satiny, almost like pajamas. Her dark red hair is in a high ponytail that sways around her much like the orange sash—and Magnus. He gets up, sits down, pulls out chairs, lifts a child all at the whim of one of her dark eyebrows or plump lips.

Ashleigh and Becca Sue wait for a moment before approaching the table. Ashleigh says, "She's mesmerizing, isn't she? So incredibly beautiful, but so... so..."

"Cold?" Becca Sue finishes. "Guess that's what Magnus wanted all along." She shudders, and Ashleigh moves to the table.

"Okay, Emerson and Phillips. Time to go."

Phillips slumps against his sister and says "No!"

Emerson slides off the chair and walks to Ashleigh, taking her hand. Phillips also slides off the chair, but onto the floor. Magnus leans over to pick him up when Olivia clears her throat. The older man straightens up and rubs his hands on his thighs. She turns herself toward the little boy and moves her purple, close to him. She clears her throat again and says quietly, "Phillips. Get up."

The toddler rolls over onto his back, then looks up at his mother, who is leaning over her shoes, still in her chair, hands folded in her lap. He sits up, then stands. Looking down at his shoes next to hers, he smiles and looks up, but no smile greets him. His mother turns, places her feet under the table, and lifts her wine glass to her mouth. Ashleigh reaches for the boy and steers him toward her and the door. The children and the two women walk out the front door.

"It is getting dark. I'm so glad Carlos gave us his keys. Who wants to ride in Carlos' car?" Ashleigh asks the children in an excited voice. She presses the unlock button, and across the street in the small parking lot, lights come up on a car. "There it is. Now, I know we don't have your car seats, but you're just going to sit still in the back seat with Becca Sue, okay? I won't drive fast and we'll be there in just a minute."

With everyone strapped in, Becca Sue in the middle and a child on each side of her, Ashleigh pulls out onto the quiet street. Driving under the posted speed of fifteen miles per hour, she finds Becca Sue's eyes in the rearview mirror. "Did you see it?"

"Yep."

"You think it's real?"

"No. But I can't for the life of me think of why Magnus would be wearing a fake wedding ring."

49

"Think I'll just stay in the car," I say as we pull into the Kings' driveway. It's obvious from the lights people are home.

"Oh, no you won't. Chicken."

"But I haven't even seen Miss Bell yet."

"Believe me, this isn't going to take long. Think I want to go in there and explain this any more than you do?" Then in a higher, more positive tone, Ashleigh says, "Here we are! Everybody out!"

Before they even get to the door the twins are jabbering unintelligibly, but one word can definitely be understood—mommy. I try to hang back, but Ashleigh grabs a fistful of my coat and pulls me forward.

Ruth opens the front door, and as I come past her, she gives me a big hug.

"It is so good to see you, Becca Sue. You and Jameson are just the sweetest couple!"

"Oh, okay. Thanks."

Phillips barrels into his grandfather's study and is half yelling, half crying as he attacks his father's legs. Eason takes the papers in his son's hands so he can bend and pick up his son. "Hey buddy. You okay?" He looks up at Emerson who is standing at the office door. She starts talking a mile a minute, but no one can make out what she's saying. But her grandmother picks up that she's talking about her mommy.

Ruth bends down and scoops her up. "Oh precious, precious girl! Your mommy misses you, too!"

Eason raises his eyebrows and smiles. "Nana had some wine at dinner. Did you have a good walk?"

Ashleigh looks at me, and I shake my head at her. She waves a hand at Phillips and says, "Why don't you go see what Nana and Emerson are doing? Okay?"

He clings to his father, but Bradley, sensing something in Ashleigh's voice, hands him off to his father. "Buddy, go see Nana for a minute, and then I'll come out and we'll play Legos."

Eason takes his grandson's hand. "Come on, you show Grandpa where the Legos are so we'll be ready."

I'm closest to the door, and when I turn towards it, Ashleigh says, "Don't you dare leave."

"I'm not," I lie. "Just closing the door."

Bradley leans back against his dad's desk. "What is it? The kids look okay. Did something happen?"

Ashleigh shrugs off her coat. "Okay, here's the deal. Olivia is here in Backwater. We ran into her accidentally over at Magnus' where they were headed to dinner. We were headed to Sylvia's, too. You know we go see Carlos, and so we all went there."

Bradley stands up. "Wait, Olivia? Olivia as in 'Mommy'? The kids saw her? She saw the kids? Where is she now?"

Slowly stretching out her arms and lifting her palms, Ashleigh says, "Having dinner?"

Bradley is suddenly across the room, and I back out of his way when I see he's coming for the door. He slams it open and turns to see his parents and children all looking at him. He stops, takes a breath, and then turns back towards us standing in the open doorway and shakes his head. His shoulders slump as he walks to the couch and sits down. "Dad, can you turn off the TV? So, guys, you saw Mommy tonight?"

Ruth gasps and sits down in the chair next to him. Eason looks alarmed, then he looks up at me and Ashleigh. You can see he's torn on staying there or coming to talk to us. Ashleigh grabs her coat and says in a loud whisper to him. "We're just going to leave. Holler if we can help with anything."

He nods at us, then sits on the other end of the couch to listen to his grandchildren.

On the sidewalk, Ashleigh and I exhale together. "I see you didn't mention Magnus' wedding ring," I say.

"Absolutely not. Now, let's take Carlos' car back to him. Then want me to go with you to Miss Bell's?"

The last light is fading in the west as I look over at Miss Bell's house. "I just wish Drummond and Mimi weren't there." Then just like I summoned them, the creepy couple come out the front door of the house. I duck up the drive to be behind the SUV parked there. Bradley's car, I assume. Ashleigh joins me, and we peek out to see them get in their car and leave.

"Well, there ya go. I'll take Carlos' car back to the restaurant and walk back here. Give you some time alone with Miss Bell."

When Ashleigh pulls out and leaves, the night is so quiet. None of the summer or fall sounds I associate with Backwater. No frogs or birds. No buzzing of bugs. And it's strange for there to be no humidity. It's almost like a presence is missing. The only sound is my shoes on the road.

Could Magnus be married? To Olivia King? Really, I'm mad more than surprised. But why would I be mad? Okay, I'm going to actually think about what I'm feeling all the way to Miss Bell's front door. Then I can stop. This just letting stuff happen to me is getting old.

I'm mad because I... I... I thought I might see Magnus tonight. Oh, no. I didn't really, did I? Yes. When I saw her on his porch I felt that, that she was, well, I felt jealous. That's why I didn't plan on where I'd sleep tonight. Magnus was always a possibility in the back of my mind.

Feels like a knife in my chest to admit I thought more about Magnus' house, the big soft couches, his huge bed, the dim lights and candles, more than I thought about seeing my cabin. Why did I even think Magnus would be here?

Because he's supposed to be waiting for me when I don't marry Jameson.

Now the knife has moved to my stomach.

I step up onto Miss Bell's porch. Thank God, I'm finally here.

This thinking thing sucks.

Miss Bell tucked me back into my room here. There are boxes and furniture everywhere, but she declares I'll always have a place to stay with her. She and I both knew she was just saying what felt good, because she'd already said without my car here, no one could even tell I was here. She tried to laugh when she said it, but...

She's aged since I left. Her house doesn't even look like the same house. Not just because of the boxes and moved furniture, but because so many of her little knickknacks are gone. She said they remind Drummond of his father, so he asked her to pack them up. She apologized as soon as she said this. "Don't think I'm talking bad about Drummond. Poor boy has been through enough in his life. This house, this should all be his. He says I always will have a place with him and Mimi. They are trying to be good to me, but it's hard. I understand."

I roll over, flipping my pillow and punching it at the same time. They've ruined her. Looking at her used to be like looking at a lit jack-o-lantern. Full of light, so happy. Now she reminds me of the sunken ones in the middle of November.

We're going to get up extra early and have a cup of tea before I need to leave. She says Drummond and Mimi won't be up, and so, again, they won't even know I was here.

"So Ashleigh and Carlos are bringing you up to the wedding next Sunday," I say as I sip my tea at a little table she's set up in her room.

"Yes, and I can't wait to see your parents again. Your father is one of my favorites, you know." She looks better this morning, and I tell her so.

"It's knowing you are going to be happy. Everyone in Piney will take such good care of you, I'm sure."

"I saw Magnus last night."

"Oh, Becca Sue!" Her face falls. "He's not good for you. You shouldn't have come back here. You and he have such a pull on each other, and I know firsthand how destructive that kind of pull can be. Look what it made me do to Drummond." Then she frowns at me and even snorts a bit. "I know all about you having one more little fling with Magnus that night of the party here. Down in your half-finished cabin rolling around on the floor." She plops her cup down into the saucer. "You need to leave now. You can't resist him and he can't resist you, so before you mess things up with Jameson, you need to go."

"Miss Bell! I did not have another fling with Magnus. It wasn't him."

"It wasn't? Then who—no, I don't want to know. And you're probably just covering for him, anyway. That kind of obsession can be a blessing, but it can also be a curse. When you have that connection with someone, it's so hard to walk away, even if you should. Luckily, you found it again in Jameson. I think your attraction to Jameson began because you had such a spark with his brother. They are quite a bit alike."

"Caleb and Jameson? Alike? Not hardly."

"Oh yes, they don't appear alike at first, Jameson so reserved and Caleb so... so wild. But remember, Caleb is who Mr. Bell and I dealt with building this house. We got to know him quite well." She sips her tea and looks at me over the brim of her cup. Her eyes fill with tears. Probably because mine are full, too.

"I didn't mention that much before because you were still so sad. I see now that Jameson has healed that sadness in you.

Being back in your hometown has given you some peace. As much as I will miss you, you need to be at peace. And you need to be happy."

Reaching out, I take her hand into mine. "But I want you to be happy, too." I look around at her large master bedroom, now stuffed with boxes and mementos from the rest of the house. "This isn't right."

She lays her other hand on top of our joined hands. "Shhh, I'm finding being happy isn't as important as being at peace at this age. You're lucky to have learned that at such a young age. Peace must come first." She pulls her hands away. "Now, you need to get on the road and not worry one bit about me."

We stand up, and as I lift my empty cup and saucer, she says, "Oh, put that down. I have something else for you to carry." She reaches behind her and lifts up a full beach bag. "Just some things you liked in the house. In your new home up there, they'll remind you of your time in Florida. Your other things, summer clothes and such, are in boxes, and you can get them another time. That way I know you'll be back!"

I hug her and then we tiptoe through the house to the front door. She steps outside with me. "There's Ashleigh coming to take you to your car. Perfect timing. There are two bags of biscones on top in the bag. One is for you to take to your parents, and the other is for Ashleigh and Carlos."

We hug again, and then I run out to the car.

I have a wedding shower to get to.

50

"Well, where is she?" Pepper demands from beside the diner's front counter.

Brenda Cousins rolls her eyes and moves around her. "I don't know. I assumed she was with her fiancé when she didn't come home last night." She takes full plates of food from the kitchen pass-through and turns. "Have you checked with him? Surely he'd know where his *beloved* is?"

Pepper growls and stomps back to the office. "I *wish* she was with him. Might as well try him again." She slams the office door behind her and then dials her phone. Her growl turns into a purr. "Hey sugar, you ready for the shower today? Everyone is so excited to celebrate you two. How's Becca Sue this morning?"

She frowns and keeps her voice light. "Well, have you even tried to call her? Maybe she'd like to hear from you."

After listening to Jameson, her voice falls flat. "Okay, I'll let you go, then. Tell your mother I said hello and that I'll see her at church."

She hangs up, and the growl is back. "Becca Sue, you are on my last nerve. Where are you, woman?" Opening the office door, she stomps back through the diner. As she passes Brenda, she says, "I'm going to church. If that daughter of yours shows up, tell her she needs to get her tail to church, too!"

Brenda watches the petite blonde woman pick her way

through the gravel in her high heels and throw herself up into the front seat of her vintage truck.

"You folks ready for the check?" she says to the table across from her. As she selects it from the other checks in her pocket, she mumbles, "Run, Becca Sue. Run as fast and as far as you can."

"It's a Valentine's Day wedding, so of course we decorated with hearts," the elderly lady worrying her hands says to Pepper.

"Well, it's tacky as all get out. Looks like a fifth grade dance. Let me guess, pink punch, too?"

"With maraschino cherries frozen in the ice rings," the lady says with a growing smile. "And the games all revolve around hearts and love, too. It's going to be so sweet!" She claps her hands in delight.

Pepper turns away. "Sweet as a rotten peach laying in the sun. Carol!"

Carol waves as she walks across the hall. "Hey, doesn't it look..." Her face falls as she studies Pepper. "What's wrong?"

"This? Can you not see how tacky this is? I thought you had taste."

"It's a church basement," she whispers. "And the ladies, well, *this* is what they do."

Pepper dismisses her. "I knew I should've done it myself."

Carol catches up with her and bends her head down to the shorter woman. "Pepper, this is a *church* shower. There's a committee of ladies that are in charge of this, and they worked real hard. It's a church basement shower, what did you expect?"

"Is it called the Tacky Committee? Or maybe Hillbillies on Parade? First things we're taking down are these streamers. You get that end."

273

Carol grasps Pepper's upper arm, causing her to turn and look surprised at the usually calm woman. Bending into Pepper's face, Carol's dark hair falls on each side so her anger is shielded from anyone watching. "You will not touch one inch of that streamer. My mother is on the Tacky Hillbilly Committee, as you call it, and this is what. They. Do. And they do it with more grace and heart than you'll ever possess." Carol stands up straight and drops Pepper's arm. Her chin lifts while her lips compress, her eyes never leaving Pepper's.

Pepper breaks their eye contact first, pulls herself as tall as possible, puts *her* nose in the air, and marches out of the fellowship hall. Jessie, who'd watched the scene from behind the photo booth setup, sashays up to her friend. "Bless her heart. Poor thing should know—you don't mess with church ladies."

"Daddy, you're coming to the shower, aren't you?" Becca Sue asks as she comes out of the trailer's bathroom.

"I'll be there with bells on and hoping the building doesn't cave in. Look at you! That's a pretty dress."

Becca Sue turns around and smooths her hands down the dark blue dress. "Thanks. Ashleigh found it on sale and bought it for me. Pepper and I bought a different dress for me to wear, but that one feels too fancy for church."

"Don't you mean too slutty?"

"Daddy!"

"Well, girl, I see how that Pepper dresses. Everything tight and short, low-cut. Not saying I don't enjoy it, but that's not you. You're more what I'd call classy."

"Well, then I know you'll be there to see what Pepper is wearing, right?" She laughs and leans over to give him a one-armed hug. "And Momma is getting off work to come." Becca Sue picks up her purse and slides into a long, lightweight coat that matches her dress.

Her daddy looks up at her as he takes another drink of coffee. "How were things in Backwater?"

She stops before opening the door. "Interesting. I think Magnus got married to this woman who already has two kids, twins. Me and Ashleigh watched the twins for their daddy and they were so cute. Ashleigh has the baby bug real bad."

"How about you?"

She sits on the arm of the couch. "You know, I did a lot of thinking on the drive this morning, and I'm not sure I want kids."

"Really?" Her father's eyes widen, then narrow as he nods. "Does Jameson know that? I mean, not having kids might be a deal breaker. Would be for a lot of men. Especially when they're from a family like the Masons."

"Oh, *I know* Mrs. Mason is looking for us to have kids. That's the main reason she's so okay with us getting married."

Rick leans forward in his chair. "Hon? Are you sure about that? Not any other reason she's so gung-ho about you marrying her one and only son?"

"Well, and she's getting old. Wants to see him happy." Becca Sue slides down off the arm of the couch and onto the couch cushion.

"Probably some of that, but there are rumors about... things."

She sits still for a moment, then suddenly stands up. "He's a Mason, Daddy. There are always rumors about the Masons. Remember how everyone always talked about Caleb?" She pulls open the trailer door. "I've got to go. Don't want to be late to church." Before she can close the door, her father calls her name and she leans back inside. Big smile in place and eyes open wide in question.

"I do remember the things folks said about Caleb. Also remember that they turned out to be mostly true." He winks at her and looks back down at his newspaper. "See you later."

She pulls the door shut and screws up her mouth. Out of the side she says, "Can't start listening to rumors *now*, can I?"

"Mrs. Mason!"

Pepper's voice is all honeysuckle and sunshine as she greets Piney's matriarch at the front doors of the church. "You looks absolutely stunning this morning. Everything is ready for the shower. The ladies, bless their hearts, have done their best."

Mrs. Mason pulls in a long breath through her nose and then releases it slowly as she moves to the side of the brightly-lit welcoming area. "Pepper, please," she says as she motions the young woman to follow her. She faces the corner and says, "I'm concerned about my son. He's not acting, well, right. This wedding *is* going to happen. Isn't it?"

"Absolutely. He just has a little case of cold feet. That's all."

"Well, you know he broke his engagement to Cecelia Mattle, the governor's daughter, last summer, so we cannot have another broken engagement. *People will talk.*"

Pepper blinks and then looks into Mrs. Mason's eyes with wide-eyed concern. "Yes, I know. There have been some rumors going around..."

The older woman puts her hand to her forehead. "I knew it." She drops her hand and reaches it out to steady herself on the wall. "I'll be so relieved when we get past next weekend." She laughs a bit and sighs. "Somewhere Caleb is laughing himself silly that I'm so anxious to get Becca Sue back into the family."

"Leave it to me, Mrs. Mason. You just count on me." Pepper pats the woman's back as the older woman lifts her chin, stills her shaky hands, and walks back into the stream of people entering the sanctuary.

Pepper looks to the ceiling and breaths a quick prayer, "Lord, help me get through the next week." She straightens her tight blazer, turns to the wall so she can resituate her boobs, then whirls around to face the front doors with a big smile. A smile that disappears into anger.

"What are you doing here?" she blurts as she stares at the shadow darkening the doorway.

51

"Hi there," I say, answering my phone.

"Hey. Guess you know everyone and their brother is looking for you this morning?"

"And so they all called my fiancé thinking he might know where I spent last night?"

Jameson laughs. "That's about it." He pauses, then asks, "So, where are you?"

"On my way to church. Just turned onto the blacktop."

"Oh," is all he says, but I hear more.

"You were kind of hoping I was in Florida, weren't you?" He doesn't answer, because it wasn't really a question. So I ask, "Where are you?"

"Sitting in my car in the church parking lot. Way at the back by the creek."

The conversation stalls there. We don't hang up, but we don't talk. Finally, I say, "Wait. I'll be there in a minute."

The road to the church winds through small hills, so no empty fields, just woods and a few houses. At the church sign, I turn in and keep to the perimeter of the large parking lot. I circle around until I'm behind the church. After I pass the playground, I pull in next to Jameson's car.

"Good morning," I say as I get into the passenger seat of his big SUV. He gives me a sideways smile, and I give him one of my own. "Jameson, I've missed you. Missed talking to you. We seemed closer when I lived in Florida."

"I know. I feel the same way." He puts his hands up on the steering wheel and flexes them. "This has gotten so mixed up. I'm not sure how we got here."

I reach for his closest hand and fold it into both my hands. "Talk to me. What's going on?"

After a minute, he turns to face me. "You look beautiful in that color. With your hair down. You look so grown up." He smiles, saying, "You really, really are good for me..."

"But...?" I question.

"But I don't want to be like Caleb."

I drop his hand. "And being with me makes you like Caleb? Is it that only someone like Caleb could marry trash like me? I'm good enough to be your friend, but not your wife?" Tears threaten, so I jerk open my door. He reaches to hold me in the car.

"No, Becca Sue. Not like that. I don't want to lie. You know he lied to you all the time, right? The hunting lodge? You romanticize it like it was just for you and him. Your little hideaway. But it wasn't! He took girls there all the time." He releases me and turns to look out the windshield. "It's just not right. I don't want to do that."

"*You* take girls to the hunting lodge?" I snort a cruel laugh as I slide off the high seat. "As if." I stand in the open doorway and catch my breath when I see that he's crying, too. "Oh. What are we doing?" Leaning against the open door, I hang my head and try to just breathe in and out. I hear him doing the same thing, and finally I look up and smile. With a deep sigh, the truth comes out. "You don't want to marry me."

He smiles at me and shakes his head. "And you don't want to marry me."

We both laugh a bit and then take deeper, easier breaths. Just then the church bells begin to ring. I look up at the church. "But what about the shower?"

Jameson shrugs. "Don't want to disrupt the worship service. Guess we just wait until everyone gets downstairs and tell them all together?"

"Think that's the only choice we have. However, I do know

where my mother is so I'm going to go tell her." I take a step away to close his door. "You going into service?"

As he turns the key in his ignition, he says, "No, think I'll just drive around a bit. See you back here in an hour?"

I nod. Then I close that door with a good solid swing.

Momma called Daddy and he met us at the diner, which is why I have them both by my side, walking into the church's fellowship hall. We are purposely a bit late, coordinated with Jameson, so that we'd have to do very little small talk before making our announcement.

Jameson walks up and shakes Daddy's hand and hugs Momma. He then turns and raises a hand, asking for everyone's attention. As most folks are looking at us, the sound in the room does diminish a bit. Then Pepper comes striding towards us.

"No, no, no. Not yet. However, it is nice of you two to show up!" She exclaims with a tight laugh and a cut of her eyes at me. "We had to go ahead and have the pastor bless the food so folks could eat. We have *special* seats for the happy couple right over here." She takes my arm and pulls me away from my parents toward the other side of the room. Jameson reaches out and takes my other arm to hold me back. So I'm standing in the middle of a heart-strewn room crisscrossed with pink and red streamers, my arms splayed out in opposite directions.

"Stop!" I yell. "We have something to say." Well there, *now* we definitely have everyone's full attention.

Neither lets go of my arms, but they both step towards me a bit so I look, and feel, less like a wishbone at Thanksgiving.

Jameson clears his throat and announces, "Becca Sue and I so appreciate this lovely shower. Everything is just perfect.

However..." He pauses and suddenly Pepper drops my arm and turns away from us.

She shouts as she points and marches across the room. "You! I knew when you showed up you were here to cause trouble."

Being tall means I can see over Pepper's poufed-up hair and see that she's pointing at her sister, Riley. Riley is standing beside the punch bowl with a little glass cup of pink punch. She has on a very short, very white halter dress, but it's her huge grin that catches my attention. If Pepper was screaming at me like she is at her sister, I sure wouldn't be smiling. I'd be looking for somewhere to hide.

Riley shrugs and, with the hand not holding the punch, ruffles the back of her short, dark hair. Then she drops her grin as her eyes widen, and she becomes the very face of youthful innocence.

The crowd on my other side parts as Mrs. Mason joins us in the middle of the action. "Pepper! Control yourself," she demands before she turns toward her son and me. "Jameson, explain what is happening."

But before he can answer, the area around Riley erupts. Riley's dress is now partially pink and her bangs are wet. Drops of punch fall across her face, which has lost any look of innocence. Pepper lets the now-empty punch cup shatter on the floor and prepares to meet her sister in battle. My other arm is abandoned as Jameson rushes to stop the melee.

At least that's what I thought he was going to do. Instead he grabs Riley and wraps her up in his arms and calls her darling. He pushes her wet bangs off her face and kisses her cheek, her other cheek, and then her mouth!

Pepper screeches, "No, Jameson! She is trash. Pure trash. And I should know, she's my sister." She reaches for Jameson, but she doesn't get to him as Mrs. Mason grabs her arm and shouts, "Pepper, what is going on? You told me he was gay!"

Now *that* got Jameson's attention. "What?"

Mrs. Mason steps toward her son but suddenly remembers where she is and how many people are listening. She draws herself up. "Jameson, let's go home and discuss all this. Let go of that *girl*." She turns to leave, with only one blistering look in Pepper's direction.

"Mother, no," Jameson says, but it doesn't even cause her to hesitate.

Louder he says, "Mother, *this* is the woman I should be marrying."

That causes a bit more than just a hesitation. It causes the turning around of the woman growing older before our eyes.

Pepper literally growls and folds her arms. "That's a mistake. A huge mistake."

I step towards Jameson and say softly, "Actually, um, Pepper might be right. You see, well, I saw Riley at the hunting lodge and..." He meets my eyes and nods.

"Wait." My mouth drops open. "She was with *you*?"

Riley nods and reaches her hand up to caress the face of the man I woke up this morning planning to marry.

I'm stunned as I say with complete assurance, "She was with you at the hunting lodge."

Mrs. Mason sighs loudly, then shakes her head as she turns again to leave.

"Where are you going?" Pepper demands of her. "Come back and tell them this is never going to happen. Tell her she will *never* be Mrs. Jameson Mason! Where are you going?"

Calmly, the matriarch of the Mason family, owner of Mason Farms, and my ex-mother-in-law, says loudly, "Where am I going? I'm going to burn down a hunting lodge."

52

"Come on in. That rain is cold," Jessie says holding her front door open to Becca Sue. "I came right home from church and put on a pot of coffee. Martin took the kids to an indoor playground for the afternoon since I was going to be busy with the shower. Can I get you a cup of coffee? Or I've got iced tea or water."

"No, coffee would be wonderful. Can't seem to get warm." Becca Sue sits at the dining room table in the windowed alcove Jessie points her to. Rain streaking down all the windows makes the space feel small and cold. She shivers and rubs her arms.

"Sorry, I had the heat turned down. Weather's been so mild. Should warm up in here quick."

They sip their coffee for a moment, and then Becca Sue says, "So, is all this what you were trying to warn me about?"

Jessie nods her head. Her curly hair is even fuller with the humidity. "Yes. Well, some of it. I don't know, and some of it is I'm just so over Pepper Johnson. Anyway, around Christmas, Martin and I saw Jameson out with Riley, and it was obvious to me he was crazy about her. But then I decided maybe it was just *lust*. She *is* twenty years younger than him. Not many men could resist *that*."

"But nobody said anything at all to me? Everyone seemed so happy for us."

Jessie pulls down the front of her sweatshirt, twisting her

hands in the hem. She tucks one sock-covered foot up under her in her wooden dining chair. "You know, well, when it was Caleb no one said anything either. Masons have always kind of done what they wanted and we all let 'em."

"Yeah, Caleb. But Jameson isn't like that. Is he?"

Jessie shrugs. "Who knows? Although I do think that's why he was struggling with marrying you. You said before that you and he hadn't been together, hadn't slept with each other, since you came back up here. Right?"

At my nod, she says as she shrugs, "So, maybe he *is* different."

We sip our coffee and listen to the rain for a bit, then I ask, "What about Pepper? I honestly liked her."

"She is pretty likable—at first. She really brought a breath of fresh air when she came back to Piney. Then she opened the Shoppes and they've been a great boost to the economy and just how Piney sees itself. But man, does she hate her sister!"

"Why? They are so far apart in age—are they really in competition with each other?"

"Want a piece of zucchini bread? I have some I pulled out of the freezer." She goes into the kitchen area, then returns with a saucer of bread slices. "I warmed it a bit. Here's the butter if you want it." Jessie takes a piece of bread and holds it in front of her. "Okay, I'm going to tell you something you can't repeat. Martin will have my head if this gets out."

Becca Sue nods as her mouth is full. Then she croaks out, "Sure."

"The Shoppes and the diner are mortgaged to the hilt. Martin says at the bank they are fighting to keep them open, but they may have to foreclose. Apparently, Pepper and Bruce moved here because they had worn out their welcome up in Atlanta. Left behind a string of failed businesses and lots of unhappy creditors."

"So it's all a lie? They aren't really rich?" Becca Sue shakes her head, but then stops. "But wait, what would that have to do with Pepper and Riley?"

"Pepper is jealous of Riley, first of all. She wanted Riley to treat her like some family savior when she came back here, but no go. Riley can be pretty mean. Mostly, though, Pepper was actually interested in Jameson herself when she first came back to town. Before she moved back, she'd come here to visit and always talked like her marriage was falling apart. She even told me and Carol that marrying Jameson was her plan B. *She actually told us that.* About that time is when Riley moved in on Jameson. So Pepper went after Mrs. Mason as not only an investor in the Shoppes, but also as an ally in keeping Riley from getting the coveted last name of Mason. Pepper and Mrs. Mason became fast friends, which we all thought was totally weird. Now, I'm thinking Pepper was filling Mrs. Mason's head with stuff about Jameson being gay. You know it's been a rumor for a long time around here."

"I know." Becca Sue sighs. "Caleb was one of the main ones that spread it. I think he thought it made all his running around look better. Gotta admit it hurts thinking my future mother-in-law only wanted me because she didn't want folks to think her son was gay."

Jessie pauses and then looks straight at Becca Sue. "Honestly with what you knew about her from your marriage with Caleb, how did you think anything good *at all* about her? She had her son snipped so *you* wouldn't get pregnant, then let him get unsnipped when he was with a girl whose father owned property she wanted." Her voice raises. "While he was still married to you!"

"Oh, everyone knows about that?"

Jessie rolls her eyes and spits. "Everyone that wanted to know. It's rather easy to not know stuff in a small town if you'd rather be blind. Come on, you knew who Mrs. Mason was all along. You just chose to be blind. Some people really prefer to be blind."

Becca Sue's hurt shows on her face. "But I thought she'd changed. I thought..."

Jessie looks down and takes a deep draw of breath. "What did I tell you? Piney is still Piney." She lifts her head, and her eyes are sharp. "Honestly, those of us that knew about Jameson and Riley figured if you were coming back for more Mason drama, you deserved what you got." She sits back in her chair and watches her guest. Despite the heat having kicked on, the room is chillier than ever.

Becca Sue stands up and lays her folded up napkin onto the table. "Thank you for the coffee and the bread. I knew you could fill in some blanks." She walks toward the side door she'd entered earlier. Jessie follows her. At the door, Becca Sue turns around. "You and Carol are still friends?"

"Of course. We will always be here in Piney, and we will always be friends."

"That's good. I mean, that you have each other." Becca Sue looks out the glass door for a bit, then looks back and asks, "You and I wouldn't be real friends if I moved back here, would we?"

Jessie shrugs. "Maybe." She leans past Becca Sue and opens the door. "But Piney is still Piney."

"Olivia, it's me again. Are you really here in Backwater? The kids want to see you. We'll be at my parents' house all day. Call me when you get this." Bradley pushes the end button and holds the phone out at his mom. "There, I left another message. Are you happy?"

Ruth tsks and shakes her head. "I just don't understand. How could a mother do this?" She's talking low even though Emerson and Phillips are around the corner in the living room with their grandfather. She startles when the doorbell rings. "I'll get it. You can get lunch started."

At the door, she peeks through the small window. Her mouth drops, and she looks at her son before she opens the door. "Olivia. Magnus. Come in."

Bradley beats the children to the door. "I've been leaving you messages."

"And here I am. So obviously I got them." Olivia shrugs at him and then squats down to hug the children.

Magnus reaches over her to shake Bradley's hand. "Good to see you! Hear you're hitting some bumps in the road with the pot place."

"It's not a pot place, and you know it. Besides, what do you care? You pulled out, remember?"

Magnus stretches to shake Eason's hand, too. "Eason. Won't ask about the business venture. Apparently it's a touchy subject." He grins. "Probably a good thing we didn't go into business together anyway, don't you think?"

Bradley shoves his hands in the front pockets of his jeans. He's barefoot and wearing an old T-shirt. Olivia is dressed like she's heading for a ski chalet in knee-high boots, light brown leggings, and a long cream sweater. Her hair is held back by a cream headband and as she straightens up, she is taller than him.

Bradley dismisses the older man. "Yeah, whatever, Magnus." He focuses on his ex-wife. "So, you here to take the kids for a while? You can see we haven't even had a chance to get dressed. It'll be nice to not be on kid duty twenty-four seven."

"Bradley!" his mother says. "The children are right here."

Her son takes a deep breath and calms himself. "Yes. I mean it's, well, how long have you been here?" He tries to make it sound like a pleasant query, but there's a hardness to his words. Emerson comes to him and wraps her arms around her daddy's leg. Phillips is sitting at his mother's feet crying to be picked up.

Eason steps forward, opening his arm up toward the living room. "Why don't you come have a seat? Can we get you something to drink?"

Olivia speaks up. "Apparently, the nannies from last night didn't tell you anything." She weaves her right arm into Magnus' and holds out her left hand. "Magnus and I are married. We've been enjoying a little alone time this week in his house across the lake. That's why we didn't tell you we were here. However, we did want to drop in and share our happy news on our way to the airport. We're headed to Europe for a *real* honeymoon."

Eason and Ruth don't move a muscle. Bradley lets out his held breath and then laughs. "Well done, Olivia. He's richer than Mommy and Daddy Baets will ever be. And congratulations to you, too, Magnus. She's obviously able to bear children, possibly even in multiples." He steps forward, smile wide, with his hand outstretched. "Let me shake your hands. You both got exactly what you want." When their hands don't extend to meet his, he drops his hand and his smile hardens. "And you both got exactly what you deserve."

Magnus puts his arm around his wife and takes a step back. "Then I suppose it's a good thing we can't stay. Our trip will give you time to calm down."

Bradley steps to the side and says quietly to Olivia, "I'll fight you for the kids. They don't deserve to be some vague second thought to you."

She tilts her head and raises her eyebrows. "Oh, no worries. I've had the papers already drawn up. You'll have full custody. I only want visitation."

Ruth gasps and raises her hand to her mouth. Then she recovers and bends down to Emerson. "Sweetie, tell your Mommy goodbye. Phillips, here, stand up like a good boy. Give Mommy a hug."

Bradley stumbles back to a chair next to the front window and sits down. He watches Emerson give her mother a tight hug and start crying, then his jaw slackens and tears fill his eyes as his son goes into full meltdown, ending up laying at his mother's feet. Ruth and Eason struggle to pick him up, and Bradley finds himself unable to get up and help them.

Magnus is horrified and quickly opens the front door for his wife. "Honey, let's go. He'll be better if we just leave."

Olivia looks up and locks eyes with Bradley. Her eyes are also full and she mouths, "I'm sorry."

Bradley swallows, nods, then pushes himself up. "Go. We'll be fine."

As the door closes, Bradley kneels beside his son on the cold tile floor. Emerson leaves her grandmother's side and comes to lay her head on her daddy's shoulder. Bradley moves off his knees to settle onto the floor, he pulls his daughter onto his lap and lifts his son to join her there. "Daddy's here, Daddy's here," he repeats over and over until the sobs become deep, ragged breaths and eventually soft snores.

Emerson pats her brother's arm. "He sleepin'," she whispers.

"Yes, sweetie, he is. How are you?"

She lays her head against his chest and lets out a deep, deep sigh. Then her little voice wonders, "Daddy i cream?"

Bradley laughs and hugs his children tighter. "Yes, we most definitely can go get ice cream."

53

I left Jessie's and drove around thinking. Now I'm sitting in the parking lot of a bank along the highway, across the street from my grandmother's house. I don't know who lives there now. Momma seemed surprised that I even asked her if she knew, when I first came back to town. Seemed even more surprised when I asked her why she didn't move there when her momma died.

"That old house? Why, honey, it was falling apart, and besides, your grandmother didn't own it. Your Granddaddy Wayne rented it to her for just a bit. Not like he would've gotten much from anyone for it. Lord knows he don't put anything into any of his rental properties. Especially for *my* mother." Then she laughed. "You thought your grandmother owned that place?"

Guess I have chosen to be blind. Rain coats my car windows, and I have the heat turned up high so the insides also have a layer of fog. Feels real private sitting here.

Shouldn't I feel more of a tie to this place, this town, than I do? When I moved away last year, it was more like running away and I thought... I shiver and put the car into drive, too much thinking. Cab and Maggie are home from their trip, and they're going to meet me at the burger place at this end of town.

Darting out of my car through the rain and into the small

restaurant, I'm hit with the smell of grilled onions before I open the door. I'm starving all of a sudden.

Cab waves from in front of the counter and says, "Want a number one? Maggie's getting our drinks.

"Sure." After getting my cup from the counter, I join his sister at the drinks area. "Hey there. How was the trip?"

Her eyes are dimmed and tired. She leans onto my arm. "It was amazing, but I'm so tired. Jet lag is awful."

I bump her head off my arm and laugh. "Oh, it's jet lag, is it? Why, bless your tiny little world-traveling soul."

She laughs and turns toward the tables. "Hey! I'm working on my excuses for teachers tomorrow. I didn't do any of my schoolwork. Here's our table."

We sit down as she rambles on and on about the trip. Cab brings our tray of burgers and fries, slides into the chair beside Maggie, and they both talk while we eat. The windows are fogged here, too, and it feels like we're in a cocoon as we laugh and talk and eat. I'm beginning to wonder if they know about the wedding being called off when finally Cab says, "Sorry to hear about you and Uncle J."

Maggie blurts out, "But it wasn't right. You know it wasn't right, don't you?"

Cab shoves his sister with his body. "Mags, shut up."

"I will not shut up. She knows it wasn't right or she wouldn't have called it off."

"Wait," I say with a hand held out across the table. "What exactly do you mean, it wasn't right?"

Cab shrugs and picks up a french fry, then he looks at his sister. So I look at her, too.

Maggie chews on her straw, and her green eyes are wide. "Becca Sue, you don't belong in Piney. It's not right for you. Remember, we saw you in Backwater. We know you there and we know you here. People act like Piney is the only place on the face of the earth!" she exclaims then lets out an indignant huff.

Cab nods. "We're Masons so we're kind of stuck here, but you're not."

Maggie bangs her cup down on the table. "No, Cab. Grandfather Worth says we are not just Masons! We are also Worths and can be anywhere we want to be. Well, when we grow up." She grins. "When I grow up, I'm going to live in London."

"London? Well, guess that means I'll have to come visit you there, right?" I reach out and lay my hand on Cab's arm. "Honey, you're not stuck here if you don't want to be. Roger is right, you are not just Masons. Listen to your grandfather. He's a really smart man."

The tall boy who is so like his father nods, then says, "I know, but I want this. I *want* Piney. I *like* being a Mason and having a farm." He seems to have grown up in the time it took to make that statement. I squeeze his arm and then remove my hand. He looks around the restaurant, and his look says this is his home. Then he elbows his sister. "Come on, Mags, I haven't done any schoolwork either."

As we clean up our table and get our jackets on, we end up at the door. I hug them both, and Cab runs out into the rain. Maggie hangs back and hugs me again. "Even though it wasn't right for you and Uncle J, I still wanted you to live at the house with us again."

"I know. I did, too."

She runs out of the door and jumps in the car her brother has pulled up to the sidewalk. She waves from the window, and I watch as they pull away. Then I run out into the steady rain and get in my car. I pull out, but turn the opposite direction.

Taking lots of turns and side roads and side trips, my journey to my folks' trailer takes longer than it should. The day is turning from light gray to dark gray by the time I get there.

"Hey, I'm home," I say as I enter the trailer. No one is visible. I take off my jacket and shake my damp hair. "Y'all here?" Their cars are outside, where could they be?

Stepping into the hall, I look down it just in time to see their bedroom door slam shut. Momma yells, "We're busy!"

"Guess the doctor gave his heart an all clear," I say with a chuckle. Then the door opens a bit, before closing right back, and Squirrel comes running out.

"Oh, so you were in the wrong place at the wrong time? Come here, sweetie." I pick up my kitten and then sit on the couch. "Here, let's turn on the TV for some cover noise."

With the light from the television and the voices from the actors, it's easy to ignore the sounds coming from the bedroom. I cuddle with Squirrel and relax. The trailer is warm and dry, and feels like, it feels like home.

This is pretty comforting after my strange drive though Piney. It was like a place I didn't know. For the first time since I've been back, I know what I've been feeling. This town isn't my home anymore. This trailer is, though, and then I suddenly realize why. Momma and Daddy are here. For the first time all day, I'm warm. My fingers aren't cramped and stiff with chill. Even my nose is toasty, and the conviction settling in deep feels more and more true.

Piney is my hometown.

But it's not my home.

54

"What if I say no?" Roger Worth's words on the phone cause Becca Sue to take a deep breath. He continues before she can let it out. "What if I say you left me, and Backwater, high and dry? What if I tell you how presumptuous you were to play like you were getting married and moving to Georgia? Did it cross your mind that the cabin you were so in love with just a couple months ago has been sitting idle all this time and that I put money into it because you are my *onsite* partner? What about the other work that simply came to a standstill because you were off playing around in Piney? Did you give even a second thought to what would happen to Backwater? This is not how I do business."

He waits, and as Becca Sue waits with him, she stiffens. She clutches the edge of the sofa cushion and searches for words to fill the silence. Finally she says, "Roger, I don't know what to say except... you're right. You're right about all of that and I understand."

He still waits, so Becca Sue lets out a long breath before mumbling, "I'm sorry."

"For what?"

"What? I'm sorry for everything."

"Not good enough. Sorry for everything means nothing. Try again or hang up."

"Um, I'm sorry I just ran off. I'm sorry I let you down. I'm sorry I let everyone in Backwater down. I'm sorry I acted like a kid and not a partner." Her voice gets stronger as she works through the list. "Wow, Roger. I really let you down. How did I not see this? It honestly never occurred to me how awful I've been."

"Exactly. It's time you grew up, Becca Sue. You've been given a rough hand to play with for most your life, and I appreciate that, but that's the past." After a moment, he chuckles. "You sure tried to reclaim that hand with your little foray back to Piney, didn't you?"

Becca Sue laughs a bit, closes her eyes, and lays her head back against her parents' couch. "Yes, yes, I did. Roger, I want to come home. I want to work for you, with you. I want to live in my, well, in the cabin."

"Good. It's been almost impossible to not show up in Piney and shake you real good. But I understand, better than most, that hometown ghosts have to be dealt with. Especially when leaving wasn't exactly your choice."

"Ghosts. Yeah, ghosts." Becca Sue looks around her parents' trailer and then stands up to walk around. "Roger, I won't let you down. I appreciate everything you've done. If it's okay with you I'm going to sleep in the storeroom at the office. Guess it was Cab's room when we lived there. Living at Miss Bell's probably isn't such a good idea right now. Plus, I need to take care of myself."

"Now, you don't have to sleep in a storeroom. I'm sure there's a condo—"

"No. I appreciate that, but I need to grow up. I just appreciate you letting me come back to work."

"Becca Sue, you are my partner. I'm not 'letting' you do anything. I just expect a great deal from you."

She smiles before she says, "Well, guess it's about time I started expecting something from me, too."

55

"You're back!" Ashleigh shouts when she opens her front door. She pauses with some suspicion on her face. "For good?"

I hug my friend and nod. "Yep. Back home for good. I'm settled into the storeroom with a blowup mattress, and work crews will be back out at the cabin first thing in the morning." Ashleigh leads us into their little living room, where she has a heater plugged in.

She leans over and switches it off. "Let's go somewhere and get dinner. I'm frozen stiff."

"Frozen? With this spring-like weather? But I do want some seafood. And I do want to see the ocean. Think Miss Bell would want to go with us?" I ask as I take out my phone and dial her number.

Ashleigh puts on her shoes while I ask Miss Bell to join us. "We'll swing by and pick you up in a few minutes." I push the end button and frown at my phone. "She had to ask permission! Those people!"

"It's a mess, but she says she knows what she's doing. Thanked me for my help and then basically told me to mind my own business—but in a nice way. Okay, I'm ready. So, how did things go last night? Did you see Pepper?"

We leave out the front door, and by the time we get in my car, I've thought through the last twenty-four hours. Sunday night is when I talked to Roger Worth, then Monday morning

I started to wrap everything up in Piney. This morning I hit the road at first light to go home.

"Yes, I did see Pepper, and no, she's not sorry for anything. Don't believe that's in her nature. She's denying everything and is now Riley's biggest supporter. Crazy. She's pushing for Riley and Jameson to take our spot and get married on Valentine's Day."

Ashleigh's mouth falls open. "No way."

"Yes way. She's a piece of work."

"But how does that make you feel?"

Turning onto the blacktop, I smile at her. "I don't care."

The palms along the road sway in the late afternoon sun. It's brighter here, and the sky seems bluer, more open. The smell of sulfur water is like an exotic perfume, and even a clutch of buzzards beside the road makes me happy. It's all so Florida.

"I honestly do not care," I say again. "Jameson is head over heels about Riley, and if she makes him happy, then I'm happy. Plus, she's Mrs. Mason's worst nightmare, well, except apparently for her son being gay, but a mouthy, trashy girl, practically still a teenager, is probably a close second."

As we pull into Backwater, I say, "Home again, home again."

Ashleigh finishes, "Jiggity jig!"

We laugh until we see the group of people standing on Miss Bell's front lawn. This does not look like a friendly neighborhood gathering. Ruth is crying and holding the twins a bit away from the others. Eason and Bradley are toe to toe with Drummond and Mimi. Drummond is laughing out loud. Miss Bell is back in the shadows of her porch, wringing her hands. We park and jump out, then dash towards them, me toward Mrs. Bell, Ashleigh toward Ruth and the children.

"You've ruined me!" Bradley is shouting.

Eason is madder than I've ever seen him. "You lied on the application. It wasn't a mistake. You lied!"

To their shouts, Drummond laughs again and puts his arm

around his wife. "Darling, let's go get dinner. They have nothing new to say."

Miss Bell steps away from me and the porch. "Drummond! You stay right here and talk with the Kings. This all has to be some misunderstanding."

Drummond's laughter dies immediately. "Virginia, there is no misunderstanding. You seem to think *everything* is a misunderstanding. We must bring that to your *doctor's* attention, mustn't we?"

Eason roars, "Don't you act like she's not altogether here! You've been insinuating that all along, and we all know she's of very sound mind. Much more than you two!"

With a shrug and a raised eyebrow, Drummond answers, "Of course she's of sound mind. She did sign all those papers, didn't she? Thank you for verifying her soundness."

Mimi smiles and pats her husband's arm. "Yes, now that you mention it, I am hungry." She turns and walks toward the porch, moving past her mother-in-law, not even giving her a glance. "Come along, Drummond. Virginia, maybe you shouldn't go out tonight. It's been a rather stressful day for you. Come inside so we can set the alarm."

"No."

"What?" Drummond says as he looks back toward the house.

Miss Bell shakes her head and says louder, "No, you've hurt my friends. I did sign those papers to give you control, but only for the money from your father's accounts. But this is my house. You are my guests, but only until you find a new home. After all, you have your father's money to buy one now."

Mimi turns and demands of her husband as she strides toward him, "What does she mean this is still her house?"

Drummond shrugs. "She only signed over the money. Figured we'd deal with the house later."

"You lied about the house?" Mimi shoves him.

Miss Bell's laugh is dry. "He tends to do that. A friend of mine looked into how he ran your father's business into the ground. I have money from my family and this house. Everything Mr. Bell left is now in Drummond's name. If you let him ruin you again, that's your choice, Mimi. However, I would stop believing anything he says."

Miss Bell steps forward and touches my arm. "Mimi is right about one thing, I am tired. We'll have lots of time to talk and you can plan to move back in here with me next weekend."

I grab her hand, "But Miss Bell if you knew all this, why did you let it go so far with them?"

She sadly smiles at me. "Guilt made me want to believe him. He looks so much like his father. Giving him his father's money has relieved my guilt. Your room, you *original* room, will be ready for you this weekend." She motions toward Drummond and Mimi. "They'll be moving into the guest room until they move into their new home."

Mimi pulls herself up and stomps to the car. "Come on, Drummond, if you're coming." She reaches into her purse and pulls out her keys. "And I'm driving."

Drummond stares at his stepmother and opens his mouth just as his wife starts the car. "Virginia, I, uh, we'll be home later. Then we can talk." He strides in a hurry to the passenger car door, but looks back when Miss Bell calls his name.

"Drummond. There's nothing left for us to talk about. However, I do have a new lawyer that is looking forward to an in-depth conversation with you. Ruth, Eason, I'm sorry, but I really am worn out."

She enters her home as the shiny black car pulls out before the passenger door is fully closed.

I turn to face the King family and Ashleigh. Ashleigh's face is grim as apparently she's been filled in with what's going on by Ruth.

Eason puts his arm across his son's shoulder. "Drummond and Mimi lied on the application for the medical marijuana dispensary. They also filed completely made-up financial records. It was all to get control of Mrs. Bell's accounts."

Bradley moans and then walks toward his kids, saying loudly, "Yep, ruining me was just a bonus and sounds like to me she would've given him the money if he'd just asked."

"Son, you're hardly ruined. You'll work things out," Eason says. "We can't do the dispensary, but we'll come up with something else. You and the kids are together and you know you are welcome here in Backwater. Ruth, let's get the children home. It's time for dinner."

The twins run down the driveway, corralled by their grandparents. We watch them for a moment, then Ashleigh taps my arm and walks past me. "Let's go. I can't go to dinner. I need to get started on this story."

I scurry to catch up with her. She's on her phone and getting into the car, so I get into the driver's seat.

"Take me home," she says then finishes talking to someone about timelines and deadlines. When she hits the end button, she twists in the seat to look at me. "Bradley wasn't joking. This could ruin him. He likely will never get another part of a marijuana dispensary. Legalities of those places are incredible. Huge hurdles to jump through and huge fines if you mess up."

Starting the car, I ask, "Are you the person who filled Miss Bell in on Drummond and Mimi's past?"

Ashleigh grins, "Some, but she's smarter than she sometimes acts. She's hoping to salvage a relationship with Drummond and Mimi, but I don't think they'll be open to it."

A knock on my window causes me to jump. Bradley stands there, his head bent to look in at me.

"Hey," I say when the window is down.

"Hey. Um, so Ashleigh says you're moving back here?"

"Yes."

He straightens up and puts his hands in his pockets. "Okay, good. See you around."

Before putting the car in gear and pulling out, I look over at my friend. "You've been busy, haven't you?"

She flips her hair and grins, "A little. Someone has to keep this place running. Now, I have to get this article written ASAP. Sorry we can't go out. Maybe tomorrow?"

"Maybe, but I have a full day of work in the office." I chuckle, but end on a sigh. "It's actually good to be back to work here. Don't think I'll be itching to wait tables any time soon!"

As I pull up into Ashleigh and Carlos' dirt driveway and park, Ashleigh drops her phone into her purse. She opens her door and lumbers out of the low seat. "Thanks for the quick trip. It was quite a ride." As she walks around the hood of the car, I put it in reverse. Then she holds up a hand and motions for me to roll down my window.

She leans on the open window and smiles at me, with one side of her mouth lifted in a bit of a smirk. "So, tomorrow. When we go out to dinner, wear those shoes again, okay?" She winks and pats my arm.

"Okay," I say as I look down at my feet and my brand-new, just-out-of-the-box, Sperry Top-Siders. Bright white soles and leather thong ties.

It's good to be home.

And, you know, it's good to be me.

The End

CPSIA information can be obtained
at www.ICGtesting.com
Printed in the USA
FSHW021000150620
71205FS